THE MARK OF
THE
GALILEAN

To Basil—
with much regards—
I hope this is a contribution
to the new paradigm.
Ed

E. Noah Sarath
april 19 2000

THE MARK OF THE GALILEAN

E. Noah Sarath

To order additional copies of this book, contact.
Xlibris Corporation
1-888-7-XLIBRIS
www.Xlibris.com
Orders@Xlibris.com

CONTENTS

This book is dedicated with love and gratitude
to those enlightened masters from every age, clime and tradition
who from time immemorial have acknowledged and affirmed
in their own lives the highest qualities of God's humanity.
We can rejoice in their achievements of the past
as we recognize our own promise and future.

AUTHOR'S NOTE

I am not an amanuensis. I have no sense that what I write or the words I use or the style of my expression is the work of a hidden voice, one not mine. Yet I do not feel a proprietary relationship to the thoughts and the ideas expressed here. They surface in my awareness, during my daily meditations, as I enter and leave that charming and sustaining transcendental realm into which I am guided by my spiritual practice. But in those other times, too, when quietness overtakes the tumult of the day's activities and one falls into the poet's "blessed and serene mood."

The thoughts arise unbidden, often remembered, but sometimes reaching the crust of my consciousness only to burst and disappear like a child's blown bubble. But since they are not my creation, and I can acknowledge them without knowing their specific origins, I am not constrained to attest to their literal certainty.

But unabashedly, I warrant their evocative power. No more need we wallow in a sea of sorrow — our shared illusionary birthright — as these most subtle of whispers, inchoate murmurs from the deepest recesses of being, release the soul's transforming waves of bliss. These words and thoughts are of a time far from our own though that too is an illusion, for the past is memory and with memory how distinguish yesterday from one a thousand yesterdays ago?

The people I write of flow out of my imagination but of none of them could it be said that there was even a tenuous connection to a person living now or living then. Can that be true? I myself cannot believe that. For as I was telling their stories I sensed a time reached when they would begin telling their own, and though I wanted one person to say one thing he would say another; and when I wanted another one to do this she would insist on doing that. So where they came from I cannot with certainty say, but they came alive in the writ-

ing; why else would I cry with them, laugh with them and fear with them?

But of one that cannot be truthfully said, the Galilean, so called outside his country, or perhaps Master or Rabbi as the case may be, depending on who would be the caller. He came to me from a deeper source. Beyond memory or imagination or experience, a transcendent place whose location can only be felt as a presence, his presence, and even this conjured up out of an ocean of silence. Who and what is this presence? It was a mystery then as it was ever a mystery and remains a mystery to this very day. But it is not a mystery to be solved, only to be known and in that knowing is its power.

He and they lived at the beginning of the first century although it could not have been known as such to them. The place was in that benighted though holy land, blessed by God but cursed by men, which sat as a bridge between the rival empires of the East and West. Its fate was to be the trophy of the dominant military power of the day: Rome. *In that ancient time they were part of a people even more ancient again by more than twice those years, Jews they were called although that was not their first appellation.*

It was a tiny populace in the scheme of the world and one born out of the slave pits of Egypt. But through the love, guidance and promise of their God they were raised to a mighty nation and given the land on which they resided and from which they were fated to be cast out. Their God was just but demanding, perhaps patient even more than that, for over and over they remembered their covenant with Him and were raised up, and over and over they forgot it and were cast down; despite it all their God kept them a people, His people.

The lesson was clear but never learned — not yet learned by any people it could be said — when thrown into the mud and despair of the world they cry for deliverance and then in the lap of comfort and pleasure they forget their Deliverer. So it was in this time of which we speak. The nation was burdened by a double oppressor, one home grown and of their own blood, and the alien other even more cruel, bred to conquest and brutality, and both stood astride a people desperately searching for salvation.

But it was a search that took many forms in that troubled time; a time of wandering teachers and philosophers from all climes and cultures, East and West, mystery schools from Greece and Egypt, with their gods of healing and magic and star gazing. Within this maelstrom, however, there remained always the core teaching of the Jews, the high moral and social Law given to Moses by their God and accepted in Moses' name by His people.

And now in the generation of which we speak, after tens of suffering prior ones, a new prophet arose whose first task was to uncover and reveal again from this holy teaching the way to deliverance, both personal and of the nation.

But, dear reader, I cannot tell you more of him than this; I can only commend to you the following pages in which to find him. In them you will find the people who knew him best, whose lives and fortunes were changed and elevated by his being. And may their stories enliven in you as you read them, as they did in me as I wrote them, of these still living souls whose only goal is to guide us safely into that interior kingdom that exists to shelter and nourish us all.

First you will meet Jonathan, the aged hermitic gnome, as the solitude of his long life was shattered at its very end and his reason for living it was finally revealed. In him resided the tale whose safe transmission from generation to generation is vital to man to find God's design and humanity's purpose on earth. We learn from him his beginnings and the nature and lives of his people in that time.

Different were their lives from those that came before, and different from any that would come after, but for one constant: their instinctive need to know and satisfy the desires of their mysterious, invisible God. Like the flower that follows the sun in its daily travels, they follow this craving in their hearts and minds though, and this is the most exquisite irony, they look away from His true residence.

Then we come to know Aaron, the boy whose adolescence and innocence — not to speak of uncountable future lifetimes — are fated to end, but who is still to find fulfillment in a few short days as the power of divine knowledge works its transforming magic. Thus in this centenarian and in that youth we see the complete, unfiltered transmis-

sion of the workings of time. And we see nothing is lost, not a jot nor tittle, nor thought, nor word, nor deed. Though this place where the world can be recovered cannot be known, it can be entered and so we have our stories.

Through these two will be revealed the life of Sara and her time. As a girl and woman she was remarkable for her strength and will, her strange abilities, and the qualities of her mind. Chosen to love and be loved by one she could not have, loved by one who saw he could not have her, and loved by another to whom she was joined by a stronger power for its own uses — though benign — she made her life her own.

And we come also to know Jacob, known not only as Sara's husband but also as a complete man of his time. He was born to the country and farm, a true son of the Judean people, but torn from these moorings and sent out to school in the sophistication of Roman Jewry. There, the seeds of his discontent were sown as the learning to which he was exposed cast an opaque veneer over the lore and tradition learned at his mother's knee.

Because of this, for many years he was unable to surrender in his heart to what his eyes could see and his mind told him. But through him we learn of the earliest expressions, teaching and deeds of the young Master whose being even in this unfinished state could not contain its manifestations. Through Jacob's travels, also, we learn of the ways of that land and others in that time, their sufferings and yearnings and the interior struggles of men and women.

Joseph comes alive too, the first disciple, the messenger of the Messenger, to whom was revealed the new guide at the time of the Teacher's emergence from silence. Through Joseph, himself, we learn of his instant and certain surrender at the first sight of his Master, and Joseph's later steadfastness when these two and others were cast out from their cloistered enclave for disputing the accepted Rule and Teacher.

Around them circled other orbs in that divine constellation. The wise Jewish physician, Alexander, with Greek ways and name, who first understood Sara's special quality, and who saw Jacob's needs so clearly that he served as an unwitting instrument guiding his friend's destiny.

And Jason, the sagacious counselor whose stars brought him from boyhood slavery in a tiny Greek village to the scholar's home in Athens, thence to the heady center of Roman Jewish life. And finally, to the distant Eastern land of the Buddha where his "Greek head, Jewish soul and Buddhist heart" found realization in the message Jacob brought him, though Jacob himself could not yet hear it.

Tomas, too (the first Christian?), plays his part in Jacob's life. This donkey driver, the least of Jacob's servants, saw deeply and immediately into the "presence", his life seemingly lived only to make this discovery. Through Tomas, too, we see the workings and movements of God's supportive and loving hand when one is content to do His bidding.

There are others, of course, who play their necessary roles in this story, like little Anna and Ruth whose tales tear at the heart. And many others too, named and unnamed who affect and are affected by the vicissitudes of life, no different than those who live on the periphery of our own. And like those of that day, who will know when any one of these seemingly minor players will leave that outer orbit and enter the center of our fate? Truly, there are no insignificant souls.

As our story opens, only the twisted Jonathan remains to give credence to and to preserve for posterity the meaning of the lives of those who loved and sustained him. Important for him, clearly, but equally important for us, the posterity for whom that preservation was intended. The knowledge of these lives and deeds and their message of love and fulfillment illuminates their presence in our hearts and nothing so purifies and uplifts our own souls than the shining light of others.

CYPRUS I

By the reckoning of our people it is the year 3868, eighty and five years since I received Master's final blessing, and the fourteenth year of the reign of the Emperor Trajan, Rome's present ruler who extends ever farther his nation's brutal reach. His hand is felt also in my isolated cave overlooking the tiny Jewish village that cares for me. Even this poor community, although hidden at the foot of the mountains on the eastern tip of Cyprus' finger, does not escape Rome's influence.

Since I was brought here many years ago, spirited out of Galilee after the imprisonment and disappearance of my Master, the village has enjoyed an uncommon well being. The seasons come on time, the crops are ample and the Law is fulfilled. For this reason, each year after harvest the village selects a family who is honored to provide me with my one scanty meal a day. There is water from a nearby mountain stream and, although dry at times, there is always enough for my meager needs.

The village properly thanks our invisible God for their peace and plenty, but in the way of spiritual innocence they attribute to my presence a special beneficence, a more substantial and visible sign of God's approval. I have long given up the attempt to dissuade them from these ideas. I am satisfied that I was able to resist their blasphemous attempts to make of me an object of veneration. I know only too well the fate of prophets, saviors, and wonder workers. I have seen their suffering and I have suffered with them.

These thoughts came as the call, low as it was, shattered the beautiful stillness of my dark mountain shelter: "Father . . . , father, I am here with your food. And I brought a visitor."

I at once realized it was a different boy who called. Could a year have already passed? I have no sense of time but for the slow change of seasons. Except for the boy who brings my food, whom I do not often see, I have had little human contact over the years. What could anyone want from me? My time in the affairs of men has long passed and, although I sense the importance of those turbulent, worldly years, I do not dwell in their memory.

In this I am content. Although alone I am never lonely except when, as now, an alien intruder enters this quietness. But at ease as I am, I am equally ready to pass from this world with no desire to return, the prospect of return being one which some of our teachers hold out for sinners.

With some difficulty and with the help of my staff, I hobbled slowly from the deeper recesses of my cave to a point where I could see my visitors, but where I remained not easily seen myself. I had long ago learned how my appearance affected those who came upon me for the first time. The two had taken a few tentative steps in from the chamber's opening, the man following the boy whose boldness spoke of an earlier familiarity.

"Who are you?," I asked, "Why are you here?"

"Father, I am Aaron, the boy who brought you your food three years ago. I brought it once more today because I was asked to bring Simon, your visitor, to you. Do you not remember? You allowed me to speak with you at times. I asked you to heal my twisted leg."

Ah yes, the bright boy whose twisted leg, accidentally broken and never properly healed — was that the reason for my special feeling for him? Was that three years ago? Of course I could not heal his leg. Look at me! If I could heal would I not have healed myself? And even Sara, to whom God gave the gift of healing, could do no more for me than this. It is the healing Master gave us, the healing of the spirit, . . . Ah, no matter now. A visitor? What need do I have of a visitor? What need he of me? At this thought, Simon said quietly: "Father, please excuse my intrusion."

He spoke haltingly in the common language, as if he were more comfortable with another tongue.

"I was sent by the Jews of Salamis who are mired in a terrible dispute that threatens to rend their congregation. It was thought you would be able to resolve this problem."

"How is that possible?" I replied. "How do you know of me? What do you know of me? What can I know of your disputes?"

I was so unused to this kind of contact I unthinkingly moved forward to see my visitor better, forgetting that by doing so he would get a clearer look at me.

As Simon replied, I realized my gnome-like appearance meant little to him. My initial resentment at his presence melted as he spoke to me in the same even manner of those few I had known and loved, they who were able to see past my body into my heart. The thought of my beautiful Sara flashed into my mind, especially how, in those terrible days as I was coming to manhood, she would say to me: "Jonathan, you may be a half-man in form, but you are a giant in soul and wisdom."

"Father," Simon began, "a Jewish evangelist recently came to Salamis to preach a new faith. A Jew who speaks to Gentiles as well and speaks to them of our Law and in the Greek language. He is part of a new sect, Christians the people call them because they say our Messiah has come. He preached to a long dormant cult among our people, one that was founded by another evangelist preacher who came long before this time, a Tarsus Jew named Paul — a Greek name because of his hellenistic style — who came in the time of Claudius.

"Paul spoke of a man who was killed by the Romans for calling himself, or allowing others to call him, our promised Messiah who would free the Jews. Paul told them this new king was hanged on a cross, was buried in a tomb and then rose from the dead. He called him *Christos Jesus* as they would refer to him in the Greek language."

Those words startled me, dispelling the growing torpor Simon's account was causing. The name of my Master was Jeshua and this name could be sounded as "Jesus" in the Greek tongue, though few would call him that, only Sara, who knew him as a boy and man; Jacob, Sara's husband who spent that fateful time with him; and Joseph, the erstwhile monk to whom was revealed Master's return and who became as if his right arm. All others knew him as Master or Teacher, which he truly was.

How long I was silent I do not know. So unused to conversation I had become and so long ago were these things of account it could well be my visitors thought I did not hear. At length I felt their discomfit as long forgotten stirrings rose in my breast. Messiah? Though some had considered this so, neither he nor we ever thought of him as such. Moreover, he was watched carefully by the Temple leaders because of the interest in his teaching throughout the villages of Jewish Palestine; the fear Temple authorities showed of these areas, especially the wild region of Galilee, made the ever present talk of Messiah and wonder workers most dangerous.

I felt myself tiring and losing interest. I had long passed the need to engage in these disputes. Had I not found the Way and had it not lightened my long life? Nevertheless, with some effort I pulled myself out of my languor. I must rid myself of these visitors, I thought. "You cannot be talking of my Master, Simon. He was a man and men do not rise from the dead. You know these Romans well, Simon, and they make no mistakes when they want to kill. Do people rise from the dead, Simon? Is that what you are asking me?"

"This is what our people believe Paul taught, father. At a time not long after the events, this Jesus appeared in a vision to him and directed him to preach to the world beyond Israel. His preaching, he was told, was to be that the Messiah, the Christ of the Jews will soon return for everyone and the people must prepare their lives for this second coming. Paul provided instruction for this preparation and those who accepted this instruction and lived their lives accordingly would be saved. The others would be cast aside to pay dearly for their refusal to obey."

From somewhere I felt a surge of strength. My irritation grew apace as what I had been hearing failed to awaken any new memories of my Master. I felt resentment at this disturbance of my comfort and that resentment itself was an added burden. I replied with a sharpness that surprised me and that I had not expressed in many years, but which I did not attempt to restrain.

"Simon, be still! What has this tale to do with me? You come and tell me a fanciful story of the coming of a Jewish king who will save the Gentiles and desert our tradition, of a prophet, another false one on the face of it, who will bring to the Jews a new Law, what else can this instruction be? What more do we need than what we have been given by the Lawgiver? If this is not enough, you tell me that among our people there are those who will leave our house to follow one who has risen from the dead and will return again in the flesh to rule the whole world.

"Is this what you came here to speak to me about? I have no interest in these arguments. Since Moses led the people out of Egypt, Jews have been disputing these issues. What will they talk about if answers are ever found? For me these questions are settled. The teaching of my Master takes me out of the mud of this world and permits me to satisfy my life's purposes here and alone. You are disturbing that desire."

"Did your Master live in a cave, father?" His sharp tone measured mine but his change of tongue caught my attention. "I think not. It is about your Master we have come to learn. I have no wish to upset your solitude. But I am here now sent in good faith by our people. We must know what you know of those times. There can be no further peace for you until that is done and I say that with full respect for your needs."

For a moment I did not realize he spoke in the Greek language. In his agitation it came more easily to his mouth. How many years since I heard those words. I understood it well, I had learned it early, but I was so unused to speaking it some time elapsed before I could respond as I could not as readily bring the words I needed to my lips. It was Aaron who broke the silence, disturbed I am sure at the temper of the meeting.

"Father, this is my fault. During the dispute in Salamis, one elderly man remembered the talk of a teacher, a Galilean Rabbi. Some said he was our Messiah but one who came and went unrecognized save for a few because the people looked for him in one place and he came in another. The elder remembered hearing of a hermit living near my village who was one with that teacher.

"When he described the hermit as a 'half-man' — excuse me father, those were his words — I realized he was talking of you. Forgive me father for my boastfulness, but I couldn't keep from announcing it was my village they were talking of, and that I served you as a boy, and that I knew how to find you. I was proud of the impression I made. When they asked if I would guide Simon to speak to you, I agreed. I know now I should have asked permission first. I see you are disturbed and I am sorry. Please do not be angry with me."

Aaron's words gentled the atmosphere. After a moment, I spoke to them both: "I am not happy with this disturbance. My life has been tranquil for many years and I have not thought of these things that so agitate you. But Simon is right: my Master did not live in a cave. Nor did I when I lived in his time and with him. Leave now and come tomorrow. We will talk more then until I have no more to tell you. But I warn you, this is a waste of time. My Master is with me often but never in the flesh, and who else would he come back to if not to me?"

The echo of their footsteps down the mountainside faded. But the blanket of silence that fell in its place provided no comfort as it became the background and shocking contrast to the destruction of my tranquillity. Emotions flooded my being that I had thought were burnt to ashes in the fires of my long hermitage. How delicate was the stillness of my mind, a silence so long nurtured, so long taken for granted, now drowned in the thoughts of the world, a world I had believed had been successfully discarded. How fragile, Oh Lord, is your peace!

I noticed the bowl of food left by Aaron, but I had no thought of eating. I picked it up and brought it over to my little stream, washed out the bowl, and took a taste of water. I would do any-

thing to divert my thoughts, but I soon found that was not possible. As thoughts of Master, Sara, Jacob, and Joseph waxed and
waned, I could not free my thinking from the idea of my Master as
king. When Simon mentioned it my response was the habitual
denial our sect ingrained in me at the time of his ministry.

Chief among the deniers was Master himself. Nevertheless, he
was often called such by the poor villagers of Palestine, so desperate were they for deliverance, and we often found it difficult to
resist that designation. We knew its dangers and our fears were not
unfounded.

As the afternoon ebbed, I made ready to resume my normal
routine. The preliminary activities, fixed by so many similar uncountable days were largely automatic and they were now serving
a calming purpose. I retreated to my accustomed place and collected myself as Master had taught, and as I did so my mind moved
to the thought of his instructions. I closed my eyes expecting to
enter that holy interior silence grown so familiar and so constant a
presence in my life, when a most extraordinary event took place.

As I felt the familiar, intimate core of serenity emerge out of
the dark clouds of the day's unusual activity, a vision entered my
consciousness that overwhelmed my heart, my mind, and my soul,
such that I lost all sense of time and place.

I found myself looking at the highest of mountains in a place
far distant. But the "I" was more a point of awareness than a being
with form or substance. In this I sensed an ultimate personal freedom with but one flaw: the presence of the mountain. It was, I
thought, the final obstacle to a completeness the nature of which I
could not know but just sensing it stirred a deeply hidden feeling
of joy.

These thoughts required but a fleeting instant to pass through
my mind and my attention remained fixed on the sight that inspired them. It took a moment for me to note the movement of
the topmost peak of the mountain. So slowly did it begin to fall
that it was well underway before I realized what was happening.
Then the next layer began to crumble and I knew the mountain

was disintegrating before my eyes. As each level followed the one just above, it smashed and dislodged the face of the mountainside creating a monstrous landslide.

A river of stone, large rocks and boulders formed and began to follow a dry gully that I saw was going to pass directly below me. It appeared at first as a slowly moving stream of molten sludge until the leading segment of it came closer to me. As it did so I saw each stone as a distinct unit with its own size, shape and quality. I heard no sound and I felt no fear as I watched this mountain come down piece by piece, then flow past me and disappear into a far off veiled ocean.

Vaguely, out of a deep void, I felt more than heard Master's words: "We have each accumulated many mountains of sin, Jonathan, but there is infinite forgiveness for them if only we reach for it." It was then I felt the last tenuous strand dissolve connecting this life to the things of the world.

As the mountain tumbled I saw a vast, luminous world behind it. Its brightness lit the entire cosmos and I saw revealed the nature of God's world as God must see it. Without knowing how or when I once again felt myself as substance, and I began to expand outward, in almost a bursting, as my body strove to fill all of space.

And I perceived once again that sensation of absolute peace, well-being and security that I had known those countless years ago when Master first showed me the way into the Kingdom. In time, the mountain became a plain and the river of stone ceased its flow. But the blissful effects remained as I slowly regained my normal state of awareness.

I opened my eyes and saw a new day was at hand. But not only the day was new. I saw the world with new eyes; I heard it with new ears; indeed, its very odor was transformed. I looked to my morning needs, such as they were, and settled myself in the comforting sun, still enthralled by the night's events. Deep inside, I knew they had a connection to Simon's presence and his mission, but I could not fathom the reasons for it. I felt a curious anticipation for his return, one so unlike my usual antagonism toward strangers.

It was midmorning when I heard the gravelly sound of approaching footsteps. Simon came into view, alone, carrying a small bowl. I was set back in the now shadowy section of the cave's opening and he could not make me out easily until his eyes adjusted to the light. He did not call out, but waited until he could discern my form and then he addressed me without preamble.

"Father, I was sent with some dried fruit. Aaron was not permitted to come. It was with reluctance that the village leaders agreed to this new visit. They were upset at your reaction to our presence here yesterday. They are solicitous of your well being and desire for privacy. Were it not for the persuasion of some who recognized the importance of what you can tell us, I would not be here."

He fixed his gaze directly at me, his authoritative demeanor was somewhat contradictory to his awkward and indirect apology. The more I contemplated him, the more I found him agreeable. As I did not respond, he continued.

"These people also, father, when they learned of the new preaching, what this new evangelist is saying about salvation, see a link with your arrival here and the story of those fateful days that are in contention. They remember the stories told when you first were brought here. You were one of those with the Galilean whose life and fate they now dispute. It was said that his servant, Joseph, taught some in this village of the teaching of your Master and it was they who agreed to shelter you at Joseph's request.

"They spoke also of a woman, one whom the priests claimed was a sorceress, an abomination, who was the source of corruption of this Jeshua, proving, to them at least, he was not the awaited One. She was captured by the Temple authorities, given to the Romans who planned to send her to Rome for display. Somehow, the story goes, she disappeared with her Roman escort on the way and was never heard from again. Can you help us find the truth of these stories, father? Do you not see their importance?"

As he spoke, the thoughts and images of those times pushed into my mind and now at last what Simon was saying had a peculiar resonance and I recognized the skeletal outline of lifetimes in the past. Vague impressions surfaced of the last days of the people who gave purpose and value to my life and to the times in which they had lived. Are those meaningful and substantial lives now to be reduced to myth and conjecture? Are these stories, indeed, of my Master, Joseph and Sara and Jacob? What is it they are saying of them?

"Simon, I need to know what is being said about these matters. But I must tell you I feel differently now than I did yesterday about your visit. You make me see an importance about these questions I did not see before. I feel a need now to tell you of my knowledge of these events, of my Master and the others. But tell me, what is this new preacher saying of those times now?"

"First," Simon began, "he fixed the time of these events as the time when Herod Antipas, the Tetrarch, ruled Galilee. This is remembered by the people as the time you came here, although the new missionary has indicated no knowledge of you. But strangely, he talked less of the teaching of the Galilean than that of the evangelist, Paul, who came long after your time and the events we speak of. It was Paul who wrote and preached essentially, if not in exact words, as follows: 'All beings come from one God, the Father, who gave us Christ Jesus to die for our sins. These sins were buried with Him and remained buried after He, Himself was raised from the grave in pure spirit.'

"Moreover," Simon continued, "it was to Paul that Jesus entrusted the mission to the Gentiles, and to those Jews who would heed his voice. That he, Paul, would bring the 'Good News' of salvation. Paul's vision and leadership would prepare, in Christ Jesus' name, circumcised and Gentile alike for final redemption at the time of return, a time Paul assures is imminent. That, father, is the core of this new doctrine."

"I must tell you, Simon," I replied, "I hear echoes in your words of the times in which I lived and of my people. But abroad in our land then, as now I am sure, knowing our people as I do, there were many preachers and who could know them all? Could that woman of whom they speak, the 'corrupter' of Master, be the Sara who nourished and saved me? If that is what is said of her there is corruption in this but it is not hers.

"Moreover, it was my Master's presence among us and what he brought into the world by this presence that left it a different world. He spoke, true, and taught with words, true, and those words are still a power in the world, but unless they lead to finding within ourselves the Kingdom he spoke of, they are empty and useless. I am beginning to sense now, Simon, why you have come to me for I feel it is time for the times of my Master to be told. This is the final purpose of my life though I may have forgotten it in the long span of years."

"Thank you father, I know too this is my purpose. We have closer ties than you think. Let me now tell you more of the teaching now being preached. It adds to the 'Paulist doctrine,' if I may call it such. It makes of Paul's Jesus a man of flesh and blood rather than a spirit, born of a woman called Mary, a man who had a father and siblings. It was said he was a poor working man who became a learned Rabbi and led a multitude of Jews. He healed the sick, worked miracles and preached the establishment of a new Kingdom, a Kingdom of God. He was persecuted and crucified, then raised from the dead.

"It was when the elders heard this later message they thought of you. For they now remembered the circumstances of your exile, that you were present at those tumultuous times and were a follower of this Jesus though they did not know him as that. If this is the case, father, only you can sort out the truth of these teachings and prevent a calamity from overtaking . . . "

"But, alas, I cannot, Simon," I interrupted gently, and I let these words fade to allow their import to reach full measure. "I was brought out of that country before Master's disappearance and I heard of no death, let alone a physical return. It was through Sara's husband Jacob we have the strange tale of Master's final hours, and how Jacob, himself, was caught up in the frenzy of those times, hauled before the Temple council and charged with serious crimes. He escaped execution only because, at the end, he accepted and defended Master, though resisting him for so many years. Jacob's story also must be told.

"I know this because some time after I was brought here, a servant arrived with these last messages from my country. Through Jacob's effort, this messenger said, Sara found earthly and spiritual protection with a remote conclave of our sect. And it was this same messenger also who brought me the last words from Master: 'Tell Jonathan, bide his time.' I treasure those words but waited all these years to understand them."

Is this the time for which I wait? That thought struck my heart like a clapper calling God. The question itself was its own answer and I now looked at Simon with new eyes; perhaps he feels himself the inquirer of those days, but for me he became the new herald bringing me Master's last message; "Now is the time."

I was now filled with the joy of anticipation: My time was drawing to a close and my final healing was at hand. Whatever hostility or resentment I felt toward Simon disappeared. I realized with him a common purpose to enshrine Master's teaching, his life, and his being, into the bodies and souls of this new generation thus sending it down to the ages to come. I continued my discourse, trying to cover my new understanding, thinking not to divert Simon from his mission while the way to accomplish my own unfolded as I knew it would, though I could not then know how.

"So you see, Simon, whatever I say about Master's last days I cannot say as a witness. Therefore, anything can be preached without contradiction. You are a thinking person, Simon, you know that in these matters people believe what they will. But I find I now need to know more. When this strange Jew came into the city how was he greeted? How did he get the attention of the people?"

"When it became known he was in Salamis," Simon began, "a number of members of the congregation who, as I mentioned yesterday, kept alive the memory of the earlier teaching, asked that he be permitted to lead services and preach the new message. The synagogue's leaders condemned the teaching as blasphemy and angrily refused permission. The disaffected Jews then decided to find another place in another quarter of the city where this word could be heard.

"I speculate now, father, but I believe the leaders of this faction knew they would be denied permission to use the synagogue. For when the other meeting was held, not only were many of the Jews from the congregation present, but their numbers had increased because of the noise of the dispute. But also many Gentiles came who, it soon became clear, had also been in contact with this teaching and nursed it for those many years.

"The result of the meeting, father, was a new community: Jews who accepted the validity of this new preacher and Gentiles who accepted salvation by the Jewish God through this same instrument. They are now being called "Christians" by Jew and Gentile alike as a form of the Greek word, "Christ," or the anointed one. I hear there are like communities throughout the Empire."

I listened intently to what Simon was saying. And it was the word "Christian" that now reverberated in my heart. That time comes back to me when I first heard it expressed. Jacob's servant, Tomas! Ah yes, "Tomas the Christian" he was called in the Eastern country where he and Jacob found themselves after Tomas fell under Master's glance and became Master's voice in that land. Tomas himself told us of this when he came to us at Jacob's farm.

"You know Simon, our people have been waiting for and planning on the coming of this 'special' one for many centuries. In all this expectation there have been many descriptions of him, many forms, many deeds, but never had he been one for other than our own people. Some believed only a violent, cataclysmic act led by a divine leader would establish God's Kingdom. Others thought his simple arrival would signal a world renewal, the end of this earthly trial and the realization of the glory of the Garden. I know I have been cloistered here for many years, but I do not think I would have missed either occurrence."

"You say that, father, but you could have easily missed both. While safely sheltered in your 'cloister', as you call it, the world you were once part of disappeared through catastrophic upheaval. The Temple was destroyed, the country also, and its people strewed to the ends of the earth. While you were busy counting the days, madmen ruled the Empire, visiting upon your countrymen horrors so terrible that even Romans cried out in fear. Did your Master and his teaching come and go, father, as if he had never been here? You cannot want that, you say his times must be told us, but only you can do that."

Only now did I begin to see a new level in Simon's character, the new purpose in his visit. I detected a subtle shading of expression that caught my notice, but which for the moment remained in the back of my mind. I was more interested in what relationship his quest had with my Master and I felt closer to that end. Is this Christian Jesus truly Jeshua of Galilee, my Master? I found myself entering into Simon's thinking, sensing we were reaching new levels of understanding as I was beginning to think of things so long forgotten.

I felt my desire and need for solitude and privacy diminish and a new interest in this social intercourse arise. Now the nagging question in the back of my mind came to the fore as I detected new dimensions in Simon that I could not express. He had revealed a strong, authoritative manner, not the apparent supplicant or simple agent by which he initially introduced himself.

"Who are you really, Simon? You do not talk like a man confused by these questions, and what do you know of my Master? You talk of him as if you know something of him. Were you really sent by the people of Salamis? I do not doubt the boy, Aaron, but you are not telling me the complete story of yourself. Simon, you are not honest with me."

"You are right, father, but be sure I have no intention of deceiving you. What I have said about the disputes in Salamis and elsewhere are accurate. There are a number of evangelists preaching the 'Christian' doctrine as I have outlined it for you. They are a growing sect and tend to be fanatical in their beliefs. They had originally been centered in Judea, and after the death of their Master they dispersed throughout the Empire. They insist the teaching of Paul is the true teaching of Jesus. But I know now, from the little you have said, that their Christian Jesus is the one you followed, and, I must now tell you, my Master as well."

I could not credit my ears with what I was hearing. Again, Simon had lapsed into the Greek tongue, one he used more easily when he would speak with passion, but I almost did not realize that because of the import of his words.

"Simon, how can this be? You do not know the fate of my Master, and you do not know the fate of either Jesus if, indeed, there were two."

"This is what I came to find out, father, and this is the reason I was sent to you. Although the people of Salamis, with the help of Aaron, made this last leg of my journey easier, their needs and interests are not central to my mission.

"I come from a place in the upper reaches of the Egyptian desert where I was brought as a small boy and raised in a community of believers who embraced a hidden teaching that permits a personal spiritual union with our Lord. The founders of this community came here as a refuge from the persecution of the early Greek occupiers of our Holy Land, the Selucids, who would not permit our studies and practices. Later, after they themselves were expelled by victorious Jewish fighters, these new Jewish rulers maintained our exile. I am sure you remember well this story, how the new priesthood would not countenance our peoples' return. They, too, felt a danger from these beliefs.

"In your time and well before mine, an exile from the Temple trials which were searching out blasphemers, your Jacob it must have been, came to our village speaking of a Galilean, his Master, as a person thoroughly learned in these mysteries. Jeshua, Jacob told them, is one who spent many years in the Eastern countries bringing together the simple truths contained in all sacred teachings and making these available to those prepared to accept them.

"Jacob came to live out his life in our commune, forbidden to return to Palestine, and content to bring us the story of the one who became his Master."

As I listened to Simon I felt transported to another time and place. My mind again flooded with images of those I loved and who loved and succored me. I was compelled to interrupt, so overwhelmed was I with these unaccustomed emotions.

"Wait Simon," I blurted out, now also speaking in the Greek tongue to more closely identify with him. "You are like my past come alive. Are you Jacob returned? It is as if my Sara is once again explaining his comings and goings. Do you know, too, of Master's teachings?"

"This, father, is the core of my mission and, thankfully, I now know it will be successful. You are without a doubt the person of whom it was said lived in Master's time, who knew him and heard him speak. The one of whom Jacob spoke, yes Jacob spoke of you and others when he came to us, but forgive me if I was not so forthcoming earlier. I had to be sure.

"We must resolve the doubts the new Christian teaching is raising in our midst. It denounces the traditional practices and knowledge as heresy and insists our understanding of Master must be on their terms. For this reason we have scribes collecting the stories of Master's teachings and preparing a written record. I am one of many sent out to find those who can provide information and knowledge before it is gone. You can put to rest these doubts and provide an authentic version of his life and teaching."

During this conversation Simon would sit close to me looking directly into my eyes with an authority that could not be denied. Other times, he strode back and forth almost as if talking to himself. For my part I remained seated and still. I did not know how to answer him. To gain some time for thought I arose and went to refresh myself at my small stream. Returning to my place I noticed a quizzical expression on his face.

"Where is your staff, father? Forgive me, but yesterday you could hardly walk. Today you seem a person much, much younger."

Immediately my mind went to the experience of my morning awakening: my sense of the world's newness and the lifting of the burden of age. What could I tell Simon of this? I saw him now as a brother in spirit but I was not ready to bring out the sacred events of the previous night.

"Your presence brings me new life, Simon," I replied, trying to dismiss the question lightly. "I have listened carefully to what you have been saying and I am prepared to help you. The life and teachings of my Master — and on the face of it, your Master also — plumbed depths that few if any of us were able to explore completely. True, when I hear the stories of his rising from the dead, visiting with his disciples, promising another return, I do not associate that with the man I knew. And I know he truly was a man. For were he not a man, of what use would he be to men?

"But now, with thought, I realize my knowledge of Master is limited by my own limitations. In matters of this nature it would be unwise for any to insist that only they have the complete truth. Let us learn more about each other, and then we shall see if a greater truth can emerge."

I felt a new energy as I again grasped control of the discourse. Since the dissolution of the "mountain" the previous night my detachment from the world became more complete. But strangely, despite that reality, decades of living an interior, isolated life were rapidly coming to an end. As I began to again move outward into the world I realized no passage of time. It seemed like yesterday that I thanked my escort for safely bringing me to this place of shelter.

Simon made arrangements to return to Salamis. He decided to tell the people there I could be of no help to them in their dispute with each other, that I could neither authenticate nor disprove the new Christian teaching. This he felt — and I agreed hopefully — would convince them to leave me in peace. More important, however, was the secret message he planned to send to his people: he had found a true source for the life and teaching of the Messenger they hewed to and he would stay until it is committed to memory and parchment.

To this end, Simon had already asked Aaron if he would come each day until he returned. He, Aaron, was skilled in writing in the common tongue and in the Greek and he would be pleased to record my thoughts. These were skills he learned perforce as a consequence of his twisted leg. I found this prospect agreeable; Aaron was a comfort to me.

But there would be no need to burden him with the chore of parchment and ink. I possessed powers, seldom used but yet intact, to enable Aaron to find directly the record of my life and thus the account of the others. That night, as I prepared for the evening's rest, my mind returned to the beginning days in a bizarre mixture of time and place. I watched then as it slowly settled into an orderly and comprehensive pattern, dreamlike, more a vision than a fantasy. I saw myself looking into an infinite mysterious void and watched a head emerge from it, with two faces back to back, one young and one aged. As the old dissolved slowly and the youth took on a greater clarity, I knew I was going back to my beginnings.

GALILEE

As sleep departed I was left with a momentary discomfit, a sense of leaving something behind and it flashed through my mind that I was awakening to an earlier time. But I knew I was seeing that time through ancient eyes and I wondered as I slipped back into its reality what those eyes would reveal. As I wondered I saw and I heard and lived it as a boy again.

The early morning sounds of our Galilean village brought me out of my slumber. I kept my eyes closed pulling the cover over my half-clothed body. I savored this morning time before daylight broke, for at these times I didn't need my body, that hated body, broken and grotesque. But more important, this was the day Master was coming, and finally I would get to see him and hear him as for so long I have been hearing about him.

It was a miracle I was able to sleep last night, so excited was I as the day approached. Because of our "family" we knew earlier than the others of our village of his coming, and my excitement mounted as news of his presence in nearby villages became known.

I have always known that those that sheltered me had known Master in his boyhood and youth. I would hear soft talk of him over the years when Sara and Jacob and others of their sect would speak of their teachings. Then one or another would recall his presence with a wonder that increased in the telling. In those times, talkative Sara would become quiet and taciturn Jacob would hold the listeners with his tales.

Sara had grown up with Master in her ancestral village — he coming to live there late in his boyhood because of his father's misfortunes. Jacob found him as Master's awakening reached a new level and Jacob's life was destined thereafter to be directed

into pathways beyond his control, often against his desires. It was
Jacob who last saw Master as he, Master, disappeared into the
eastern land from which he now returns.

We knew of his return only recently. The pious Joseph came
here from his dry desert community in which he had lived his
austere life in the company of holy fathers. He came seeking Jacob
and Sara and his message to them was a simple one: "Jeshua has
returned, he greets you both with love. For now, as for the past
many months," Joseph explained, "Jeshua remains at our community where he has shelter and where he, as he says, finds entrance
once more into the lives of his people."

That news came to them like a lightning bolt. I saw a flash of
joy light Sara's face upon hearing it and I thought then he had
never been far from her thoughts. Jacob seemed no less pleased
but his response was tempered with questions.

"You both knew," Joseph continued, "that for many years he
was in Eastern lands living in a seclusion he could not find here.
He has now returned and brought back to us a new understanding
of the hidden wisdom in our own ancient books. He speaks very
little of his days here in Galilee or his family. But he knew of your
new home and that you continued to make your presence felt to
our community and to teach and practice the new covenant. He
asks you now to accept and trust my guidance into a more complete instruction in his name until the time he can again meet
with you. This new teaching, he tells us, fulfills the promise of the
old."

Answering Jacob's unasked questions, Joseph went on, "You
must realize Jeshua is no longer the person you knew. I say this
with confidence although I did not know him then myself. I suspect you recognized a special quality about him when you knew
him as a boy and youth, but what you may have seen then was
only the first sprouting of a seed that has now become a mighty
tree."

Why I was watching Sara and not Joseph as he was talking, I
do not know. But when he mentioned Master's boyhood and youth,

an unusual expression crossed Sara's face, an expression impossible to decipher. Its explanation awaited another time, but the event stayed deep in my memory.

Joseph's softened voice sharpened our attention. "I first saw him entering our enclave from the surrounding hills where he had spent some solitary time before coming to us. We do not yet know the circumstances of his return to our country. I spied him first and he appeared to me as a returning prophet. His presence was magical. Although I am learned in the law, and despite my youth considered a spiritual elder by our community, I felt compelled to prostrate myself before him. I knew instantly this was the teacher I was seeking.

"He raised me up," Joseph said, now hardly able to contain himself, "and he said, 'Joseph, come with me.' I had nothing to leave behind, but I knew had I everything I would not have looked back."

But Joseph was asked to give up more than he thought. Accepting Master's teachings meant entering another path, embarking on a mission different than the one to which he had up to then given his life. His special work had been to seek out the widespread but loosely connected families and groups and communities that held to the traditional beliefs of our sect. Although there were small circles in the cities that needed nurturing, it was in the countryside, among the landless workers and marginal farmers, where the hunger for a return to the protection of Mosaic social law was most real. Like few others of his time, he knew the Jewish world of Palestine and Egypt as well.

But now his new Master had another message and teaching. It was one that was directed less to the mind than to the heart, and one that permitted access to a hidden transforming kingdom that fulfilled and completed the teaching of the holy books. It is a personal salvation Master taught that is the basis for the creation of a just society. Without it nothing will come of their great plans, their detailed organization, their fasting and deprivation, nor will God send them a fiery instrument on His behalf to smite the enemy. But with this teaching, all things will be possible.

This message caused much consternation in the community with calls for expulsion and shunning from the brotherhood. Joseph remained resolute. Many others, too, accepted the purification and initiation rites offered by this new messenger who, some whispered, was indeed the awaited one. Joseph, with a few others who were deemed able, received special instruction enabling them to preach and minister in Master's name. Thus Joseph first came to Sara and Jacob bringing Master's message, though for Jacob, years of confusion had to pass before understanding arose.

It was from that time Joseph made his home with us, although he was often away. Since Joseph's first appearance I waited and now my patience was to be rewarded. Joseph did his work well guiding Master to the people; too well, as it turned out, for a people overripe for any promise of relief from their double oppressors: the Roman overlords on the one hand and the Temple authorities on the other.

Though his mission, in the beginning, was primarily intended for those few of the pious that already were seeking it, it could not be contained. His words were the simple teaching of Moses that God's favor is as close to us as our hearts, that His kingdom is found within ourselves. But there were preachers aplenty in those troubled times and words began to lose their power.

At first Joseph guided Master throughout the land seeking those of their sect for his message. But his presence alone caught the attention of a multitude wherever he went and before he finally cloistered himself in retreat with his chosen disciples, his eyes blessed every part of this land. And in time people would claim just this gaze on them would bring solace and the stories of healing and miracles would follow as the wake of a boat.

People called him different things but in our group we knew him then as Jeshua though it was Jacob's habit to speak of him as the "Rabbi." The "others," as the general Jewish Palestinian population was called by us, talked of him as a healer or miracle man. And in the city, that is, in Sepphoris or Jerusalem, people spoke of him with disdain as a "magician" though no one could say what magic he performed. It was soon clear, however, that it was his message, and his special presence that led us to call him Master.

Because of the closeness of Joseph and the understanding of Sara and Jacob, I was well aware of the nature of Master's words. Joseph would repeat over and over the refrain: "Personal salvation, finding the kingdom within, that is the foundation for a more orderly world."

But this message entered the consciousness of the larger population on another level, and in the context of the understanding of the people it became a teaching of social liberation, of healing, of miracles, and because of the power of Master's presence he was seen as divinity in flesh. The beauty of the message was so seductive, that lost to many was that there existed a method of its achievement. The habit of looking outward was too deeply ingrained to be easily overcome.

I must confess I too was carried away by this notion and, despite cautionary suggestions from Sara, I could not give up the hope of physical healing from Master. For good reason, it was not his words that interested me but the stories of his healing. I had all the "teaching" I needed, but the healing, ah yes, the healing caught my attention. No one had more need of healing than I.

It had been eight years since the occupiers rode so imperiously through the narrow, winding streets of our village. Lost they must have been, because it was so foolhardy for the hated troops to enter the labyrinthine Galilean villages. Although it had been many years from the time they last encountered physical resistance from Jew or Gentile, the reputation of Galilean volatility put them on more than a normal military alert.

It happened as my mother and I were walking home from the market. Just as we heard the bizarre commotion of horses in our neighborhood, the troop turned the corner into our tiny street. There was room enough for a single file, but as they tried to form one we were caught by the trailing horse as it was held back by its rider. We squeezed against the wall as tightly as possible, breath held, motionless, with mother holding my little eight year old hand in hers. But still there was not room enough.

The hindquarters of a trailing horse lurched, crushing my mother against the wall and somehow throwing me forward into a tiny opening under the door sill of a nearby house. I was told later she died instantly and I was left lying like a discarded rag, legs broken, back twisted, and thought dead.

I was not dead, but I was surely broken. My back was deformed so as to grow outward — I never grew but a few inches taller — with an ever enlarging hump between my shoulders. My legs learned to carry me, not straight but with a side to side motion and remained spindly and crooked. Nothing grew normally thereafter but my undamaged head. Large, fully formed, it only exaggerated the freakish nature of my body. But thank God for the head; the body was surely useless for man's labor.

And thank the Lord, too, for the childless family, not born to our village, who took my broken and useless body under their care and added me to their strange household. In reality, my childhood ended that day and my life never again concerned itself with childish things.

If not for Sara I would have been more blessed to have joined the poor woman who bore me. For one year, no less, she was the center and sustainer of my life, ministering to my body and soul. I could not have been more carefully caressed and tended to even in the womb of my natural mother. The slightest motion meant terrible pain but the balm of costly herbs, oil and wine was always ready to soothe me.

Every day each crevice and fold of my body was cleansed. She brought from Jerusalem her former tutor and friend, Alexander, a Jewish physician despite his foreign name, who was trained in the Greek ways, to set and bind the broken ribs and arm.

More than that he could not do. The shattered legs were in an impossible condition and his fear was that to try to straighten them further could cause unknown and dangerous consequences. They spoke quietly — I remembered later, more like equals than supplicant and benefactor — over the small cradle-like bed that Sara had had Jacob make for me:

"You know what to do," the physician said, "your hands are better than mine. I cannot believe he will ever walk, but his upper body will heal. That he is alive is itself a miracle."

"No miracle," Sara replied. "There are signs some only know as signs, but their reading simply awaits the learning of their language. I know in my heart Jonathan was sent to me to care for and in this caring I do God's will."

"But is Jacob of this mind, Sara?" the doctor asked. "First there was Anna, with her crooked back and misshapen face . . . "

"Don't speak of Anna as a burden, Alexander, you know better than that." The interruption was sharp and the doctor knew he had overstepped a boundary. "She was sent into my care by Jeshua, as you well remember because you were called to my father's house when Jacob himself brought her to me. You know the story of her survival as well as I do, how Jacob was charged directly by Jeshua to bring her to me.

"And don't mention Ruth. It is not my doing that this house fills with these castoff children. Can you of all people ask me to let them die? I know what is said about you in Jerusalem. You minister to the most despised and even here I hear the talk that other patrons are dropping away from you because of that. Poor Ruth who was brought to me by desert nomads who found her near death after she was left in the Samaritan wilderness. They found she could not hear nor talk so they had no use for her. For me it is an omen that they simply did not leave her to her fate as is the usual case. True, she can neither hear nor talk, but a dumb creature she is not. You know how able she came to be in this household."

Contrite, Alexander tried to change the course and tone of the discussion. "This boy may prove to be different, damaged as he is. I confess, Sara, I do not wonder at your compassion, but I marvel at your strength of will. I think at times heaven itself would obey it. My concern is Jacob. His steadfastness is not yours. The expense is the least of it though not little, but this boy will also require all your time. I'm not sure . . . "

"Don't worry, Alexander, my friend," Sara said with her characteristic chuckle, signaling a softening of her mood. "Jacob has never thwarted me in these matters. In more than name he is a patriarch everywhere in our village, but not inside this house. Ah well," she sighed, speaking more to herself than to him, "you know his heart better than I, you both share that same failing, you seek, you see, but then you close your eyes to the light."

Despite my pain and discomfort, I was surprised at the physician's laughter and the informality into which they lapsed, an informality, I learned later, which was born from long acquaintance. But a more somber mood returned as Alexander began to take his leave.

"You must watch yourselves more carefully," he told Sara, "there is talk beginning about your sect. You talk too openly about your disdain for the authorities. Restoring the ancient laws is one thing but when it means giving up property, forgiving debts, freeing slaves, caring for the poor — we fought wars over these things — people get upset."

"But you should know more than the rest," Sara replied, "living the life in Law will not come from violence and hatred. First the people must recover the way and the old teaching."

With an expression of resignation, refusing to start a timeworn, never resolved dialogue, Alexander took up his meager bag. He could not further tarry to meet again with Jacob with whom he had spent the previous evening. He was planning to return to Jerusalem with a local group going to market in the city. He faced a three-day trek to the south; although in a reasonably protected area, the trip was much too dangerous for a single traveler.

"I'll be back in six weeks unless you need me earlier," he told Sara. "You and Jacob, stay well."

When he left, Sara turned her attention to me.

"He is one with us in spirit," she told me, "though he keeps his formal distance."

She spoke to me as it is her nature to speak to everyone. She made no concession to age or status and I would have expected her to address the High Priest himself in that same confident, authoritative manner. As the next several years unfolded and I came to understand more of the lessons she taught me, I learned from her very being the greater lesson: this poor Jewish villager had realized within herself, and accepted without thought or question, the universal human expression of divinity.

Jacob came in shortly after Alexander left and asked what he told her.

"His upper body is broken," Sara said, "but the ribs and arm will heal although they will be painful for a while. He doesn't think the boy will ever walk but how much worse it is he can't tell now."

"He's crippled then," said Jacob. "How can you care for him?" His voice revealed the unsaid thought. "Besides, his mother's sister . . . "

"Sister-in-law . . . " interrupted Sara.

"Sister-in-law then. She looked in on him. She said she'd take him if need be."

"She has four children," Sara replied quickly, "if he goes into that house he'll die."

Before Jacob could reply, Sara grabbed his arm and pulled him over to where I lay. Taking my chin in hand she moved my head so I looked directly into Jacob's face. "Look at him Jacob, look into his face, into his eyes, and tell me to send him away."

I never knew what Jacob thought in that long instant of contact. But I later came to know Sara let her husband make a decision he already knew was made; my fate was decided by her will. Jacob never said another word against my presence. Nor did he grumble when Sara took another servant girl from the village to help Anna and Ruth with the household while she took care of me.

Our house was located on the edge of a small, unwalled village of about 200 homes. Perhaps half the village was Jews. The Gentile population was a mix of Samaritans, settled Arabs, and Peraeans from our neighboring country to the east. No matter, it was all ruled by Antipas and taxed equally by the Romans and the Temple.

Jacob's house was somewhat larger than most in the area. Built under his direction, out of the mud bricks common to the surrounding land, it sprawled into a three room, half-rectangular shaped construction with an elongated center room. Soon, Jacob planned, he would add rooms to complete the rectangle forming a large interior courtyard. Inside, walls divided it such so there were two private end rooms separated from the long center room that contained the general living area.

It was in this center room that the life of the household took place. The back wall of the long room, on its other side, served as the back wall of a long, shed-like structure that sheltered their few goats, Jacob's donkey and those sheep culled from the flock for their especially clear fleece. Jacob built the house and it sat on land given to them upon their marriage, but in truth, it was possessed and ruled over by Sara.

As in the other houses, cooking was done over a fire built in the earth floor. The fuel was more charcoal and dried brush and not the dried dung used elsewhere, which was forbidden for Jews to handle. Bread was made every day, and one of Sara's few indulgences was the use of ground flours that Jacob would bring home from his marketing. This was much to the delight of the servant girls who were relieved of the grinding chores common in other homes.

There was, nevertheless, always enough work to fill the day. Cloth was woven from material at hand in our Galilean countryside. Flax from Jacob's field yielded fiber for linen and his sheep and goats provided wool and goat's hair for our plain daily clothing. Foodstuffs were dried and otherwise stored in the many jars Sara carefully collected. Beans, lentils, peas and other seasonal vegetables joined with dried fruits to provide our two simple but ample daily meals. And of course the olive, which, next to bread, was the staple of our lives. Its oil entered all our food and gave us our light in the dark of the night.

Although not wealthy by city measure, Sara and Jacob lived better than most of the surrounding villagers, and functioned, as I learned in time, as leaders and teachers to many Jewish families.

But they were also looked to by the other villagers as leaders and intermediaries for their business with Jerusalem. They were truly a treasure to the village. Sara, with her learning and native wisdom, her self-assurance and competence, soon became the one looked to for guidance and support by all the women of the village. She succored all, Jew and Gentile alike.

Jacob could not hide his formal education even had he a mind to. But his Roman citizenship, so rare in a village farmer, and his contacts in nearby Sepphoris and more distant Jerusalem, made him a figure of suspicion. His open sympathies with Sara's sect and her attempts to instruct the Jewish women in its teachings brought both of them to the attention of Temple secret agents who were part of all village life. And on the other side, the Galilean zealots and Jewish patriots agitating for deliverance from Rome cast a wary eye on him for his hellenized manner, thinking him an instrument of the Temple collaborators.

In other ways as well they were odd. Now married for many years, they had no children. Some thought it was God's punishment for evil ways and for proof they looked at Anna and Ruth as the expression of the evil one taking shelter with her. Others, more favorably, thought they were as the pious ones and did not live as man and wife as God ordered the less holy. In fact, they suffered for many years obeying scriptural demands and instructions for procreation. Finally, Sara agreed to seek Alexander's advice and he sent her to a woman healer he trusted who was expert in these matters. She found no obstacle in Sara to prevent conception or birth and there the matter rested.

I would see the household awaken at dawn from my raised bed on a small platform just outside Sara's room. She would be first up to see to the servants who brought their water-filled containers from the well and replenished the water jars in the house. The cooking fire would be started to heat water for my washing as Sara started the women about their duties. Then, before turning her attention to me, she saw to Jacob's needs as he started for his work.

In this way, my new life began. In the very early days I could not move. A deep breath would cause pain in my side and back. Sara would first wash the night waste from me. Then she would most gently rub a mixture of herbs and oil over the exposed parts of my body. I could not feel when she moved my legs — the movements I learned later were of the smallest possible increments — but I knew when she would massage, nay caress, them as I came to love the euphoria, the almost imperceptible pressure, her hands would induce.

Alexander returned periodically as he promised seeing to the mechanical needs of bones and sinew. I always felt it was Sara he came to visit since there was little enough he did for me. Indeed, it was God's work, through Sara's miraculous hands that first brought feeling, then movement, then function to my legs. Each independent motion was accompanied by the simultaneous experience of pain and triumph.

But as the days passed, the pain lessened as did the feelings of achievement, replaced now by the consuming purpose of my existence: to strengthen my legs and to walk, however ungainly. At some point, her determination and confidence infused my own being eliminating those twin enemies of success: fear and doubt.

In those first several months I was completely helpless in her hands, those strange hands possessed of a magic I cannot fathom to this day. There would be a localized sense of warmth in the area of her touch and this would slowly seep into all parts of my body. As I fell into a state of quiet bliss, she would begin a humming. This was an eerie sound that swallowed the world; one I never heard her make in another circumstance. I remained awake, but swimming in that sound, seemingly without body and without mind, certainly without care or fear.

Only Sara was permitted to minister to me in that early time, later Anna would help her. I could not be fed, washed, seen uncovered by any other including Jacob. I slept in my small cradle at the end of the large room just outside Sara and Jacob's room. In the morning I was moved by them, bed and all, into her room where my daily needs and her healing activities were privately accomplished. Later, I would again be placed in the large room where I could watch the household's daily activity.

In time, Anna and Ruth became as sisters to me, but the servant girls from the village came and went as Sara's and their needs dictated. Because of this, it was not long before the entire village was aware of the strangeness of my growth. General acceptance and knowledge was never easily tolerated for the two impaired girls but in my case it was even worse; I was looked upon as a freak of nature. Although Jacob's early misgivings in accepting me into the household were of more earthly concerns, he was now faced by those whispers that we sheltered agents of the evil one.

Because of the nature of their beliefs and teaching, Sara and Jacob were not without enemies. Their tradition permitted, if not encouraged, the education of women in the ancient language and teaching of our people. In our country, in those days, many of our people could not read the laws of our fathers given to Moses by God in our own holy language. In order for them not to lose all contact with our tradition, it was decreed that these holy books be translated into the language of the Greek nation whose culture continued to leave its mark long after its physical presence was displaced by the Roman occupier.

But Sara's sect resisted this abasement of our religion and demanded allegiance to the sacred word not less than to the social laws, even above the religious laws so beloved by the Temple leaders. Consequently, both Sara and Jacob stopped work every day in the afternoon to teach the servants. Jacob taught the men where suitable to their work and Sara the household women in the big room she converted to a classroom. There, the language and meaning of the books of Moses were taught. In time, these small groups expanded to include other members of the village, Jacob preparing boys for entrance into Jewish manhood as sons of the law and Sara teaching those few girls whose fathers would encourage, or at least not prohibit, forbidden learning for their daughters.

Those in our village who were uneasy with these efforts were wont to spread tales of evil spirits and sorcery. On a worldly level their concerns were real enough, that their relatively stable position — balanced precariously between the landless poor and the wealthy priests, the large landowners and their lettered retainers — would be threatened by these teachings. And since they were sure their privileged position was a sign of God's blessing, it was clear that condemnation of their status was blasphemy; and proof that the evil one was present in these teachings was to be seen in Sara's household.

In truth, most villagers would have nothing to fear if all the Mosaic Law were implemented tomorrow. It was through Moses that God proclaimed the laws of a just society: both wealth and poverty have their limits. The wealthy, it was written, have but a custodial relationship to God's bounty and the primary responsibility is that the least of the nation's members have a share of it.

But the nation had long fallen away from God's requirements and was now suffering the results of its apostasy. Interest was charged and loans never forgiven, not in the prescribed seven years, or seventy or seven hundred if the truth was to be known. Land was taken from families and never returned, not in the lawful fifty-year jubilee, or a hundred years, or a thousand. The social laws requiring the care and security of all the people were more and more ignored as the landless, the servant, and the slave population were increasingly exploited.

Without obedience to the law, the wealthy were accumulating greater wealth, with a correspondingly growing attachment to it, thus tying themselves into an ever tighter bondage to the demands of the world and its foreign rulers. The poor, in turn, were sinking further into despair and dissolution. The special quality and cohesiveness of the people were being maintained by placing exaggerated emphasis on the rules of authority and the specious argument that it is God's will, and different times, that dictate the present order. Only national and spiritual destruction await this departure from the teaching of Moses.

Time and again the Lawgiver was required to admonish his

people in the desert as he returned from his short absences. Now, once again, his presence was needed, and indeed, a new Moses, a new Messenger, a new Teacher, a new Admonisher, was preparing to return the people to their covenant. It was this disturbing word — seductive to so many, but a foreshadowing threat to so many others — that was being spread in the countless villages and cities of Jewish Palestine.

This was the teaching I received from Sara before Master's return. As she tended the needs of my body she instructed my mind and quieted my soul. It was a disappointment to her, not yet in my awareness, that the body responded only in a limited way to her efforts. Later, I learned she counted this as a personal failure, believing it was the sins of her early life that made her an imperfect conduit for God's unlimited healing energy. In time, we both understood the nature of this prideful and so very human misunderstanding. Although we know better, we often forget, God's will is not for us lesser ones to manipulate.

But what response my body could not make to Sara's love and intelligence was more than balanced by the ability of my mind. It was only enough to hear her words to understand their import, to find their relevance, to have them engraved eternally in an unfailing memory. Day after day in the countless private hours we shared, I absorbed the knowledge of our people and the wisdom of the ages like the earth absorbs new rain at the end of the dry season.

On one level I was still an injured and needy boy with the fears and questions of all boys. But in these philosophical and historical areas I was her equal, discussing and opining, suggesting and speculating, my taking for granted what I knew and she, pleased, amazed, but little perturbed at my uncanny precocity.

"Jonathan," she once said to me, with that slight knowing smile to which I never failed to respond, "I believe you can't be taught anything, only reminded of what you already know. Don't think about it for now, child, it is enough for you to know that I understand."

As days melted into weeks and months, God's healing force,

so powerful in youth, worked its way into my broken bones and torn sinews. It was Anna who first noticed a movement in my leg, and from then feeling and control returned, slowly that day then in a rush in the days ahead. Finally, Sara and Anna were able to have me stand and take that tentative step which signaled the beginning of the end of my absolute dependence on them.

Sara understood the need for care in introducing me to the household. Because of her insistence on shielding me from any close observation, no one else except Anna, neither Jacob nor the village servants always about, had an inkling of the bizarre child I had become. My normal head perched atop of a mostly invisible body filled with that strange combination of ancient wisdom and childish innocence posed an unnerving sight to one unused to it. But surely none, certainly not I, expected what came.

When my more active participation into household functioning could not be put off any longer, Sara gathered Anna, Ruth and the local girl servant into a group in the large room. At her call, I hobbled into their sight, proud of my ever-improving ability, and started to move toward them. As soon as their sight of me registered, I saw Ruth's mouth open in what must have been a forlorn wail, silent as it was, and her hands flew to her face. But worse than that, the village girl shrieked with either laughter or fear, I never knew which, and fled from the house.

It took but a moment for me to realize I was the source of this horrified response. Poor Ruth, who could not flee, turned away from me and burst into tears. But Anna, God's chosen for sure, rushed to me and with her body covered me with her embrace as our tears mingled. "My poor, beautiful Jonathan, I love you, I love you . . . " she sang over and over, "don't fear, don't fear, I love you."

Sara came only an instant later. Kneeling down she cradled both of us in her strong arms. Gradually the sense of shock dissipated and some order returned to my thinking. But a desperate sense of despair grabbed at my heart. In time, I found my place in the lives of these people, but that incident never left me and forecast the future shape of my life.

So when talk of this new healer and prophet began to circulate in our area, I listened with a special interest. When his disciple, Joseph, came to our house and revealed that this Master was the one known and loved by Sara, who left and had now returned, I believed in my heart that deliverance from this burden was now at hand.

I was able to disclose these thoughts to Joseph. He said to me: "Jonathan, Master will be here, in this house, and before he leaves he will minister to your needs. But deliverance takes many forms. It may not be what you expect, but you will not be disappointed. That I promise you."

That was all the promise I needed.

CYPRUS II

Yes, I thought, nothing was lost as those beginning days so long ago faded. The doors of my senses opened and I re-entered the present time and place. Soon after, I heard Aaron's steps as first light broke the early morning sky. Because of his dragging leg, his footsteps were distinct and I knew it was he long before he came into view.

He was burdened with a large inkpot, parchment and a few writing tools. After his greeting he told me the boy whose family was providing me with my food would come as usual and would bring rations for Aaron as well. Although Aaron was clearly enjoying his new status, it came home to me now that my former life was gone. I wondered that I felt no sense of loss. My mood was again one of contentment similar to that of my days of solitude. It brought to mind Master's words: "When asked what is the sign of your Father in you? Say to them: it is movement and repose."

"How is it," I asked Aaron, "that you are skilled in writing and also in the Greek. Your speaking would not give one to believe you are a village boy."

"It is because of the leg, father," he replied. "I am a farmer's son and this work was too difficult for me after my accident. A cartwheel rolled over me and crushed my leg. It is only a miracle, I am told, that I didn't lose it altogether. I was a good boy, father, to be punished so. There was a learned man in our village who led the synagogue. He died only last year. He taught the young men and since I couldn't work he kept me with him during the day. I became very good at writing our common tongue and in reading in our ancient books.

"When he thought he could teach me no more, he suggested

that my parents allow me to go to Salamis to study with scholars there. He knew a family there with whom I could stay. It was there I learned the Greek, which is more readily spoken than the common tongue, and in time I was allowed to teach the children. My Rabbi thinks I can become like him."

"You speak of your talents with satisfaction and pride, Aaron. There is a danger in such pride for it hides the source of this talent, sometimes cutting off access to higher teaching. What would you be doing if your leg had not been crushed?"

Aaron looked at me steadily but with a puzzled expression. I was taken by his poise and his growing confidence in our relationship.

"Why, I would be working with my father, I am sure."

"And then what of your talents, Aaron? I can see you spouting Greek behind the tail of an ox. Sometimes God pulls, sometimes He pushes, but always His will remains unfathomable."

Ignoring my preaching, Aaron brought me back to his mission. "Can you tell me more of your Master, father? This is why Simon asked that I come here. I am ready to write what I hear, but I'm not sure what he wants from us. Would you tell me about Master? How he taught, what he said? I'll write his words as you remember them."

The memories crowded my mind. How he talked? What he said? Does that matter? It was enough to be in his presence without hearing his words. His glance alone would remove fear and doubt. Those of us, once in living contact with him, have his existence imprinted in our hearts, but what of those who know him only by the words out of someone else's mouth?

It appears that if, indeed, he did not survive the grave, he possessed a power that surely did. A power that shows itself in these Christians who now weave such strange tales around his name, and in those like Simon — and now Aaron — who know him in a different way.

"I can tell you this, Aaron," I began, "the first time I saw Master he was huddled with Joseph and Sara in that dark room in

Sara's house, lit only by a fading lamp. I was expecting him the coming day and I slept fitfully that night.

"Toward morning I became aware of faint voices in Joseph's room and I listened for a few moments until I realized Sara and Joseph were together with a third person whom I initially thought was Jacob. This would not have been strange and I normally would have gone back to sleep.

"But this was not a normal morning and I resisted that urge to stay in bed. Quietly I made my way toward the other room and as I approached I sensed that it was not Jacob but a stranger. Could this be Master, I thought. I inched to the open doorway and as I peeked into the room I came face to face with him.

"I knew then, Aaron I had found my Master. To describe his appearance is useless. Not only because it would change over the years, but also because I recollect him now not as a person but as a presence in me bringing to me today the same sense of tranquillity and peace, of oneness with our Father, that overwhelmed me in that first meeting. Needs, desires, concern for my body, all dropped away in that moment of silent communion."

"'Greetings, Jonathan,' he said, 'Sara and Joseph told me of you and I am pleased we meet.'

"Those were his first and only words to me that day. I could not reply. I simply stood there and said nothing and the thousand questions I thought I would ask either fled my mind or were answered by his glance, even now I know not which. A moment passed and Joseph spoke:

"'Master will be here several days, Jonathan. He will speak to the villagers each day, to those who will hear him, and before he leaves he would want some private time with you'.

"Private time? I thought. With me? Without Sara? What could that mean? But nothing mattered then Aaron, I was captured by the moment and in that instant of time there was nothing else and when it passed I was sure my life had already been changed."

At this point Aaron spoke: "Was there a special teaching, father? Simon, too, spoke of this private time when we traveled together. He said for those who truly seek there is a way into the interior life. He said that in his community there are those who know these instructions and teach the people as they become ready.

"When I asked him further about this teaching he told me to be patient. That if who we were going to meet — speaking of you, father — is who he thinks you are then we will be able to show that our path is a correct one; and where the other leads we cannot know. Do you know what Simon means, father?"

"Perhaps, Aaron, but we will talk of that later. With Simon, I ask you to be patient. You are fortunate in finding him. More and more I understand what I originally felt about him; Simon is an old and wise soul. But now let us do what he asked us to do. Do not fret about writing what I say. Put your materials aside, listen and breathe in my words. Trust me Aaron, you will not forget."

As Aaron discarded his writing materials I drew him close to me. I collected my thoughts. Where best to begin but at the beginning?

"It was Master's habit," I began, "to seat himself in Jacob's courtyard in the middle of the morning and wait for a number of villagers to come. For those men and women who planned to attend, morning chores would be completed by then and the children attended to. Master would start talking, quietly forcing people to pay attention and move closer to him. Although his presence was gentle and comforting, his early words would be in the form of an exhortation or a preaching. He would say:

"'Brothers and sisters. There are scattered among us, in our villages and in small isolated communities, people all of one mind who live pious lives keeping to the ancient laws. They understand and teach the reasons we are now put upon by suffering, illness and confusion. They propose a new covenant, which is really our old one, that would say: ... *those who reject the commandments and the rules shall perish. ... Days are coming upon you and upon your people and upon your father's house that have never come before, since the departure of Ephraim from Judah, that is, when the two houses of Israel separated ...*

"'These days are now upon us', he would say, 'because of the falling away from the commandments. Nay, not a complete falling away, for the priests and scribes at the Temple insist on those rules that keep the Sabbath and holy days, and their own authority. But a falling away from those laws that concern the earthly lives of the people, those laws that were also given to Moses by God.

"'The new yet still old covenant our pious brethren propose restores to our lives these social laws for our well being: *Each one must love his brother as himself, and support the poor, needy, and alien. They must each seek the welfare of his fellow, never betraying a family member according to the ordinance. Each must reprove his fellow according to the command, but must not bear a grudge day after day.*

"'It is good, brothers and sisters, that we have these wise words for we know then that our lives can be ordered and fruitful and protected. But I tell you, without denying a dot of this old truth, that another kingdom awaits us, a kingdom of the spirit that will feed our souls as our good works will feed our bodies.

"'Indeed, what I have learned from our Father, and what I tell you now, is that entering this kingdom, this kingdom of God, is the beginning of personal salvation and the foundation of social peace. This is the meaning of the first commandment given us by Moses. For entering into this kingdom puts the one God before all gods and does not allow our entrance into any other.'

"Then Master would continue, describing the nature of this kingdom and those who would enter it. The peace that dwelt within him was seen in his countenance by all. I would seclude myself in a shadowy place and listen to him and watch the people. There were many who were just content to be in his presence, just that, accepting the message because of the messenger. They came every day to do no more than be with him. When he finished they would leave quietly, talking little among themselves, seemingly fulfilled.

"Then there were those who paid close attention to every word. They were usually people with some learning concerned with a point of law or tradition about which they had questions. Master would speak to them, simply repeating only what he had said, perhaps worded a little differently, and leave them to further discussion among themselves.

"But always there were some — Joseph said this was true in each village Master visited — who asked about the 'kingdom' Master spoke of. In one way or another they wanted to know how to enter it. These, Master would have speak to Joseph or to Sara, one with the men and the other with the women. Then a time would be arranged for Master to visit with these groups alone. For them there would be a special teaching ending with instruction for many, an initiation or baptism we would say, into the hidden mysteries.

"In this way, in every village, and in some towns and later the cities when others beside Master were entrusted with this teaching, there would be small groups left behind with the new teaching, people who could keep it alive and nurture it."

It was my practice to pause at different points to allow Aaron to catch the last words. I spoke slowly and impressed my thoughts on his mind. He was gifted for this knowledge but still a rest was needed from time to time. At these times also, he would interrupt to ask questions. He listened attentively and was alert to everything I said.

"Father, where is Jacob in all this? And you, listening in the shadows?" Aaron asked.

Yes, about Jacob, I thought. How to speak of Jacob. He who spent so much time with Master as part of his early growth when Master, himself, was grappling with and confused by his own nature. That long trip together to the East when Jacob saw with his eyes and understood with his head the special quality of this boy who was almost a man. But, as it became clear later, Jacob resisted acceptance almost to the end causing great sorrow to himself and Sara.

"About Jacob, Aaron, I must speak with sadness mixed with joy. For reasons known only to God, there are some whose ears are so sharp they can hear the bleat of a lamb in another country but still they cannot hear the shout of the Lord from two paces away. Of these, Joseph would say: 'there are hidden sins from an immeasurable past that close their ears to this truth. They must wait for a more auspicious time, and this causes sadness.' Joy comes from knowing that Jacob's favorable time did finally arrive, a spark of light in a deeply troubled time."

Again I wondered: what can I tell Aaron about Jacob apart from Sara's life? Is this a story for his memory or for parchment? Does he need to know how Master's teaching cleaved the bond between Sara and Jacob? That what Jacob could not accept of these teachings she entered into with body and soul. From the time of Master's return her life was changed. He became its center and its purpose; his will and his needs became her will and her needs.

In those few times Master would be in our physical presence Sara would attend to his physical needs as the servants attended to their household duties. When he was away she would tend to the spiritual needs of his small group of village disciples. Few understood Master's purpose as clearly as she. The new life he brought to her ended her old life with Jacob.

And then in time, she assumed her special role. It became her task to minister to the women who saw their lives take on new meaning in Master's teaching. Sara's gift first unfolded with the few women in our small village who came under Master's spell. She alone understood the full range of change in these women, seeing emerge in their awareness the feelings and thoughts with which she, herself, had been grappling all her life.

Following their baptism into the new covenant they felt a power and freedom but also bewilderment and great fear — shared by their husbands and encouraged by tradition — that this was the trap of the evil one. Though she remembered it well, Sara had long banished those fears from her mind and now through surrender to the personal guidance of Master's teaching she took on his authority and strength to guide others to this same understanding.

It was Joseph who first saw this need for and use of Sara. He was the first in those early days to be allowed to gather disciples

and teach in Master's name and with Master's blessing. He knew
and was known in the far off and isolated Jewish villages and communities that Master first wanted to enter with his new word.

And when he found that many would drop away because of
fear and confusion, and he had no access to the women, he asked
Master for guidance. How it came about that Sara learned of this I
do not know: I know only that one day she took us aside to say
simply that she would be gone on Master's business for a spell.

The signs were there, how well I remember, when Master gave
to Sara a new teaching to prepare her for new work, but only Joseph then understood its import. When others would complain
that Master loved Sara above them all, Joseph would tell them
only: "She was Master's first test, first instructor, first disciple."
Then a certain time came when Master had Joseph take the extraordinary step of having Sara accompany him on a missionary
journey of special importance: to meet with secluded, unworldly
souls living isolated lives in desert enclaves of which only Joseph
knew.

It was Master's wisdom they were charged with giving these
souls, fulfilling a promise they had once received that the special
messenger would come to them. Master has built a new room in
God's mansion, they were instructed to say, and these holy ones
were now ready to enter. Sara has the key to unlock its door. When
we learned of this, long after, we then knew of Sara's place at Master's
side.

Jacob could not accept this nor could he affect it. As Sara's life
was becoming completely entwined with Master's work, she lived
more and more apart from her worldly concerns. Anna managed
the household, cared for Ruth, and now had servants of her own.
Jacob's farm flourished supporting all of them and he found respite in the work. As Master's influence grew, Sara's distance from
Jacob grew likewise until, finally, they ceased sharing their room.
But of whose concern is any of this? Certainly not Aaron's.

Still, there are things Aaron must know. The task Simon gave
him showed he is one of us in a way I did not see before. I must

talk of things that should not be lost. Sara once told me that if even one soul remembers, death is cheated.

I began again. "Aaron, listen carefully to what I tell you and remember. You must know of these things and tell them in time to another so they will not be lost. To know about Jacob you must know about Simon whom I know will become more and more important in your life.

"There are sages we know of who talk about sojourns between death and rebirth. I am beginning to feel my long secluded hermitage was of that nature. Although I remain in this body with memory intact, I think of myself now as one reborn. The past is so clear, Aaron, it is as if it were yesterday.

"When Master came out of the wilderness and accosted Joseph at the edge of his small communal encampment he appeared as the one they were promised. For Master, this was a return to his spiritual home. This sect and its creed were the one that his parents followed and Sara's parents as well and also Jacob in a fashion, after his marriage. When Master entered that enclave and made himself known, there were some who remembered that it was here that his parents had brought him on the day he became a son of the law.

"These elders were not so fast to accept a Teacher of such humble origins. However, for many generations, in preparation for this coming, they had lived a special life and they rejoiced in the possibility of his appearance. Soon, however, it became clear that this new teacher proposed an extraordinary departure from their long held doctrines regarding the awaited Teacher of Righteousness and their struggle against the Children of Darkness.

"It was always believed that entry into this new covenant was a long and arduous period of initiation and instruction and sacrifice. It was this idea that Master challenged most of all: he taught that the Kingdom of God was so beautifully described by our teachings, and so thirsted after by so many of our people, that the goal itself had been mistaken for the path. When the congregation would ask him about this kingdom he would say:

"If those who lead you say to you, see, the Kingdom is in the sky, then the birds of the sky will precede you. If they say to you, it is in the sea, then the fish will precede you. Rather, the Kingdom is inside of you, and it is outside of you. When you come to know yourselves, then you will become known, and you will realize that it is you who are the sons of the living Father. But if you will not know yourselves, you dwell in poverty and it is you who are that poverty."

"What does that mean?" Aaron interrupted, " . . . the birds and fish will precede . . . or to dwell in poverty? What is this poverty and how does this depart from the other teaching?"

Once again I was struck by Aaron's alertness. He seems to grow in understanding before my eyes and he brings out of me that desire to see this growth continue.

"Aaron, my son, I have heard those questions asked so often that they and their answers are engraved in my mind. They contain within themselves the whole of Master's teachings and Joseph never tired of explaining their meaning, for he never tired of seeing the light kindled in the eyes of the questioners. Listen carefully: if the kingdom is in the sky, the birds, whose nature it is to be in the sky, are already there. If it is in the sea, the fish, whose nature it is to be in the sea, are already there. "Likewise, if the kingdom is inside you and outside you then you, too, are already there. But of all creatures made by God, only we, Aaron, can hide this kingdom from ourselves by failing to know ourselves. As for poverty, Aaron, you can see now that this is the spiritual poverty that comes from ignorance of the light. These poor, I am afraid, we will always have with us.

"This is what instruction is for, to show us how to come to know our nature as living with God in His kingdom. It need not wait for grueling years of sacrifice. It needs only the seeker's desire. For this teaching, Aaron, Master was cast out.

"But there were many among them, who with Joseph, accepted Master's teaching as not a departure but as a fulfillment of the traditional promises and indeed, the only true way for salvation. It was these who formed the core of his first group of disciples as they followed him out into the world and into his work. Master and these first few went into a retreat where he taught and prepared them with secret teachings for their initial mission: to go out to the far flung communities of the Jewish Charter and bring this message to those ready to hear it, 'Good news, the messenger has arrived.'

"Many of these communities had settled in various wilderness enclaves according to a Charter of Laws to which they vowed obedience. Others, however, lived in villages and towns scattered throughout Jewish Palestine, obeying the Charter as it applied to those living worldly lives. It was to this population that Master's disciples first went and this was the occasion of Joseph's entrance into our lives. It was to both of these groups that Master was first to appear after they were prepared for his coming.

"In time, Aaron, it was Master's teaching that found the most fertile soil for growth. He provided new life and meaning to the doctrines of his earthly father and showed how they can be not only a vision but also a living reality. Now Aaron, I know it is this teaching you so ardently desire. For the last time I ask patience from you; your time is close."

"I trust you father, and I feel content in what you say. Master's words soothe me somehow. Is there more you can tell me about Jacob?"

"Yes, but first Aaron you must see how this teaching would appear to many from the community who spent years preparing for a king of this world to lead an army of the righteous against the forces of darkness. They were convinced with the blessing of the God of the covenant they could overcome the might of Rome and establish the true kingdom. And all, including Gentiles, would look to it for salvation.

"These, and their allies in other sects and bands, disdained the 'easy yoke and mild lordship' promised by Master, and as for repose, either inner or outer, they could only see this as weakness. And far from being weakness, Aaron, Master's teaching provided the strength to move mountains. But they were so boiling with rage it was impossible for them to hear words of peace. And since they could not hear words of peace, how much more difficult it was to see the unfamiliar symbol of love.

"Jacob was not truly one of these, he was, after all, embraced by Master and loved by those who too were blessed to know the absence of hate. In many ways, his was the bitterest draught. He yet refused to go into the kingdom but, unlike those who had no knowledge of it, he glimpsed its majesty and yearned to share it. Alas, the rancor for the oppressors long burning in his heart was fueled and refueled at every turn and because of this his days of torment and conflict worsened.

"Jacob's friends became Master's enemies and therefore Sara's too, even more so than the Temple authorities. These former associates saw in Master a force for peace and their needs demanded a world of violence.

"Although he could not surrender to Master, Jacob could not oppose him and certainly could not hate him as some others would. He loved Sara and she him but their lives were no longer joined. In truth, Aaron — and this will perhaps become clearer to you at a later time — even had Jacob accepted Master and joined with him, his life with Sara was over. In those last days before we separated she told me, although I sensed it long before then, that her worldly tasks were completed. 'I live now,' she told me, 'only to do God's will as Master reveals it.' "

I mused about those last words that I told Aaron. I remembered that time and how she actually told me her worldly tasks were almost completed, and I wondered then what was being held back. It was not a time for questioning. Sara's childhood boldness never left her so I was sure her exception was not a simple matter of modesty. Ah well, it was a mystery then and so it remains.

"After Master's coming," I continued, "a strange transformation began, first in our own lives and then in all the land. It was not as clear to me then as it became later. Just as a fish cannot know the whole of the sea in which it swims just so I was unable to see the nature of the air I breathed. Master's very presence awakened all of the conflicting forces in the world straining to escape their sheltering wombs to begin their independent lives."

What can I tell Aaron of the Galilee we knew, gone now along with Jerusalem, drowned in the flood of blood spilled by Rome? It was always a country of mixed peoples that Judeans would like to call "the land of the Gentiles." A crossroads for trade and commerce, not to mention armies and brigands, patriots or bandits, called so depending on whom they attacked, pillaged or raped. Its location and roads gave access in all directions to the outer world that meant, of course, entrance by the wider world into its institutions and thinking.

Those institutions and that thinking contrasted sharply with Master's teaching of the kingdom within, a doctrine that really taught the futility of violence and spoke of the power of God working through the internal tranquillity of individual lives. But I see now it was this very contrast that in a perverse way seemed to give new life and strength to these zealots. Their strident cries, directed toward the dispossessed and discontented, served to drown out the hidden glories which, after all, have few external signs. Oh, how hostility and rage blinds the eyes and deafens the ears!

My thoughts ended: "More and more Jacob found himself caught up with these groups but he also suffered distrust and contempt from them because of Sara. By sharing their house, a physical connection was maintained with her who was now known as a follower of Master. And it was clear to all that Jacob, although her husband, was not her master. This fact, that a woman was in her position, could not be hidden from the population and it caused gossip and fear of her in some places.

"Gradually, Jacob found reason to spend increasing time in the nearby city of Sepphoris, a Greek abomination rebuilt by Herod Antipas — do you know of the tetrarch, Aaron? No need, rightfully he is lost to the world — and later we learned he helped form some conspiratorial groups that were drawn into the fighting that led to our dispersion.

"To Anna and me then, fell the greater responsibility for managing the farm, though my influence and decisions were made through her. It was surely Master's grace that no sorrow, no conflict could stain the innocence of Anna's heart. Anna's love for Master was unbounded as it would be for one who brought her back from the dead, though she knew of that event only through Jacob.

"For Sara, Anna also would have given her life, for what Sara was equally as much as for what she had become. Anna's affection for Jacob remained undiminished: she simply could not find fault with any. She had become expert at managing the internal affairs of the household and those skills were now transferred, by necessity, to its external operation.

"Aaron, we were an alien household in this village. The master of it away, its mistress now a holy woman with mysterious teachings and powers, its overseer a young unmarried, misshapen woman but with man-like ways and an unseemly competence. And I, Aaron, must have been strangest of all. Though most villagers seldom saw me, most knew of me through gossip and rumor. The Gentiles heard the whispers of those few of them who had business with the house and would catch sight of me on occasion.

"Among the Jews there was a mixed attitude. Those who believed in Master's teachings and came into contact with him and Sara, knew of their love for me and found, after a time, they could converse with me as you and Simon now do. But others, though not as frightened as the more superstitious among them, considered me with misgiving. How could a body such as mine, they must have thought, house a human spirit? Even my aunt once told Sara it would have been better if she had left me to die.

"Master's work had a life of its own. He was bringing his message and teaching throughout our area, spending much time with special disciples to whom he would impart knowledge not meant for the multitude or in silent retreat where he could not be found.

"Joseph was tireless in his behalf. Unlike other advanced disciples, he was unencumbered by family; his life was Master's work, a lamp, in a way, that also lighted Sara's path. He would minister to the ever-growing congregations of followers throughout the Jewish countries. He brought to them new knowledge and patiently, over and over as necessary, explained how Master's words illuminated the experiences of their instruction. Thus, each center in each village grew stronger and stronger with individuals everywhere becoming capable of guiding them and themselves.

"It was no wonder, then, Aaron, that Master came to the attention of the Temple authorities. Their greatest fear was influence out of their control and this fear was increased by their confusion about his message. What could the 'kingdom within' mean and how could it affect the 'kingdom without' which was of course theirs?

"Although the Romans had little interest or knowledge in the religious affairs of the Jews, any talk of kingdoms meant kings and this caught their notice. And whatever caught the notice of the Romans, Aaron, was of interest to Caiaphas. Do you know of the High Priest, Joseph Caiaphas, Aaron? You do not? Good, he, too, should be lost to the world.

"It was easier for them to associate Master with the violent dissident sects they were accustomed to dealing with. They chose to consider his teaching as codes for revolt and social unrest, for although wiser heads would counsel them differently, they could not fathom peaceful dissent. They sent spies and troublemakers to watch us and spread slanderous falsehoods.

"Of course, Sara was a natural target. They spread tales of witchcraft and worse about her and when it was revealed that she had lived in Jerusalem in her girlhood days, sent there by anxious parents because of strange practices, the authorities ordered an inquiry to determine if there were any violations of the law."

"Father, what was Sara like?" Aaron finally broke his long silence. Could he have found that long dissertation of interest? But of his question. What, indeed, was Sara like? I cannot tell him what Sara was like, only she can tell as she once told me that long ago evening when our minds and spirits were so merged and she said that talking to me was like thinking out loud. Did she tell me that to say things she had to speak out and could only do so to me?

Whatever she told me of those early years, and I can repeat what she said word for word as she told me, would she have told Aaron?

I asked her one time as Aaron asked me, "Sara, how did you come to be here? Married to Jacob? Knowing of Master and his knowledge as you do?" These unasked questions had arisen often in the past, but they had become more insistent lately after one particular meeting — which turned out to be our last with Master, although we did not know that then — where she and I were together with him. My sense then, which now came to my mind's surface, was that there was a special bond between them. When with him, I saw signs in her of a shyness, a more pronounced modesty that would express itself in lowered eyes and uncharacteristic restrictive bodily movements. Never immodest in her attire or behavior, even with Jacob or me, in Master's presence there seemed a greater attempt to withdraw.

"I can't answer you now Jonathan," she said quietly, "except only to say we were children together. To say more would be to tell you things I am not ready to once again bring to the Lord's attention. But I promise you, one day you will know me as I think I know myself."

I could not ask more of her. From her reply I knew the time would come when I would know it all. We have long recognized our own peculiar relationship, seemingly of one soul sharing two bodies and minds. But, though the line between her understanding and mine had the fuzziest of edges, I could not intrude into her life without her permission.

For my part, my surrender was complete. From the earliest days when she ministered to my every need, carrying this care through what demands adolescence could make on my poor body, into an adulthood of sorts with the needs of an adult, my confidence and faith in her love for me was unconditional. When I tried to express this to her once, she said, "Hush Jonathan, God gave us to each other, our love is but a mirror of our love for Him and Master."

The time came as I knew it would when she was ready to

speak to me. I was awakened one night, the quietest time of the early morning, by her stirring about near my bed preparing to call me.

"What is it? Sara, is that you?"

"Yes, come to me Jonathan."

I went out to her and she took my hand and led me to an area outside the house at the entrance to the animal shed. An early moon eerily lighted the chilly night, but the warmth of the animals wafted out, supplying a measure of comfort.

"I decided to tell you this story, Jonathan, because Master charged you to tell his and you cannot do so without mine. Besides," she said with her little knowing smile, "what secrets can I have from you? I sometimes believe we are two persons sharing one body. I often feel when speaking to you I am speaking my innermost thoughts out loud."

That night came back to me in all of its detail. I sensed once again the calming perfume of a world in repose, that special time as night just ends and day not yet begun. I felt the silence, as I did then, broken only by the quiet whisper of Sara's voice, as almost trance-like, she began to tell her story. I felt her whisperings shutting out the clamor of my mind and I pulled Aaron closer to me.

"Look into my eyes, Aaron, deep, deeper. Go deep inside, lose yourself Aaron. Sara's there, see her . . . hear her . . . "

SARA I

I awoke that night and could not resist the impulse to go to Jonathan. I somehow feel the days are fewer that we will be together. Jeshua hints that trials are coming and what I vaguely sense he, I am sure, sees more clearly. The time is now then for me to answer the questions that I know are in Jonathan's mind. Joseph is surely right, Jonathan will survive us all.

It seems only yesterday that his broken body was brought into our house, more dead than alive. His mother now gone, his father too, only a few years before. What miracle did these people expect when they brought him to me? What kind of a person did they think I was? I was no more than they and they worried me with their expectations. But whatever thoughts I may have had of abandoning him vanished in that moment when he opened his eyes and I looked into them.

If I ever had questioned God's wisdom in keeping Jacob and me childless, his gifts of Anna, then Ruth, and then Jonathan, banished those doubts. As time unfolded, revealed with the beauty of that favor was Jonathan's understanding, compassion and strength that mirrored Jeshua's own. Like a bucket in a deep well, he draws inexhaustible love from all of us.

I cannot speak for Jacob in this. His disappointment that I could not give him sons was clear though he tried to keep it from me. I marvel, and give thanks also, that he cleaved to my side in those early barren days, and then later when my life was given over to Master's work, he accepted contempt — how that must have hurt him — rather than denounce me.

I surely do not deserve this devotion. But I no longer question the working of this power in my life. I am filled with it now as I look toward a darkening future. Jonathan must know my life; how else can he know Master's, how else can he pass it down? Ah, where to begin?

If I remember rightly, Jonathan, I was not yet ten years old and Jeshua as we knew him then was three, perhaps four years older when he came to our village. It was in the early days of the Tetrarch, Antipas, and I recall the talk of him and the hopes for a just rule. Jeshua's father was a landless farmer, newly impoverished, who was brought here by my father and given a small house on father's land.

He was to be an overseer for whatever building father needed and to be hired out for other wealthy villagers as needed. He brought his wife and another younger son. Jeshua was already a handy worker as farmers are, knowing how to work with timber and he was much needed by his father.

Father was a successful farmer and landowner by the standards of our village, with several servants and field hands from the village who worked by the day. Nevertheless, he held to the old teachings of our people so similar to Jeshua's father. I do believe his lodging with us was due to father's previous knowledge of him in connection with this sect. They were both part of that holy community of brothers and held to the laws of that community regarding those who lived in cities, towns and villages.

Therefore, father would own no slaves and would tolerate no abuse of his servants. Where possible, he helped fellow farmers prevent foreclosure and loss of their land. When their loan could not be repaid he would accept less and at times forgive the loan entirely rather than see a family destroyed. "God forbid," he would say, "if once again children would be sold into slavery to keep their families from starving." I didn't know it then, but these were dangerous beliefs and deeds and they did not go unnoticed.

I had a younger sister and no brother at that time to father's consternation. But because of that, possibly, my willful nature was better able to emerge than if less responsibility fell my way. But it was my nature, I must confess, no other can be held to blame for it. To the despair of my mother, I was a bold and confident child rather than the modest and dutiful one she tried so hard to produce.

I instructed the servants and my sister and assumed decision-making obligations if I for a moment suspected mother of indecision. In her efforts to restrain me, mother received little help from father. He did not encourage my brash ways, but I sensed no disapproval from him.

Like you in many ways, dear Jonathan, I understood things I was not taught and knew things I should not have known — I never fail to wonder how much God made us the same in those things of the mind and heart. Unlike you, however, I had to learn a sharp and frightful lesson about pride and I am not too sure that lesson has yet been properly learned. In this, dear one, you have much to teach me.

In those days, as I know you have heard, it came over me that I understood the thinking of our animals. Not their thinking in our words as we know it, but more how they sensed the world, their fright and affection. I would feel as one with them and I could not restrain from talking aloud to them knowing of course that my words could have no meaning. I knew in some strange way how they suffered when they were sick and I understood that my caresses and presence brought them comfort just as my presence and caresses brought you comfort. With comfort, dear Jonathan, comes healing. Mother at first dismissed these tendencies as childish fancies that I would soon outgrow. Later, however, they brought unhappiness and danger to us both.

One day she came upon me cuddling a sick kid. Its mother was nuzzling it gently as I cradled it in my arms. Mother would later tell father I was oblivious to my surroundings, seemingly possessed and chanting in some unknown tongue, if it were a tongue. Mother was frightened but remained motionless and silent. In time, the kid struggled a bit to release itself from my arms and strolled off to its own mother, apparently well.

I cannot say my state of mind returned because I was not aware it was gone. I do not know how much time elapsed from

when I first embraced the sick animal to when it freed itself. But I
know I was not aware of a break in time. What I mean, Jonathan,
and listen carefully, is that in my mind there was no interruption
in time from when I went to the kid and when he left my arms. So
when mother told me she was with me for longer than it would
take our small pot to boil a full measure of water, I was overcome
with confusion and the sense of peace and well being that I was
feeling was now tinged with her fear.

What happened was observed by a goatherd and house servant, as well as mother, which meant the entire village would soon
know of it, although that thought and its consequences would not
have then entered my mind. I began to realize the serious nature
of what I had done when mother sent for father. She was not satisfied to wait for the usual end of his working day when he would
normally return to the house. And father's reaction was consistent
with mother's fears.

He questioned me deeply and I felt his seriousness and concern. But his questions were strange ones I couldn't understand
and I was unable to express my feelings; I had so little understanding of them myself. On the surface of things, I knew less about the
actual happening than the people who witnessed it. But on some
level I felt I had touched a hidden world, one it seemed everyone
knew of, whispered about, tried to placate, and were terribly frightened of.

What father was thinking I do not know. But after the first
questioning he ignored the incident, although I later learned he
instructed mother to call him immediately if this happened again.
I was happy as the experience faded into the activity of household
routine.

But what did not fade in my memory was the sense of calm
and peace present at the time awareness returned. I felt that whole-
ness, Jonathan, that we sometimes talk of with Master, especially
in those moments of rest between chores or that delicious time
just before sleep comes, or those times just after our private meditations.

One day the mother of one of our village servant girls came to the house with her small child in arms. I can only guess at what her daughter told her about what I did with the kid. She asked mother if it would be seemly if I held the feverishly fretting little boy in my arms as I did the baby goat. Mother was shocked and confused but even before she could answer I took the child in my arms and went to sit on a floor mat in the corner of the room.

I cradled the infant against my upraised knees, a childlike protective position that even now gives me a strong sense of peace, and without thought I closed my eyes. As I did so I felt myself expanding outward as if I were to fill the world. Later, in a more collected state of mind, I had the thought I was touching God and a terrible fear of grave blasphemy shot through me. But then there was no thought at all, and in time I felt a gentle pressure as the child was carefully lifted from my arms.

I opened my eyes to see the baby's mother bringing it to her breast. He was quiet and feeding contentedly for the first time in days, and I saw the mother looking intently at me. Even now I remember that look; I was so troubled by it. I had no need for appreciation — believe me, dear friend, I acted with little forethought about consequences — but I knew from that look that mixed with relief for her child was fear. I knew too, it was a fear of me.

Looking around the room I realized that once again there was a loss of time. Besides my mother and the others who were present when the child was first brought into the house, father was now present. He witnessed most of what took place and he was more than upset; I would say he was unnerved. I knew this because he sharply scolded the servant girl whose baby brother was brought here. He seldom spoke harshly to a servant. "I am not pleased that you brought this trouble to us," he said to her. "Go now with your mother. I command you not to mention this to anyone. For your own good as well as all of us in this house, what happened today must be kept secret."

Even before they left the house he knew that that secret would not last long. More than those two knew what happened so even if it were not them who spoke of it, it could not be concealed. He was right of course. For a while, however, there was little outward sign that anyone took notice of this strange ability. I remained confused and fearful, more because of father's attitude than the thought I was doing something sinful.

It was a short time after the incident with our servant's baby brother that I had occasion to speak with Jeshua. I think now he may have contrived it so our paths would cross. This was not unusual since we lived on the same farm. But it was not often that we would come into contact for our lives were so different and we lived in different households. I heard more of him than I observed because father would speak of him. He thought him odd. At synagogue when the men would read Torah he would be outspoken in his comments, sure of himself, "a fine head for the law" father would say. More than once he would be so bold as to correct commentary from one of the older men.

Outside the meeting room, however, he would be silent; it would seem he had nothing to say about the world. On the few occasions on which we would meet, around the house or on the road, we would not exchange even a nod and I am not sure why this was so.

He was reserved when we were in a group together during our festive occasions, and I must confess I gave him little thought. So when that time came when he chose to speak to me I was surprised. I was behind the goat shed when he approached. He was carrying a kind of tool and timber for the purpose of repairing the shed's roof.

He spoke to me as if we had just been talking together as a usual thing. His voice was so quiet I had to strain to hear him. "Sara, I know of your healing. You are gifted. Did you know that our holy books tell of such things? They say that for the healer the world stops. Did the world stop for you, Sara?" Where, I wondered, did he see that? I never saw such things myself and I read well in our books. Later, I learned, he was able to see hidden things in our language. Still, just hearing his words lifted the cloud that was shadowing my life. It had caused me distress to make father worry and it made me think ill of myself.

How can I speak of that moment? Did the world stop? What Jeshua asked was exactly what happened but could I have understood it or said it that way? But most important for me was that someone else know what I feel, that I not be used by the evil one, that our holy books spoke of such things. Was it then that Jeshua entered my heart? Perhaps, for it was then that sorrow fled it.

It was not long after this conversation with Jeshua that a woman came to the house and asked mother if I could sit with a sick child. Just to sit with him, she asked, for the healing brews he was given were of no help. It was not possible to say no to such a simple plea and despite knowing the displeasure it would bring to father, mother agreed. My own confusion or fear was now largely gone for when I thought of this I thought also of Jeshua and that alone calmed my worry.

Soon others would request my presence and attention and to this day I am confounded by these mysterious workings, if I can be so bold as to call them such. At those times I felt at peace and people expressed a satisfaction and interior quieting effect by my attention. That would be true even in those cases where it would seem to be of little good — however it is that we measure good.

As I became known in our village and nearby communities — I had little knowledge of the talk though I basked in the attention I was receiving — father's fears were realized. The whispering began that this was the work of the evil one. It was said that a child possessing these priestly powers only turns the people away from their rightful guides and teachers. Father now forbade me to leave the farm. Again I felt isolated, confused and troubled. Thoughts of Jeshua and his words of comfort were not enough to ease these feelings and except for mother, who comforted me as best she could, I felt all had deserted me.

This village, Jonathan, was one in which the Temple had representatives to conduct its affairs among those Jews who had loose ties to Jerusalem. We were separated from the holy city by Samaria and lived with many Gentiles, as was the case with almost all Galilean villages.

Like them, we were Galileans with little affection for our rulers, so it was necessary that the Temple establish a presence among us. It was most likely these people who reported to the Temple authorities stories about a "magical" child and brought people to investigate. Although I was not treated unkindly by them, and I had little knowledge of what the consequences could be of their findings, I knew the tranquillity of my home was gone.

Father, however, more clearly recognized the danger to our family. He knew his activities and beliefs were suspect for they opposed the religious authority and secular power of the priesthood. The teaching of his sect proclaimed a new covenant displacing the present leadership. He knew there were people in the Temple who would not hesitate to condemn him through me and blacken our name to destroy us. To forestall this he made a decision that changed my life; I was to be sent away to my mother's sister in Jerusalem, to live there until this scandal died away.

Father managed to quiet the questions of the inquisitors. He had resources enough to make a special donation to the Temple but of more importance was the influence of my aunt's husband. He was of that class of Jews who administered the affairs of the Temple priesthood, the wealthy landlords, the merchants and Romans whom father despised. Without them no records could be kept and Rome could not manage their rule. Had father known the environment in which I would spend the next number of years while moving into womanhood, I believe he would have cast me into the wilderness instead.

The day before I was to leave for Jerusalem I met another time with Jeshua. I was fearful of leaving home and its safety and this fear was worsened by the thought that I was being banished for being wicked, and I did not understand why. I was close to tears, I am sure, and alone, when Jeshua came to me. "Be of good cheer, Sara," he said, "you are special in God's eyes and he will provide you with what you need for His purposes. You will not be unduly burdened."

Do I need to tell Jonathan, I thought, how this young boy, not yet on the edge of manhood, struck me with his words? Am I seeing him as he really was then or through the wiser eyes of experience and love that know him now. No matter. It is enough that again he lifted the mist of despair and fear from which I had been suffering. How many times had just his silent presence, his glance, even the thought of him dispersed those clouds? I loved him then even not knowing the essence of that love and then mistaking it later for its most shallow nature when I thought I could stay his journey to the Eastern lands.

I know now it was as Jeshua promised. My life in Jerusalem was a schooling for what was to come later. It prepared me to become your teacher, Jonathan, until you became mine. There I grew into the kind of woman Jacob could marry, and perhaps only I can understand the importance of that union.

Father and I entered the lower part of the city at the time the afternoon business commenced. The streets were crowded with more people and animals than I had ever seen in one place. Merchandise stalls were everywhere pressed against the low square buildings in streets that were not more than walkways, even more crooked and skewed than those in our village at home. The noise was so great I couldn't hear and the stench so overpowering I couldn't take a deep breath. Father knew only to walk up toward Herod's Temple now still being finished by his sons, and I held onto his hand in terror, knowing that if we separated I would lose him.

Father left our cart with the goods he came to trade and sell with the people of his brotherhood in the trading areas outside the city walls. Unburdened then by no more than the clothes we had on our backs, we made our way to the upper city where we had to seek uncle's house.

Along with the Temple, Herod's palace and other massive projects, this section of the city was also razed and rebuilt, but in Roman and Greek style. As we climbed higher out of the city proper, the soiled and dusty road we were on spilled out into a broad avenue with the beginnings of public and private gardens.

We finally came to spacious homes that we learned later housed wealthy Jews, high priests and their families, Roman officials, merchants from many lands, and those like my uncle whose learning and talents served their needs. Even the servants, whom we did not realize were servants at first from their dress, were attired finer than were our wealthiest villagers. Can you imagine, Jonathan, the sight my poor father and his bedraggled little girl must have made?

Soon a guard approached and when father told him our mission, he himself guided us to uncle's house. But suspicious of us, he stayed until we could be properly identified which was no easy matter. We were forced to wait in the servants' quarters until they located my aunt.

For me the respite after such an arduous journey was welcome, but for father it was a mixture of relief and wonder. Was he intimidated by the surroundings knowing, as he did, the origin of the mistress of the house? This I never learned but I remember how somber and tender he was toward me. I will tell you later, Jonathan, how my aunt came to be here, growing up as she did with mother in our village, but for now let me say I am thankful she did not forget that village life.

Here, even the servants' area had stone floors and smooth walls and windows that looked out onto a courtyard. Our finest village houses were not so well-made. Later I learned that uncle's was not among the wealthiest of residences, but even so, he was able to bring into his house the water the Romans piped into the upper reaches of the city. They did so for their own needs, of course, and also to satisfy the needs of the Temple. Little was done that the wealthy did not share, though all the people paid for it.

The next days are still a jumble in my mind. It were as if I were transported to another country. I had two cousins: one, Ceil, a girl my age, who brought me into her room and life with kindness and care. The other was her older brother, Marcus, who had just returned from his studies in Greece.

My own world was turned upside down. I knew with my head that this family was Jewish but I felt I was living among aliens. The laws were kept after a fashion but not as a natural part of life, as was the case in the villages.

There were two kitchens and we Jews would eat from ours. But when Gentiles were entertained, which was often because of uncle's needs, the other kitchen would prepare forbidden foods. There was plenty of opportunity for confusion and because of that there was always a religious teacher available to warn of transgressions. Were it not for aunt's resistance, I am afraid transgression would be much the rule. This was a class of Jews for whom accommodation to the Romans was less a chore than a desire.

People here spoke Greek with ease and perfection and spoke our common language with difficulty. I, on the other hand, spoke Greek with difficulty and our common language as my mother's tongue. Until the household knew me, I would be mistaken for a servant for the way I talked and carried myself. At first, even the clothes on my back, given to me by Ceil and fine as they were, were carried and worn poorly.

Before that first day ended, my poor body, coated with the filth and dust of our journey through the countries of Galilee, Samaria, and Judea, was washed in hot water tubs such as I could never have imagined. Fresh water was brought by tubes into baths large enough for several people. And it then flowed out of waste tubes to find its way into the lower city somehow, and then into the moats surrounding Jerusalem's walls.

This bathing area for women was separate from that of the men and it was the practice to bathe without clothes and without shame. It was difficult for me at first, coming from a place where we never were without some piece of clothing covering our nakedness. This was so even when the women were alone together.

The luxury of hot water, soap and servants to help me bathe made me think of father who reviled the Jews who would accept Greek ways. Even then in my youth I felt a sense of sin, but I remember, too, how the

*sensual pleasure which came from that simple activity, was mixed with
and diminished that feeling.*

*How easily that body, which the Greeks, and Romans too, vener-
ated and thought made in a divine image becomes a cloud hiding our
allegiance to God's law. How would dear Jonathan, whose body would
never permit this transgression, respond to that thought? Over the next
several years I learned how seductive these Greek customs were and how
the evil one uses them to tempt the people away from their religion and
God.*

Both aunt and uncle knew why I was brought here but only
aunt knew the seriousness of the scandal and the justification for
father's fears. She had lived in our Galilean village until her Judean
husband brought her to Jerusalem. They were betrothed in childhood and both families honored the betrothal.

Aunt came as I did: a village girl from a remote province that
was held in contempt by the people she came to live among. Though
she believed in my powers, she knew talk of them to be dangerous
and warned me to keep them hidden. Uncle, I sensed, with his
worldly ways, dismissed the entire episode as superstition, as
women's nonsense. Indeed, he paid little attention to me. In any
case, household affairs were in aunt's hands including supervision
of Ceil's education and now mine.

Because of her early village upbringing and her exposure to
the ideas of the new covenant brotherhood, she was much more
sympathetic to the needs of our servants. Of these some were Gentiles and some slaves bought by uncle against her wishes, but none
treated differently by her. She, too, knew the consequences of violating the rigid Temple religious laws so her early education and
ability to read our books in their holy language had to be hidden;
it was not permitted for women to read the Torah.

Nevertheless, she would train and educate those servants who
showed interest and promise and at times we would have a class
with a half-dozen students. Because of her kindness, it was not
unusual for her non-Jewish servants to show their love for her by
accepting our God and secretly become Jews.

Uncle was the son of a Judean merchant who had the pre-science to educate him in Rome. This was the time when Rome favored the Jews because of their support for Caesar in his victory over Pompey. Jews in the empire were then given a special status which permitted them to practice their religion not only in the Temple in Jerusalem but also in their faraway communities under Roman rule. The Romans also permitted the rebuilding of the city and its walls, Herod's Temple, his palace and other necessary lesser projects in the area.

Because of uncle's Roman contacts, friends and Greek ways, he was able to participate in these massive building projects. The growth of Jewish influence and wealth outside Judea, the people's desire to support the center of their religious life, which was the Temple, resulted in the flow of wealth into Jerusalem from all parts of the world. The influence of this affluence was felt in high Roman places as well. And uncle was one of those who benefited from this growing abundance.

But of course, Jonathan, as Master taught, we know wealth is only a blessing when one does not desire it. Otherwise the glimpse of it, or worse the taste of it, attaches a person to it with almost unbreak-able bonds. The truth of this, though of course I could not know it then, could be seen over and over again in that household.

You have told me, Jonathan, of learned men, men also of good heart who despair of ever fathoming the works of God. The Jews, they lament, are never closer to Him than when they suffer from their enemies and with one voice they cry out to Him for deliver-ance. And then when this deliverance is forthcoming, as it was in uncle's days, they flee from His substance.

Jewish influence in Roman life was now at its height, but my cousin Marcus, now back from Greece, told us one cannot tell Jew from Greek in that country and we heard the same about Rome. There, I heard our people celebrated even Roman festivals and Jews were given permission to pray for the Emperor's well being. But we never heard of its opposite: the difficulty of telling Greek from Jew or the Gentiles celebrating Passover.

What makes us and keeps us Jewish? I thought to myself. It must be as Jeshua once told us. It is the written teaching of Moses given to him for us by God that separates us from all others. Without it we would have drowned in the ocean of paganism and disappeared from the face of the earth. There is a power in that teaching that even when hidden by a foreign tongue cannot be denied. I keep looking for it but until now only Jeshua reveals it as he revealed it that day before I was taken to this place.

Our household reflected this conflict in Jewish life. Uncle was closely connected to the Temple priests who revered the written word and understood it in their own fashion. Obligation to it was demanded from all Jews and if the priests' own power was not enough to obtain it they could always rely on their Roman allies.

But these priests rejected the oral tradition, the experience and trials of the people, and above all they rejected the prophets, new and present day, whose warnings were contained in the new covenant teachings. The priests found no quarrel with those who aped the hellenizers in style of living and accumulation of wealth so long as they held to Temple rites and religious observances.

For my part, this understanding had to await my more mature years. For aunt, however, there was an ever-present fear that our lives were in violation of the Law, and the consequences of this sin would be visited upon us. She never lost contact with the teachings of her parents and the new covenant sect that had brotherhood communities even in Jerusalem.

In her own way she supported the efforts of this movement and would at times bring "brothers" to our house to preach and teach to groups of our servants. Ceil and I would attend these services with mixed feelings. I found them joyful for they so reminded me of home and our village meetings with their prophetic exhortations. But Ceil was uncomfortable, disturbed actually, because they spoke harshly of the comfort and frivolity of her life.

She shared this feeling with Marcus who attended one of these meetings. With Marcus, from Greece, came his friend Alexander. It was with Alexander's family in Corinth that he had lodged. The families were close, brought together by the business and personal relationships of uncle's and Alexander's fathers. Uncle wanted a "Greek" education for Marcus that meant sending him to the gymnasium.

He could not attend such an institution in Jerusalem because this "education" was condemned for Jews by the Temple authorities. Not only because of the requirement that students participate in Greek athletics in which they trained and competed naked, and because they were required to make offerings to the Greek and Roman gods, the worst blasphemy, but also it was known these students lost all contact with our Law.

And he could not attend gymnasium away from Jerusalem either, it turned out, for aunt was uncompromising on this issue. She was a respectful and dutiful wife, Jonathan, one I fell short of emulating, I am afraid, but on some things she could not be bent. Uncle sensed when that point was reached and God gave him the good sense as well as the sensible nature to resist testing her resolve.

It was agreed then that Marcus join Alexander in Corinth for his studies. Alexander was preparing to enter a school in that city to study the medicine of the Greeks. His family too, resisted the gymnasium but the medical school could be attended separately and it accepted Jews. At that time, a scholar trained in the Greek Academy in the classical manner after the famous Greek sage was living in Corinth. He agreed to tutor Alexander in the mathematics and philosophy he would not have in medical school, and also to accept Marcus as a formal student in these disciplines.

Theirs was an unusually pious household and they regularly attended synagogue, celebrated the festivals, and studied Torah. Marcus would say he learned more about his people when living away from the Temple's sight then when living in the Holy Land itself. When living as an island in a sea of Greek culture the Jewish communities clung desperately to their Law even while they took on the trappings of the civilization around them.

Young as I was, dear Jonathan, I understood why Jews like my

father were so offended by Jews like my uncle. They valued anything Greek and were so easily seduced by the promises of earthly
pleasures. My cousin, Ceil, and the girl and women servants we
were surrounded by also fell under this influence. Sadly, I, too,
could not escape this evil net.

SARA II

How often I thanked God for His early entrance into my life. Despite all the trials brought on to us by my gifts: the healing power, the ease of understanding, the seeing into the depths of things, I always knew it was God's wisdom speaking through me though His purposes in so using me I only now glimpse. In Jonathan, too, I recognize His work, and in Jeshua, especially in Jeshua, and in that strange time when I thought I could thwart his needs and God's will. I continued my tale:

Alexander was now living with Marcus as Marcus formerly lived with him, as a full member of our household. Moreover, he was much valued for his training as a physician. In this he was happy for this is the work he had always wanted to do. Marcus, on the other hand, found it necessary to suppress his cherished desire: to establish a school in which young men could study further in philosophy.

Uncle was planning to re-establish his father's trade network as Jerusalem was becoming a major marketing center for the entire region. Marcus' ability to enter equally into the Greek and Roman world and into the widespread Jewish communities made him indispensable to this effort.

I am always reminded, when I think of Marcus, that nothing can be known of God's purposes until they are completed; can one know even then? Marcus brought Jacob into Jeshua's life and Jeshua brought him into mine. When I hear our sages say these are ancient contacts for hidden reasons I think only the ignorant could ignore this wisdom.

It is enough to know that the closer we move to Him the more easily God's will unfolds in us, as easily and simply as water flows down the mountainside, and there is no need to know the details of that hoary past. "Let the dead bury the dead," Jeshua would say when asked about these past workings in our lives.

Shortly after I arrived, aunt decided my coarse ways and country speaking made me too easily mistaken for one of her servants. Despite her own country origins, she had taken on the manners and thought of her adopted station. In truth, Jonathan, from the beginning I felt more at ease with the servants than with the others and that comfort with them never left me.

But aunt took me in hand and decreed the first task was to improve the way I spoke the Greek language for in this place it was the mark of an educated person. She planned to hire a tutor for me but when Alexander heard of this he insisted that he tutor me himself. Neither uncle nor aunt could understand this decision, this busy and learned man finding the time and interest to instruct me in better speech, but, nevertheless, they agreed.

Of course, he had his own reasons. Aunt had told him the reason I was here. In doing so she fanned a spark of knowledge lying dormant in him; but a spark continually fanned into an open flame in our Galilean villages where our Law is kept purer than in the sophisticated cities with their centers of great learning.

But still, wherever Jews congregate and study, one or another will see in our Book and its language God's words not easily seen by more clouded eyes. He heard of those mysterious promises that permitted a direct access to God's blessings and they entered his mind to stay as seeds waiting their time to sprout.

In his own studies his learned teachers often, after describing the various techniques and practices the schooled physician must use to treat his patients, would say: "In the end dear students, after your ministrations are over, you must call upon that hidden Physician within that governs all healing." He believed that the mysterious promises of our sages and the hidden Physician of his revered Greek teachers were revealed in my gift.

The day my lessons were to begin I was waiting in uncle's library where these instructions were to take place. While waiting, I noticed a book on the reading bench and I saw it was written in our holy language. I realized at once it was our Torah but I had never seen it in this form before, not a scroll but in separate leaves laid between two heavy leather covers. I marveled at the ease it would be to go from place to place in it and I began to search through its pages.

It was then Alexander entered. "What are you doing Sara?" he asked. His voice and manner were kindly and I felt at ease in his presence. "You should not be playing with that book. It is very valuable. Do you know what it is?"

"I'm not playing, teacher, I'm waiting for you," I told him "I'm just looking for some words I was told were in here and I had never seen them myself."

"But can you read those words, child? Even I have scant knowledge of them. I know them for our prayers but for Torah I must use the Greek book. And even knowing the words does not permit understanding."

"I have known them since I was a small child. Father taught other children and me. He said that to read our Book in its own language is a blessing. Other Jewish children in our village can read and I can read the common language as well, but not Greek."

"Read to me from the Torah," he asked, turning to a page at random. "I don't dispute you, child, I simply want to hear the words."

I was happy he turned to a place I knew well, which was Aaron's tale of the building of the golden calf. How the people turned away from our true hidden God to worship the false one they could see. And how beautifully it glittered and how deadly it proved to be. Father never tired of reading this to us, telling us how, just as Moses saved the people from God's wrath then, now a new Righteous man will come to save us again, because once again the people are turning away from God's Law as Moses gave it to us.

I read that part to him. Jonathan, you know how easily we read our Torah. And I repeated word for word the explanation that father would give each time we had read it together. I little knew at that tender age the implications of all I said. But Alexander,

hearing it read so well with father's words commenting on its meaning, was deeply impressed. He told me later that his decision to
improve my speaking was motivated by his thought that he could
learn from me about my gifts and this, our first conversation, convinced him that he was right.

We would meet, two, sometimes three times a week and shortly
I spoke Greek as well as cousin Ceil, she who spoke it from when
she was a babe. But our sessions together continued despite that,
not because of my need but because he so loved to teach and I
believe he thought me the perfect student.

I was curious and attentive and the years I spent hearing the
comments and disputes about our Law made hearing these same
disputes and commentary among the ancient Greek sages more a
pleasure than a chore. I would make Alexander laugh when I pointed
out that they argue as fruitlessly as our people, and sometimes
over the same things. Everything that I taught you about the Gentile philosophy of the body and mind, Jonathan, I learned from
Alexander.

In those days, there were in Jerusalem teachers and seekers of
all kinds looking into our ancient writings for the path out of
despair and struggle. Simple workers and trained scholars from
the entire Jewish world would come to the city seeking a holy
man.

There were many sects and understandings of Torah; different
"schools" were found throughout the less affluent area of the city
away from the influence of the priests and those who depended on
them. I learned then that father's people, and Jeshua's, too, were
but one of this ferment. Not until Jeshua's return from his many
years of silent exile did my understanding mature into its final
fulfillment.

But even then, one idea was echoed over and over in these tiny
halls of study, an idea that seems now part of the very air breathed
by the Jewish people: "Love your neighbor, do no harm as you
want no harm done to you." Indeed, there were those who would
say this is the whole of Torah. God's work could be felt in the

blessed words of these sages who in their way thought to make of our people the community it once was, forged by the power of Moses after their flight from bondage.

The fervor and promise of this community caught up Alexander and he threw himself into its study. And from me he wanted something else. Ever since he heard from aunt about my healing gifts he was anxious to know about it as a physician would. Now, after our time together where I taught him as he taught me, he came to believe that the teachings of these holy ones were a living presence in me. I began to detect in him a new tenderness and affection and an uncommon attentiveness to my words.

How strange is the working of God in the lives of us poor souls! This man, seeking the learning of the ages from the masters of his world and the masters of the other, flits from sage to sage as the bee from flower to flower after its nectar. Only, unlike the bee, satisfaction and fulfillment still escape him. At the end of the day more questions and fewer answers face him than at its beginning. And then, when Jeshua came into his ken, the one who reveals the source of all questions and answers, Alexander still could not see this revelation.

He remained our friend for this is his just nature, but he is not one of us. Jeshua would say of this: "The words are in the air; some creatures hear what others do not. It is not the words but the hearing that is at fault."

Because of the presence of Marcus and Alexander, uncle's house became a center for the gathering of students, scholars and teachers of all kinds. There was a large room prepared for debate and discourse and Alexander would say it reminded him of his student days. There were loud and furious disputes and we children would overhear them.

At times Alexander would discuss the arguments with me to the extent that my youthful understanding would permit and he would be pleased that he could speak to me about them. He would jest, but I think a serious jest, that I would understand more than the dunderheads with whom he had to associate.

In this way, Jonathan, I learned much of the world. I was happy in this for even then I felt as our people always felt that the search for truth and knowledge comes out of our knowing the hidden God.

But we were also immersed in that alien world, the Greek and Roman world with its seductive ways. The Romans had their passion for order and law and the Greeks their pursuit of pleasure and bodily delights. The Greeks are a strange race, Jonathan, it would seem they are of two minds. Their great philosophers, ancient and present day, were highly esteemed and their teachings extolled the virtues of a just society wherein merit was repaid in kind and social justice was the highest good and goal. In many areas our Law and theirs were alike. Even more, Alexander read to me that in a just society women who were able and learned in law and justice could attain to kingship. How noble is this thought!

But these same people sought physical pleasures of all kinds. They knew naught of sin and thought physical beauty divine. They claimed that their devotion to the demands of the flesh was not inferior than that to the demands of the mind and they sought balance in both areas. But somehow, Jonathan, balance never was achieved, it was only the demands of the flesh that were sought; the fanciful Grecian ideas about justice and the highest good had no more substance than the tall tales they weaved about arrogant gods and heroic adventurers. Did they not put their wisest sage to death?

Even in Jerusalem, the heart of our people, there would be strange festivals and contests of all kinds. The wealthy and educated young Jewish men around Marcus would make their way to these contests behind the backs of their parents and out of the sight of the priests and rabbis. Alexander, to his credit and my relief, was not among them but his influence could not deter them, nor could it later restrain me.

More than that, Ceil and her friends would gossip about the women, Jews among them, whom the men would frequent to enjoy other pleasures. To aunt's despair, Ceil had friends who would copy these women in dress and secretly paint their faces and act shamelessly with young men.

It was in this time that I passed from girl to woman. As my body changed I realized a new idea of myself. I would like to say that Ceil's efforts to bring me into her circle of friends met with resistance, but I'm sorry to tell you, Jonathan, it was not so. I noticed the change in the men's attitude and the different way in which they looked at me. I found I was not uncomely and I began to feel a strange power in my womanhood, one that made me fearful and joyful at the same time.

I listened more attentively to the talk of the women, especially when, as often, the talk turned to men. I paid more attention to my dress and the way I looked. I played with these new feelings and I learned things about men and their weaknesses. This is knowledge, Jonathan, that without steadfastness of purpose can be dangerous to men and to women alike.

No wonder we are kept cloistered and covered. These men condemn our wantonness and captivating ways but in truth, they are so easily seduced and manipulated they should rather applaud our reluctance to take advantage of them. Our Laws are clear about this behavior, but in the looseness of the Greek culture that was tolerated in uncle's household, they were all but forgotten. I recall now with despair how the use of this knowledge led me into a sinful act that, were it not for the strength and blessed character of the one who sanctified it as he turned it aside, could have destroyed us both.

Jonathan, I was falling deeper into the frivolity and decadence of this place. I would find excuses to avoid Alexander; our meetings became less and less frequent. This kindly and wise man showed his concern and it could well have been his interest and his presence that kept me from the worst temptations.

He spoke often to aunt about Ceil and me but she was too eager to accept Ceil's assurances that we would never bring scandal upon the house. Uncle and Marcus were entirely engaged in their new business and they were no more involved in our lives than to suggest finding husbands for both of us.

I realized if Ceil could not, that behind these surface pleasures and petty achievements we were ignoring the substance of our lives. Often I would think about the sessions with Alexander and the reason for his initial interest in me. In quiet moments I recalled the feelings and experiences I had while engaged in my healing practices. At times my home and Jeshua's words would come to mind and I felt a closeness to God. At such times unhappiness would overcome me and I would resolve to change my ways. Alas, I could not obey that call and I know not why.

It was then that God interfered. I received word that mother died giving birth to my baby brother and father asked that I come home. I felt then a terrible sorrow and believed that God despaired of my behavior and thoughts but had no other way of saving me. I could not bear the thought of mother suffering for my sins and at once a cloud fell over me.

No word, no deed, no thought could lift my feelings as I made my slow way home to our village. I left for Jerusalem those short years before, a fearful and sad young girl; and now I returned, no longer innocent of the ways of the world, but no less fearful and sad.

How strange I must have appeared to father's household upon my return! Dressed as I was in city clothes, my village garments were long gone. And now I was stumbling with a hesitant village speech, after speaking and thinking only in learned Greek. Those who did not know me before must have thought me backward. I understood everything, but I struggled to find the words to respond.

I arrived into a house of mourning. Mother had been buried, but all activity ceased save the most essential. The baby was nursed and cared for by a young servant woman, a new mother herself, to the relief of father who had so wanted a male child. He thought him a gift of providence. I remember now my ignoble thought when he expressed that sentiment: Did he thank that same providence that took the baby's mother?

I was well aware of the changes in myself worked by my stay in

Jerusalem the past years. But still I was unprepared for the changes in the lives of my family in that same time. I always had the sense that this family, into which I was born for God's good reason, was apart from our neighbors in many ways, and that sense sharpened with my return.

My younger sister was betrothed to the eldest son of a well-to-do farmer in a neighboring village. They did not say why they could not wait for my own betrothal as was our custom; perhaps father, knowing my nature as he did, understood that only I would make that decision and in my own good time. Whatever the reason, after mother died and I returned, it was decided that sister would live in the house of her future husband until she was ready for the marriage bed. Father's plan was that I take mother's place in the household.

It was during this mourning period that Jeshua again entered my life, though he had often been in my thoughts. Neither of us was prepared for the changes we saw in the other. I do not know what he thought in that first tentative moment when he appeared unsure of who I was, but I recognized him immediately and marked that I saw no remaining boyish quality in his bearing. His earlier shyness was gone and I was struck by the innocent nature of his new self-assurance.

I thought later, when musing about that time, when I saw him among the company from the village, how some treated him with a certain deference but others would ignore him and still others would treat him with disdain. If there were any reason on his part to provoke these responses, they escaped me.

You know, Jonathan, we often talked about this quality of his, present so early in his life, that allowed some to see deeply into his heart and soul and rejoice in its divine union with the Almighty. We feel so keenly, even now, how his very being guides our own to that goal. He is our path. And yet, at this late date, there are others to whom he can say nothing and to whom he is nothing. Some, indeed, see him as an enemy and traitor to our people.

Only our venerable Joseph, who understands these mysteries

better than most, could explain: "It is not Master who is at fault; people are made ready to visit the hidden world, the world beyond, by their own deeds, those they perform now or had performed earlier in their immeasurable past. The others are not to be condemned, they must simply await another call."

How easily I moved back into the life of the village. It was as if I had never left. I picked up the rhythms of the day and I realized I forgot nothing of the ways and needs of the animals. I was thankful the servants accepted my supervision and decisions as they accepted mother's.

I felt a new confidence and strength and rejoiced as my despair left; I could see now clearly the abyss I had been heading for in Jerusalem, and my sorrow was for Ceil whom I left facing those temptations without a steadying hand. Jeshua once told me, when I had reason to confide these thoughts to him: "You have a power and presence people cannot ignore, Sara. Regard them carefully."

As I settled into the slow and quiet tempo of village life, the heavy burdens imposed by living in that Jerusalem world became ever clearer. I no more agonized over my dress, my image, and my attractiveness. It mattered not the glance or lack of it from this one or that. I realized only then the bondage of a life spent in the anticipation of events, then in the immersion in them, and then in their fading, often into disappointment.

After that first meeting at mother's mourning, Jeshua and I saw much of each other. It became almost unseemly and father remarked about it. What drew us together was more my need of him than his need of me. Only later was I to learn the nature of his needs and the impossibility of my providing for them.

But as the influences of Jerusalem faded, once again God's will — I always believed it such — emerged in my awareness. And I found in myself questions only Jeshua could understand and I found that only to him could I state them.

I felt that old kinship with our animals return as once again awareness of their fears and pain came into my knowing. When they were skittish or unwell I would be called and just my touch or presence would gentle them. And once again this same touch and presence would bring comfort to our ailing children, but we learned the lessons well from our former trials and suspicions and we were careful in using these gifts. Aside from Jeshua, only that group of father's religious brotherhood would acknowledge this benefaction. I was accorded a special place among them.

Despite this special place, I would not be permitted to be part of this group because I was a woman. There were some, there were always some and Jeshua was among them, who would accord the not few women like myself a place in their spiritual life, but most could not; their traditions weighed too heavily against it.

But father, who felt keenly my strong kinship with God from the experience of our lives together, counted me a fellow disciple. He would share their conversations and discuss their disputes and listen to my commentary and thoughts about them. Indeed, to my delight, he would often use my thoughts to embellish his own comments and when I heard him do that, I must confess, it increased my already unbecoming boldness.

Jeshua, too, had his difficulties with them. His father and mine were devoted elders of the external community of brothers and, like me, he was brought up from childhood hearing these teachings. But from early in his life, along with his bold interpretation and commentary on the Torah in the village synagogue, he never hesitated to question the understanding of their rule and their law.

For this reason, and despite his father's desires, he was always judged unfit for initiation into the order and his position with them remained unclear. Indeed, in those days, Jonathan, if that infinite tranquil nature we have come to associate with Master were present, it was not easily seen in young Jeshua.

Nor were other things seen that a less misted eye could not have missed. Scarcely a day passes when I do not thank God for His presence, and Jeshua's pure awareness of Him on that night when the evil one made me an instrument for his plans.

Did you know, Jonathan, that Jeshua's father and mine were

of a mind for our betrothal? I did not know of these plans nor did I know of Jeshua's adamant refusal to obey his father. This well could have been another reason for their constant bickering; Jeshua was not an obedient son. Although we find it difficult to find any fault with him, even one from his early days, it would be wrong to deny his sins.

For this reason father did not inquire about my feelings. I knew nothing of this until long after Jeshua left and Jacob came to us with Anna and we learned Jeshua would be gone, perhaps never to return. I am sure, in my ignorance, I would have agreed to this union with joy.

How much ignorance and how little joy that union would have proven to be! The day I heard that Jeshua was to leave with the trading caravan my heart stopped at the thought of his absence from my life. I remember a feeling of terrible emptiness. And it was into that emptiness that Belial crawled to do his work.

Can I tell Jonathan how that idea seized me? That I could keep Jeshua with us by offering my love and my body. Even now I recoil at the thought. But those days in Jerusalem came back to me when I saw how easily men could be beguiled.

We would at times meet together in places where we could talk quietly, although not hidden places. He was always a source of solace; as others found comfort in my words and closeness, so I found comfort in his. So when he told me he wanted to speak to me with news of importance, I knew it was to be about his leaving. We made arrangements to meet that evening.

When we met I held myself close and I remember, Jonathan, a fear of what Jeshua would say to me. I could not know then what I learned later, how impossible my thoughts or desires were. Nor did I understand how his life was suffering an unanswered call from an unrelenting heavenly Father — calling for his disobedience from an equally persistent earthly one.

He told me he met by chance (could it have been by chance?) a holy man from an Eastern country. There is a remoteness and peace in that country, even now lying on the land after many centuries since the arrival of *their* Messiah, that cannot now be found here, the Monarchos told him. Though Jeshua spoke only few words with this one, he knew that that was his call: here he was dying, there was new birth. Only there could his questions be answered. He must leave the tumult of this land and the conflicts with his father. And he had contrived a way to leave without shame for his parents.

I paused. Can I reveal, even to Jonathan, what has never been revealed, how I contrived for us to meet in a secluded place? I can still see that place where I would go when the need for solitude came over me. I do not know now how I failed to see my wickedness when I made ready to meet Jeshua that night: when I covered my naked body with a simple cape and the remnants of an ancient perfumed oil.

Can I remember what he said? Did I hear him? But, alas, I do remember what I did as these soundless words faded uselessly in the night. I shut my eyes tightly to shut out the world as I allowed the cape to fall from my shoulders to the ground. "Look at me Jeshua," I said, and as I did, I thought it was another speaking, that I was not one with this person. "Take me tonight, hurry, so we will never part."

When his hands touched mine I came together again; I will never forget how my body came alive in every part of it. Every particle of it had feeling and I began an uncontrollable shivering as he gently lowered me to the ground. An eternity passed as I waited — waited for what? — I will not think of it.

Nor do I know what I thought when I felt his cloak being wrapped around my body. I opened my eyes when I was covered again and felt his hands pulling the covering together around me so tightly I could not move. How strong, I thought, were his hands.

My eyes were so full I could not see his face as he pulled me toward him. Had I been able I would have disappeared into the void. He kissed my forehead and his lips were as balm to my shaking body. What he then said is engraved on my soul. "Sara, I love you and I accept your love as you offer it. My body responds to yours as a man's should. But I cannot do this thing. I do not know who I am, or what I am, but only that I am of this world but yet see in it things others do not. I leave because I cannot live with the fetters you offer. We are joined in ways that are even more powerful but I cannot say more for I do not know more."

Yes, even this must be revealed to Jonathan. And as I make that decision I know that never in Jeshua's eyes was I less for this expression of love for him.

Our lives would always be joined, he told me, but not in the way our fathers imagined. You may think it strange, Jonathan, that I can speak of Master as an ordinary man. But there was a time everyone in our village thought of him in that way and only I knew how really extraordinary he was. And that knowledge had to remain in my secret heart.

CYPRUS III

Father, I am frightened. Where was I?"

I heard Aaron's faint voice, but it was the tightening of his hand on mine that brought the world back into focus. I looked at the sun's shadow on the wall and saw only moments had passed. How elusive is time! Does it really exist? No, not in the light of that other world, only in the darkness of this one.

"I saw a woman, father, was it Sara? When I tried to look closely she faded; I heard her also but when I listened to the sounds they fell silent. Then there was writing on a large parchment but when I went to read it I could not; I saw the words, I knew the letters, but I could not grasp the meaning. I am afraid to close my eyes. When I do so I see a jumble of images and hear strange voices. Tell me father, what happened to me? What possesses me father? Help me."

"Be calm, Aaron, you are not ill. This is all good. You entered a world that is beyond yourself, beyond what your eyes can see or your ears can hear. A place where happens another kind of seeing and another kind of hearing."

I felt the turmoil ease in him as his hand relaxed the tight hold it had on mine. But he did not release my hand, perhaps yet need-ing the security of our contact. But his touch reached deep inside me to a long forgotten time when I grasped another's hand for that same security, and the love and comfort I then received from Sara now flowed into Aaron in his time of need.

"It is a dying in a way," I continued, "a fear you may not have known because of your age, but this is what you felt. We cling to the things of this world, to ourselves, as life itself, not knowing it is just this we must lose to gain the other. Then we return as one reborn with the power and knowledge of God's kingdom, now ours in whole or in part. But doing so, Aaron, often stirs up the leavings of your past, from what eons of past only God knows, therefore your visions and sounds. Ignore them, they will fade as the illusions they are."

As I repeated Master's words I remembered his manner, his understanding of my confusion, the comfort I felt in his gaze and the joyful sensation of happiness that stole through my body. I looked at Aaron and I knew this, too, was being offered to him.

"Aaron, you reached this place through me, really as a gift from Master to whom you must give thanks, but you can now find your own way. You will see. You need only a little more guidance.

"Now you know the story of Sara as I do. It is there though you may not realize it. When the time comes that it needs to be told or inscribed you will find it. That is the way of that world, you will come to know it as you know this one, even better, in truth, though it seems a mystery.

"I remember well when Master taught us this and other things that men, then and now, call the workings of God. They would frighten some who would say leave the work of God to God — it is blasphemy otherwise. Master would answer, are we not made in God's image? If so, why would one in His image not do his deeds? Why would one not be perfect as He is perfect?"

"Father, what of Jacob? I feel this emptiness in me of not knowing him as I know of Sara. Can I learn of Jacob too, father?"

He could and he must. But for that he no longer needed me. He knew the way but did not know yet he knew.

"Come to me, Aaron," I beckoned, and as he moved toward me I touched that place in him I knew would open his understanding. "Close your eyes, Aaron. Look into Jacob's heart, Aaron, seek it, find it, enter it, and you will know the man. Stay with this thought, find Jacob."

I needed do no more, he was as I am, and he could find his way.

JACOB I

There are among our people those who see in every event, every happenstance, every meeting, an expression of the hidden workings of our invisible God. I am not one of them. Although a Jew by birth, creed and ritual, I have spent more than enough time outside the villages and towns of my people to find other simpler, indeed more reasonable, explanations of the vicissitudes of life.

When one of my donkey-drawn wagons broke down, cracking an axle and ruining a wheel, I saw no special omen, malignant or benign, in that fact. Nor did I see an otherworldly influence in the fortuitous event that it happened at the end of the caravan day when animals and people stopped their plodding and prepared for their evening meal and night's rest. I generally find no solace in the idea that bad things can be worse.

It was no more than a coincidence, I knew, if I thought about it at all, that this resting place was close to the village I already had need to visit. This was the village of the woman, Sara, who as a girl stayed in the Jerusalem home of her kinsman, my patron and friend Marcus. He, with his close companion and fellow student Alexander, made my acquaintance when upon their return from their studies abroad they were intent on exploring Herod's new Jerusalem. I, too, at this time, was fresh from my days in Rome and, like them, passed easily between Jewish and Greek culture.

I labor this point of chance because it becomes more difficult to sustain as I recollect those distant events. Clearly it can be seen now, with that clarity hindsight always achieves, that the odd encounters in the time I speak of affected my life in ways I could never have imagined.

Were those changes divinely inspired to provide me with opportunities for a great righteousness in the tradition of our pious ones, as some have suggested? Or perversely, to divert me from my long-held desire to see my country and its people free from Rome? These questions still tear at my deepest being.

Those two young men, Marcus and Alexander, from wealthy Jewish families who were newly rich, were eagerly taking advantage of a benevolent and protective Roman emperor. Caesar was intent on repaying the Jews for their earlier support for him against the hated Pompey in the civil war yet fresh in memory. Siding with Caesar against Pompey was not a difficult decision for the Jews, remembering as they did how, Pompey, he destroyed the city and profaned the Temple.

These youths slipped easily into the Greek ways that were earning Jerusalem its conflicted reputation. It was not only the center of the religious life of our ancient Jewish people and held sacred by them, but it was also the cosmopolitan and trading hub for this part of the Roman world.

Accessible by sea and land from the centers of western and eastern civilizations, it lacked for nothing that could be transported from one part of the known world to the other. There was no lack either of an alien population drawn from the hinterlands with goods and services of every description, services it must be said, often anathema to the Jewish rulers of the city. Large public displays of Greek beauty and flesh and Roman type circus and theater could not be found. But discreet activity hidden from the eyes — if not the knowledge — of Temple police and authority, and ignored by the Roman overseers, could be located in the many non-Jewish quarters of the growing metropolis.

The city teemed with Syrians, Egyptians, Persians, Arabs, Hindis, Greeks and others and then mixed with regional peoples of indistinguishable ancestry. In addition, Roman civilians with their special privileges and manner, and slaves of all hues, added to its diversity and this only begins to describe Jerusalem in the early days of Herod's frantic rebuilding. This polyglot people could be individually distinguished by their distinct dress but all had in common the Greek language. This was the language of commerce, the legacy of Alexander's conquests; just as the common people shared the Aramaic vernacular, that almost Hebraic tongue, itself the legacy of an earlier conqueror, the Persian, Darius.

But this was still a Jewish city ruled by Temple priests and their wealthy allies under the rule of the Herodic dynasty. Only they had access to the Roman procurator and they were the nominal administrators of the city and the provinces of Judea, Samaria, Peraea, and Galilee. The grievances of disgruntled foreigners would, on occasion, make their way to the ears of Roman officials. "How," they would ask, "do the conquerors permit their subjects to prohibit perfectly normal and accepted behavior that is the custom of others? Indeed," they would subtly chide their masters, "even your own legionaries are required to leave the city for distant places for their lawful periodic relief from their duties."

But Empire politics were such at the time that a delicate balance needed to be maintained to ensure stability in the area, always a problem with this volatile people. Jewish influence was felt directly in the inner circles of the Emperor himself and no procurator, whose personal fortune and future well-being depended on his ability to prevent a word of dissatisfaction from reaching Rome, could afford to alienate Jewish sensibilities. History has too often shown the cost of that arrogance.

It was because of that special dispensation toward the Jews and their large presence in Rome that I was able to reach my present position, coming as I do from a small village in southern Judea. How the early Jews found their way to Rome is part of the story of our dispersion to communities around the world. There was no part of the Roman world in which we could not be found with our special God and separate ways and, above all, with His Word given directly to Moses for our guidance.

It was Pompey's perverse fate that his defeat of the Jewish defenders of Jerusalem and his defilement of its holiest alcove would seal his future. The subsequent decision to transport surviving Jewish fighters as prisoners to Rome for sale or ransom in fact augmented

the Roman-Jewish community and, indeed, increased Jewish influence in that city. In Jewish eyes he was damned and they only
waited the time for their revenge.

Our region provided many fighters, some my relatives, for their
ill-fated defense of Jerusalem, and despite the chaos of the times
they managed a tenuous thread of communication with their home
areas as they were transported past Jewish communities on their
torturous trek to Rome. Some escaped en route and the Roman
troops, many of them non-Roman ignorant barbarians, simply
collected innocent villagers to replace them. The enmity this caused
Pompey can only be imagined.

In time, a ransom was arranged and, because of the shifting
political winds of that unstable Roman era, many of the former
prisoners were permitted to remain in Rome. This, as it turned
out, was a wise decision for Caesar — not to mention his descen-
dants. When his alliance with Pompey, as part of the first triumvi-
rate to rule Rome, broke down he found significant, some would
say vital, support from Rome's Jews and Jewish communities
throughout what was now to become the Roman Empire.

One of my kinsmen, a young warrior whom our elders still
recall well, was one of those ransomed who elected to remain in
Rome. He married into an established "old" Jewish family and
prospered as the community prospered, until finally, after Caesar's
ascension, acquired Roman citizenship, being among the first Jews,
if not one of the first foreigners, able to do this, at no little cost it
must be added.

Nevertheless, neither he nor his family-to-be ever cut their
ties to their Judean background, and unlike many of their Roman
Jewish counterparts, continued to read our Law in Hebrew and
more than most kept as close as possible to its prescriptions. Dietary laws, discreet religious observance, and a clannishness, though
subtle, marked the entire community apart.

Still, an unworldly Jewish visitor from a Jewish village almost
anywhere in the world could never have distinguished him or any
one of his class or congregation from a well-to-do Roman Gentile

by dress or speech, or indeed, household activity, so easily did they meld with the city's population.

But our ties went even deeper than this surface appearance. It was a tradition in our family that one of its sons would be sent to Rome to our kinsman's family, preferably just after the time of entrance into adulthood, for education and training. This traditional connection provided proven material benefits: for our people in Rome it represented direct contact with an area of growing importance and wealth to the new Caesar Tiberius and, of course, great benefit to my local village as ties to and influence in Rome were of inestimable value.

It was my fate that I would be chosen for this role. And in fact, although impossible then to fathom, this selection also was the seed for a terrible personal conflict that would, in the end, turn all of my life's accomplishments to dust, and then only would a new life be redeemed in glorious triumph.

It was with contentious feelings that I greeted the decision of my father and uncles that I would be the one chosen. Descriptions of Roman life, in truth, more mythical tales than fact, challenged my adventurous spirit and I felt the confidence natural to youth and ignorance, and but little apprehension. But, on the other side, I was content with village and farm life and not anxious to leave it. I was sure of my abilities with its work, understanding well the needs and qualities of our animals and the care of the good Judean earth.

Also, because of my position as the oldest son of the chief village landowner and the added benefit of a large and sturdy frame, my self-assured manner — perhaps somewhat arrogant, I now ruefully acknowledge — I experienced a valued deference from peasants and servants. Though this respect was not solely due to my accomplishments it was one, nevertheless, in which I took an unseemly pride.

I did not know then, but was soon to learn, that a big man in a small village could shrink considerably in a large town. I suspect the decision to send me to Rome was greeted by many because of a desire to see me gone, and not out of happiness for my perceived good fortune.

My years in Rome did not succeed in erasing the formative years of my life in my village; those earlier days remained the bedrock of my nature and sensibilities. But they did succeed in superimposing a veneer of "aristocracy" on my personality, a gloss that could hide my rustic beginnings. My schooling was formal and practical and I reached a satisfactory mastery of scholastic Greek and legalistic Latin. I became knowledgeable in Roman and Greek history but, so much more importantly, I deepened thereby my understanding of the history and needs of my own people.

I learned the ways of men of politics and commerce, and I took on the dress, manner and voice of a son of Roman nobility. And it is in this context I would point out, that if I, a son of a far-off Judean village, could so easily take on the trappings of this Gentile world, how even more easily a Roman-born Jew could lose his way. What kept us Jews? How powerful must our God be with no visible reminder but His Word as given to Moses.

The temper of these unstable and unpredictable times brought into sharp focus within my ken the contradictions and social forces working to tear these societies apart. Rome's transition from republican rule to emperor mirrored in a strange way the social upheavals in my native land.

The Roman drive for expansion, the city's engorgement with slave labor with its necessary impoverishment of the free worker, and a professional paid military, created revenue needs with no end. Road taxes, head taxes, land taxes, water taxes: no one moved or breathed without paying and cities and regions alike were dunned.

All of this was imposed on the system of revenue gathering already in place to sustain local rulers; for our people it was added to Temple taxes and tithes for various levels of the priesthood, and every offering required an acknowledgment fee beyond the offering itself. An army of special tax collectors grew up to be found, and hated, everywhere.

The farmer who fell behind in payments had little recourse beyond the mercy of the collector who enjoyed the power of Temple authorities buttressed by Roman rule. He could lose everything and finally be imprisoned for failure to pay his due.

True, I am the son of new, if middling, wealth and privilege, and acquiring a larger share of these material gains seems more and more to occupy the thoughts and time of my family. Yet we recognized our deep Jewish roots, our special place in the eyes of our God and our connection with the common Judean people. It was impossible, therefore, not to reflect on the mindless and pernicious behavior of those more fortunate of our people who over and over risked God's fury by repeating the misdeeds of their ancestors.

Indeed, as the holdings of my own family grew with the joining of house to house and field to field, members of my household, steeped in our Law and history, became increasingly disturbed by the subsequent impoverishment of our neighbors, at whose expense this aggrandizement took place. We could only absorb a few displaced farmers and even fewer of their own former farm hands and servants.

Villages throughout Judea suffered the same fate and the dispossessed flooded into the larger towns nearby and then to Jerusalem for what work they could find. Most sank into a servitude even greater than that of their former state, many became beggars, and, although most Jews did not buy or use slaves, it was said some fell into this category and disappeared into the Gentile world.

One consequence of this growing destitution was the increasing influence of various sects, always present among our people in seed form, that echoed the warnings of past prophets reminding the high born and newly risen of the old time of kings. They reminded them of the time when the son and grandson of David oppressed the people and squandered their wealth on temple and palace.

They reminded them how they fell out of God's favor and were shattered and dispersed to foreign lands; reminded them of their return to Jerusalem and the rebuilding of the city with God's love and grace. And reminded them over and over of how Nehemiah responded to their lamentations. After hearing the selfsame complaints from the ordinary people of his time Nehemiah said:

I reprimanded the authorities and officials. "What a burden you impose," I said, "every one of you on his brother!" Summoning a great assembly to deal with them, I said to them, "To the best of our power, we have redeemed our brother Jews who had been sold to foreigners, and now you in turn are selling our brothers for us to redeem them!"

They were silent and could find nothing to say. "What you are doing," I went on, "is wrong. Do you not want to walk in the fear of our God and escape the sneers of the nations, our enemies? I, too, my kinsmen, and my servants have lent them money and corn. Let us cancel this debt. Return them their fields, their vineyards, their olive groves and their houses forthwith, and remit the debt on the money, corn, wine and oil which you have lent them."

"We will make restitution," they replied, "we will claim nothing more from them; we will do as you say." At once I summoned the priests and made them swear to do as they had promised. Then I shook out the lap of my gown with the words, "May God do this, and shake out of his house and property any man who does not keep this promise; may he be shaken out like this and left empty!" And the whole assembly answered, "Amen," and gave praise to Yahweh. And the people kept this promise.

In this time also the leaders of the people brought Ezra, learned in the Law of Moses, from Babylon to instruct them in the Law and their behavior as Jews, which had grown lax in exile. Although the Persian king, Artaxerxes, mandated this effort to bind the people closer to his rule, something more took place. Ezra gathered the thousands in public and instructed them in the meaning and power of the five books of Moses, in its own holy language and then in commentary in their common tongue so all could understand.

They are not simply a tribe, he would tell them, nor a cultural entity, nor a subject of this king or that nation. But they are people of God's Law: in their own land or dispersed, self-governing or oppressed, they are a community governed by the Law of Moses, chosen by God to keep alive his Law.

And this Law leaves no doubt: neither king nor priest, neither rich landowner nor merchant, should impoverish the people for the accumulation of unlimited wealth. Over and over our people have felt God's wrath by violating these warnings and now, once again, they were risking destruction through greed and ignorance. And once again strident voices were heard throughout Jewish Palestine calling for a new Nehemiah, a new Ezra, to instruct and guide the people.

But there were hidden voices as well. Conflicting and dangerous voices that rallied the people to resistance causing fear in the hearts of the Jewish authorities and nervousness in the minds of the uncomprehending Romans.

These voices were so much part of my life that I cannot tell now when I first heard their whisper. Indeed, I sometimes wonder if, as some of our people believe, they came from an earlier life where they were engraved on my soul.

And they caused much sorrow and searching because of their influence. Unlike my companions, I could never enter into the seductive concupiscence of the Greek world without a later feeling of despondency and a need for penance. In time, only wine offered peace.

After each period of debauchery, when I lay spent from my excesses, the exhortations of these new prophets emerged in all their clarity, and left me with a new confusion. For two conflicting demands compelled my attention, albeit both calling me to take my rightful place in the community of God. One, stand with the Jews who resist the Occupiers and the Jewish oppressors who abet them; and the other, join with the pious believers in isolated desert communities and small urban groups. These are preparing the way for salvation through obedience and prayer as they earn God's support and await the new Teacher.

My upbringing, training and character all worked to make me feel my place belonged with the resistance. If I thought at all of my position as a Jew, as part of these people, of an obligation to them above myself, I thought of myself as part of that group.

I appreciated my material position and understood well my privileges. But I resented the Roman occupiers and their arrogance and sense of superiority. Although I knew the increasing impoverishment of our people mirrored the impoverishment and enslavement of their own common masses, I knew also it was out of their ignorance and imperial insolence they could not do differently.

If I determined to follow a purposeful life course my inclinations and desires would move me in this direction. Why then was it my continuous fate to be thrown into the most intimate contact with the pious ones? It was as if I were held by unseen bonds needing the most forceful effort to loosen; then, when freed from them, I was to be thrown into a new despair.

I determined finally I must leave this chaos and find a new way for myself. I could no longer live this dissolute life. I could see clearly in the lives of others, even those more promising than I, a disastrous end. Yet I had no access into the new world of faith calling me. I sensed its promise, I responded to its song, but so insubstantial was it that I could not find the words to express this longing, though I would feel it over and over.

I could unburden myself only to Alexander, cry out these vague musings to him alone. I knew him as a wise physician, although still young, and a friend, though surely more Marcus' than mine, but now I found him a kindred spirit with compassionate understanding. He shared neither my wanton tendencies toward fleshly desires nor my ascetic aversion to the things of the world, my two enemies, but he understood both. In temperament and training he hewed to the Greek principle, "moderation in all things." And this moderation made him a wise mentor.

He did not address the details of my lament, indeed, he seemed to dismiss them as symptoms of a deeper malady. He mentioned that Marcus was proposing a trading mission, his first extended effort since reorganizing his grandfather's business. He was looking for a person to accompany and supervise the transport. "Speak to him, Jacob. With your command of languages and your travel experience, and as a person he can doubtless trust, you should suit him perfectly. For your part it will provide a long respite from the cares you now suffer and it will offer much time for reflection."

As it was said it was done! In fact, Alexander's surmise was correct. Marcus was pleased and considered my proposal a fortuitous event for him. He was planning a trading expedition of three wagons and four camel carriers. This group would be part of a larger caravan being organized by a group of Jerusalem traders.

Roman peace and Roman military roads revived the movement of goods throughout the region. Large caravans provided security from small groups of bandits and made it possible to pay Roman commanders for protection against the larger guerrilla units controlling the wilderness.

Thus it was I found myself making my way toward the farm of my patron's kinsman. The village and countryside of my boyhood Judea and this rugged Galilean landscape could not be more different. But as I approached the village I felt a sense of growing familiarity, as I became more and more aware of the sounds and smells of pastoral activity.

Jonah's farm, I had been told, was the first to be reached from the south and by tradition his land reached to the edge of the road. His would be the first dwelling I would see, off the road a way, but clearly visible from it.

The village, a hamlet really, was located in the southern part of upper Galilee. Situated on one side of the major trade route out of Jerusalem, it headed north to a branching point near Damascus. One part of it continued to Antioch and the other turned to the east to pick up the ancient road connecting our world to the eastern peoples.

In addition, the community was in the orbit of the capital of the Galilean district, Sepphoris, which Herod Antipas was in the process of rebuilding in the Roman image. Travelers to that city included wealthy vacationing Jerusalemites, Roman military on leave, merchants intent on new business and a continuous stream of officials to conduct affairs of state in Herod's court. The people here, therefore, were not the usual Galilean rustic, but had some of the language and sophistication of us Judeans.

The main building of Jonah's farm was built with four sides enclosing a large courtyard, less typical of small villages than those closer to a town, but speaking of more than the meager resources usually seen in these areas. The front of the house facing the road had a large gated opening through which animals, carts and people would pass.

As one approached the building proper, large water cisterns and presses for olives greeted the eye, and there were vats for oil and millstones and storage areas for grain. It was clearly a well-run and well-to-do farm. I was soon to learn there were small residences for servants and laborers on the grounds and day workers as needed were employed.

In the center of the courtyard was a large shade tree. External cooking areas were strategically located and used especially this time of the year when it was still hot and dry before the onset of the new season. As I neared the gate I could see movement around the cooking areas as the evening meal was being prepared. I saw a servant notice me as I tentatively entered the yard who went to call his master. Immediately a man whom I took by his bearing to be Jonah, the master, stepped out and motioned me forward.

"Peace to you master," I addressed him. "I am Jacob, a servant to Marcus, kinsman to your late wife, God bless her."

His eyes opened with interest. "And to you peace, Jacob. You are correct, I am Jonah. And how is it with my wife's people?"

"They are well, Jonah, and send greetings. Especially to your daughter, Sara, whom they remember with fondness and pray she is well."

"She is well Jacob, thank you, and she will be here shortly to greet you. Please sit here and I will have some wine brought to you."

Before I had a chance to seat myself Sara stepped out the open door standing just behind but to the side of her father. As she came out our eyes met and for a full measure of time we looked directly at each other. And then when her gaze lowered I sensed it dropped out of custom, not out of the deference that is the nature of our women. I thought then how much I wanted to look again into those eyes.

"Your cousin, Ceil, sends greetings, lady, and hopes you are well. She sends this letter to you." I felt her eyes on me as I fumbled in my tunic for the paper I had for her. I noticed in myself a strange loss of composure with our contact, one that left me perplexed for the few moments I was aware of it. She took the letter nodding her thanks and said, as much to her father as to me:

"I'll see to our evening meal. Jacob, you must stay of course. We don't often hear news about our family and events in Jerusalem although you'll find we are not ignorant of those things."

After she took her leave and Jonah brought me to the table for refreshment, I had my first chance to speak to him regarding the problem with my wagon.

"Well," Jonah said, "you can do no better than to find repairs here. Our town is noted, as you must have heard, for the skill of our wheelwrights and carpenters." He looked at me quizzically for a moment before he continued. "Your speech and appearance seem that of a common man, Jacob, but there is about you something that leads me to think otherwise. Am I being misled in my thinking?"

"No Jonah, I don't want to mislead you. My boyhood was as yours, on a farm in southern Judea . . . "

"From your speech I gathered that," he interrupted with a snicker close to derision, "I knew you were not raised in these parts."

"But later I was educated in Rome," I continued, ignoring his interruption, "which circumstance led me to my friendship and service with your kinsmen."

"They are really my wife's kinsmen, not mine," he said, obviously not pleased with the relationship for reasons I later learned. "My interests and purpose are far from theirs."

He looked at me intently as he said those words trying to

judge, I thought, my reaction to them. I made no response but I was surely alerted to what he said.

After a moment's pause he continued. "But to your problem, Jacob. We have a man on our farm who can see to your needs and I will send for him shortly. For you he will do a service many others here can also do. But I believe he will consider it providential that you turned up at this time as you did."

Jonah then went on to explain that the man, Jeshua, the son of one of his tenants, had been called to a Jewish settlement, it was really no more than that, in an eastern country which was formerly a Greek province once conquered by the great general called Alexander. This country, he went on, Bactria it is called by the Greeks, is the meeting place where the two worlds collide, coalesce and speak to each other. . . .

"But why am I telling you this," he interrupted himself, "you know better than I of what I speak."

Indeed, I listened with surprise at what he was saying as I am not used to farm people with this understanding and knowledge of the world. More than once as events unfolded I was to be surprised at my own lack of perception and my misunderstanding of a people with whom I had little contact and about whom, I now know, I heard so much false information.

"This settlement," he continued, "is part of the larger community of pious Jews who want to restore the ancient social laws. This, I am sure, is no secret to you. We believe (and for the first time he identified himself as one with them) that only in this way will we regain possession of our own lands and earn the support of God who will send his anointed one to free us."

Yes, this was no secret to me. In Jerusalem I would hear these people spoken about with fear by wealthy and leading Jews and with rage by the Romans who were frustrated by the reluctance of the Jewish authorities to silence them.

For the Romans it was a matter of treason but for the Jews, except those closest to the procurator, in league with him as I heard more than once, it was still a matter of religious dispute. It is with good reason, I now thought, they speak of Galilee as the land of disputation whence nothing good ever comes.

But who is this Jeshua, I wondered, and what service can I be to him? Sitting thoughtfully for a moment, and then as if answering my unspoken question, Jonah began to tell me about his tenant's son.

"You may find him somewhat strange, Jacob, but as we know him for many years, coming to manhood as he did among us, we find a depth in his strangeness that touches our hearts and transforms what others find odd into a sense of joy in his presence. From his boyhood he showed an extraordinary intelligence.

"His father is of our sect and devoted to and most learned in its teachings. Jeshua's days, when not working were spent in mastering the written word, but he showed himself most apt in understanding the hidden mysteries elders of our community uncover in the ancient words of the one who led us out of Egypt.

"In synagogue during services he could explain the book and teachings in such a way that we all soon forgot his youth. At first the father's life was conflicted, for as the eldest son Jeshua was important to the well-being of his family and his father depended on his skills.

"The larger community, however, revered his knowledge and understanding and called upon his time as well. He was often summoned to the desert commune, one not far from here, where our people live in isolation for purposes of retreat and study. They esteem him highly and some are moved to say he might be the messenger we await. That the awaited one would come from one of us, one hardly a king, is scoffed at by most, and I am troubled by the talk because I have a more intimate knowledge of him than many others and I find the idea difficult.

"Sara, too, my daughter as you know, would discount that thought I am sure, though we have never spoken of him in that way. She is closest to him almost being raised together. Do you know of Sara, Jacob, why she was in Jerusalem with her mother's family?"

I nodded my head. "Slightly, Jonah, I heard Alexander, the

tutor her aunt arranged for her, speak of her so I knew of her presence but little else."

Again, the thought of Sara got my attention. I saw Jonah was going to say more about her so my lagging interest in his words took new life.

"She is in many ways odd like Jeshua." His tone took on a musing aspect as he continued. "She knows things she ought not know and understands at the first explanation of any question. She was sent to Jerusalem because there was talk of her in the village that she was a sorceress; even the mothers of those whose children she helped would not defend her.

"It was my habit to teach the village children our ancient teachings in the holy language, boys and girls alike, and it was a miracle how rapidly Sara learned her lessons, almost as if she knew them already. I am told that the Greek philosophers would say of one like her that she is simply recollecting what she knew in the past, she is learning nothing new. Is that possible, Jacob? You are learned in the Greek thinking. Do our people speak of that?"

"Yes, Jonah, I heard that as well." Again I wondered at the knowledge of this seemingly simple man. "In the city there are many scholars who dispute the different beliefs and there is one creed from the land to where I am traveling that has this tenet. But also in our books, I have heard in my own village, we have similar ideas embedded in the teaching, but that it requires a special understanding to uncover it."

Again I realized how uncomfortable I am with this kind of discussion, though it seems my destiny I am chagrined to think, to forever encounter it. Though I wanted to hear more of Sara, Jonah continued with his account of this Jeshua:

"His father, my tenant and friend, is also unhappy with this situation. Although thanking God for this gift in his son, he also fears losing him to the wilderness. There have been others, who when struck by this fever, have taken themselves off preaching a new way, scourging themselves with fasting and torments, only to end a fruitless life by self-denial or at the hands of those they

denounce. There are no signs of this frenzy in Jeshua, true, but a
father's fear is not always a reasonable one.

"It is in these ways that he is so much different than others of
our young people. And like most of our people, he talks less than
you city folk, but that is a blessing I would think."

I smiled inwardly at those words. I had seldom accosted a
more garrulous farmer than my present host.

"As you say, Jonah, my respected host. The nature of your
tenant's son is not unknown to me, please do not take offense, but
these ecstasies and transports some of our rural people are given to
are embarrassing to more sober heads, especially those who must
care for the needs of the people. And your sect and beliefs are also
no secret to me, but I must confess little interest in these questions.

"Putting that aside, though, I also admit that my heart is close
to your thinking as I have seen in my life the terrible injustices
inflicted on our people by the Occupiers. Alas, truth to be told,
our own people do no less to each other."

I realized even before finishing my last sentence that Jonah
had taken no heed of my attempt to mollify my disparaging remarks about what was of such importance to him. He was clearly
upset, thinking no doubt that he said more than he should have.
But before he could reply we each noticed a man nearing the front
gate although still some distance away.

As he approached I was surprised to see another figure meet
up with him, both of them stop in greeting, and then come toward us together with an obvious compatibility. In a moment I
realized it was Sara that met with him and as I watched them the
thought came to me they were betrothed. It was not seemly for
couples not so engaged to be so easy with each other. And then,
when they came nearer and saw they were being observed they
stiffened and separated slightly confirming me in my thoughts.

I was surprised at my reaction when I sensed this. A flicker of
resentment at the man, just beyond youth I saw, touched my heart,
then died away, but long enough to catch my notice. Before I had

a chance to reflect on this, Jeshua as I surmised him to be, came toward us, nodded to Jonah and greeted me in what I came to know as the Galilean way:

"Peace to you, Jacob, I am Jeshua. I know of your broken wagon."

He looked at me directly with no sign of deference. Are there no servants in Galilee I thought or do I appear just a common man to these people? I stole a glance at Jonah not knowing what to expect, but saw an almost expressionless face, almost but for the slightest hint in it indicating he read my thoughts.

"To you, Jeshua. Yes you heard rightly. It is most pressing that I am able to leave tomorrow with the others. I want you to gather whatever men and material you need to see that it is done."

I was annoyed with his attitude and lapsed into an imperious Greek. I thought I set the right tone to establish my authority. I prided myself on knowing the thinking of peasants everywhere and their slyness when dealing with the ignorance of city people when they are outside town walls. I now expected some regard for my position. I had spoken to him sharply and in the language of an educated person to impress him with my importance.

But his response took me completely aback. In Aramaic, the common tongue, ignoring my Greek but clearly understanding it, with a quiet calmness and assurance, he dismissed my concerns and said,

"I received Jonah's message and sent my brother to look to your wagon. As soon as he returns we will know what to do. For now I must return to my father's house for our evening meal. Afterward I will come back to speak to you. Jonah may have mentioned that I have a great need for your service."

When he finished he took his leave simply by nodding, first to Jonah then to me, and without waiting for acknowledgment he walked off.

"You say he is the son of your tenant, Jonah. Seemingly he misunderstands his father's position."

"Seemingly Jacob, but I can tell you no more about him than

I have already. But listen well to me. As time goes on you will understand what we in this village know, that this is a man called by God. What the calling is for will yet unfold."

"As time goes on, Jonah? I made no pledge to spend more time than necessary with your man. It is not at all clear to me that I can take him with me."

I realized by now, of course, that my service to Jeshua would be to carry him to his destination. It did not enter my mind then that they knew my final destination. They would know I would be going to Damascus, but how could they guess I would then turn east, and especially to the Bactrian city of Bactra, leaving both the protection and the constraints of Rome, not to say Jerusalem?

At first thought I was not pleased with that idea. I had no authorization to find a companion. I was not sure either if my documentation so carefully prepared by Marcus would allow this. That this Jeshua needed my service was clear. It would be impossible for a lone traveler to make this trek. And to pay for accommodation with a caravan was out of the question for these people. At best, like most such travelers, he could wait for a berth with a trader and work in his service. And that itself had dangers not counting the long wait it would entail.

Interrupting these thoughts, Jonah said, "You will talk with him later this evening, Jacob. Then you can decide."

I was pleased that his earlier disapproval of me somewhat dissolved. Still I was not comfortable with the way things were going because I had the disquieting notion that the situation was out of my control despite my blustering and position.

We prepared for our evening meal. The servants brought water for washing and Jonah led us in prayer. We sat down for a simple farm style supper that brought back memories of my youth. Sara busied herself with the servants and sat down for her own meal, apart from us, after she was sure we were well served. Conversation at the table was muted and people ate engrossed in their own thoughts. This was so different than the noisy and disputatious repasts I was accustomed to. Compulsively, I kept stealing glances at Sara. More and more I felt an unnerving attraction to her and I had to will myself to be less attentive.

After supper Jeshua returned, and it was as Jonah knew it would be. First Jeshua calmed my fears about the wagon. The entire rear, the axle and the two wheels must be replaced. A new unit, of fine workmanship I was assured, was already available and Jeshua's brother with the necessary servants was doing the repairs. Then he spoke to me of his calling to the distant Jewish community in Bactria.

They knew in the village, by the make-up of the caravan, that part of it was going to the East, toward his destination. He less asked to go with me than assumed I would allow him to accompany me. This was a service to our fellow Jews especially those who by their lives were a service to us, it was implied. And before I could demur, not interested in service to them nor being able to imagine what service they could provide to me, an agreement was reached I felt unable to deny. This was the first experience I had of this person, who stated his needs then went about his business as if they were already satisfied.

JACOB II

The wagon was ready to roll the next morning as promised. Clearly the new wheels and axle were far superior to those with which we had left Jerusalem. Even my inexpert eye was able to see the difference, and the driver suggested I speak to Marcus about Galilean workmanship for his future needs. I had earlier thanked my host at my departure, but I failed to see Sara to pay my respects. I really wanted an excuse to see her again; she was in my thoughts more and more.

But now, because of an event the previous night, my feelings about her were fed by a growing confusion. It had been a restless time for me. On one occasion I arose from the pallet Jonah had provided and quietly walked outside. It was in the very early morning with deep moon shadows everywhere and they easily hid me. I heard a rustle in the yard. Looking to where the noise caught my attention, I spied a form I knew to be Sara's; she was clinging tightly to a cape thrown around her shoulders making her way into the house through one of the doorways, presumably close to her own quarters.

I remained very quiet and when enough time passed for me to make my way back to my place, I did so with a sense of dejection. I still believed she and this Jeshua were betrothed, but if so, I thought, why was he to go to this distant land without her? And if this were not he she was meeting, a meeting that would not be an unusual occurrence for those planning marriage, who could it be? And, finally, why am I so caught up with this woman, certainly no longer a young girl and late in marrying?

I took my leave without seeing her but I felt a compulsion to ask Jonah to convey my respects to his daughter and compliment

her competence in ministering to his household. Despite myself, I
think I was less casual than the situation required but Jonah took
no apparent notice.

"Peace be with you, Jacob. I truly believe you are fortunate
with your company. Do us the honor of stopping here on your
return."

"Peace to you," I replied, "I will keep your offer in mind." As
to my good fortune with my company, I thought to myself as I
strode away to see to my work, well, that we will see. I was determined that I would not put up with any nonsense from my "companion," nor would I allow the interests of my master to be sacri-
ficed.

Although I accompanied the caravan at all times, my role as
Marcus' agent was an administrative one. Each wagon employed a
skilled driver and servant directly in his service. Consequently they
were my servants as well and under my supervision. But they were
experienced men needing no instruction from me regarding their
activities. They knew best how to load their wagons for maximum
weight distribution, how their animals were to be fed and watered
and how much and for how long they could pull. Perhaps, equally
important, they worked with other wagoners, Jews and Gentiles
alike, solving mutual problems and looking to the success of the
caravan as a whole.

The camel transport, however, was a different situation. These
four huge beasts and the Arab tribesmen who owned and worked
them were "hired," as it were, simply as a transporting device such
as one hires a boat to transport goods across the sea. For an agreed
fee, in gold or goods or both, they will carry a set amount of material from one place to another. They traveled in family groups and
on this journey, besides the four drivers, there were other members of their extended family including wives and children.

Other caravan agents whom I came to know expressed misgivings about a novice agent like myself — one whose manner and
bearing belied my ability to weather the harsh conditions of caravan travel — being able to control the nomads who, they assured

me, were notoriously unreliable. They warned me that if once permitted to enter the desert with their pack animals they would be impossible to locate.

I was not unaware of this problem and I raised this question with Marcus in early discussions of my duties. He knew the tribe and individuals who were going on this trip — in fact, they were of the people who carried his grandfather's trade — and he was certain of their trustworthiness. I accepted this assurance at face value and it was not, as events proved, a misplaced faith.

I knew, of course, that Marcus would not give me this responsibility out of a sense of obligation to a friend. The cost and importance of this venture would prohibit his making any but the most cautious decisions about its success. But I myself had some misgivings, wondering just how I could contribute to its well-being. I was soon to realize however that Marcus' decision was well calculated.

It was impossible to count the custom points, official and otherwise, we met during our sojourn. Since all travel permits and bills-of-lading were written in Latin and Greek, at least a commercial knowledge of these languages was required to negotiate continued passage. Documents were examined at each station and woe to the agent who had a discrepancy in what his document claimed to be carrying and what the inspector, often a retired Roman soldier whose service had earned this sinecure, found on his animals. If satisfactory explanations were not forthcoming, and in truth most problems were for lack of communication, the cost in bribes could be considerable.

It was my habit to wear the working tunic and other clothing of my early farming days, for I found them more comfortable during the long days of travel. I would, as well, speak with my fellow travelers in our common tongue with my heavy southern Judean accent. But early I learned the advantage of wearing Roman dress and using my most formal Greek when we approached these custom points. My attire, manner, and apparent high status served to unnerve the functionary and often my transport was left unexamined.

Marcus, who listened well to his grandfather's advice, had also procured letters of protection from ranking Roman officials in Jerusalem. The respect and fear a written pass could evoke even at this place so distant from Rome earned my grudging respect for Roman law, its power and military discipline.

As we continued our journey, I found much to occupy my attention. We were carrying a mix of material from Marcus' storehouses in Jerusalem. The special olive oils found only in our region were obvious in their heavy skins. And duly listed for declaration were the grains for drier areas to the north and east and cloth from our finest weavers.

Less obvious but more valuable was the work of the city's craftsmen. Fabricated in precious metals and rare stones, these artifacts were destined for wealthy Roman cities and Rome itself. These items were carefully hidden and seldom indicated in the list of material for transport. Indeed, only I among the wagoners and Arab drivers knew of their presence, and for good reason.

Because of their value, their ease of transport and disposal, they made tempting targets for the bandits infesting this area if their existence were known. We have trustworthy servants, Marcus never failed to assure me, but it is only necessary for one to yield to temptation and signal intrepid robbers. There was more than one trader who thus lost precious goods through such collusion.

Nevertheless, there were long periods of time when little alertness was necessary. I found in these unoccupied times that my thoughts would return to Sara, and Jeshua's presence was a continual reminder of her. I could not find surcease from these thoughts, I knew, until I learned the truth of their alliance.

There were times when we were thrown together with opportunity to speak, and then I fear I pressed this matter with an unseemly insistence. Despite my attempts to hide my interest, it would have been impossible for any person of normal prescience to not know of my concerns. And I knew this Jeshua was far beyond ordinary in this regard.

But these tentative queries would be answered with silence.

Could he not have known how infuriating this kind of response would be? At times I came close to berating him for his insolence, and reminding him of his position, that I was the master in charge of his present fortunes and but for me he would still be in his village repairing wheels. But no matter how I rehearsed these words they never escaped my mouth. I was simply unable to confront him, then or ever.

Finally, thinking I would never find the answers to my questions, I accepted this situation and tried to put the issue aside concentrating on other things. One day, as we were plodding along in that rhythmic state animals and men fall into on these long journeys, Jeshua sidled up to me and we fell into a silent communion. Then he half turned to me, and in a manner which indicated he had some inkling into the thoughts that bedeviled me for so long, he said:

"You could not have known, Jacob, but it was the intention of my father and Jonah, Sara's father, that we be betrothed. In this I disobeyed him, and I suspect, disappointed and hurt the others. Further, when the call came and the elders suggested I go to this desert community so far away, I agreed, again over father's wishes.

"I tell you, Jacob, I am doing things lately that sadden me as they cause sorrow in those I love. But growing in me is the notion, and it sustains my life, that I am obeying another summons to follow a different path. When I obey that summons it seems all obstacles diminish for me, but then I create difficulties for others, forcing them to move outside their chosen ways.

"It seems it has always been thus," he continued, leaving me dumfounded at both his loquaciousness and confession, "and I must say that I know you have not escaped this fault in me."

At that, I tried to protest. "No Jeshua, really, you have been no trouble to me . . . " but he would not let me finish.

"Jacob, I say this not to excuse myself, but to suggest that you may have to shoulder other burdens outside the normal range of your concerns. I say that they will not unduly trouble you, although at first they may seem to."

I could not give credence to what I was hearing. The words and their import were strange and, in truth, I believed they had little relevance to my situation. I had no interest in his personal condition, only his connection to Sara, and now that he answered that question others took its place. Was there another for her? Did he know my thoughts these days and weeks? And what further burdens is he to put on me? These questions flashed through my mind as we approached yet another Roman custom point and I had to prepare for my role as agent.

More and more I realized that Jonah's characterization of Jeshua as "different" was an understatement. My encounters with him were surreal; from the looks of him, dress and countenance, he was an ordinary village clod, but his manner — I can say it no other way — was that of a high priest.

He spoke his thoughts with a conviction of absolute surety. When he spoke of future burdens one knew there would be such. When he spoke of a "path" one felt it was a path chosen by God. In his presence one sensed a presence and no challenge could be made to him. He simply ignored the tone or words of the challenger, responded as he pleased, directly or not at all.

At night he would lie down with our little group to take his sleep but as we stirred awake with the sun he would not be among us. Instead we would see him returning from the countryside after spending some part of the early morning away from the security of our caravan. It was not a wise thing to do in that wilderness but who would caution him? And then, he was not a stranger to this land.

In the evening, after all the animals were seen to and we finished our sparse meal and prepared for our rest, he would take himself off a little way and begin reading from the holy book, which I think the only "baggage" that he brought with him. As he sat reading aloud in the softest of tones his body would move in step with the words.

He read in Hebrew and although he barely spoke the words, in the stillness of the evening his voice would carry a distance. The

Jews in the caravan would recognize the words and cadence from their childhood exposure to them, even those like me who had fallen away from them in our adulthood.

After a while, a few men would approach his place and sit near him, listening. Then more came until finally a bolder one of the group asked him about what he was reading. "Tell me, Rabbi, so I can understand the words of our fathers." And then Jeshua would read from the text in Hebrew and later translate into Aramaic so all would understand. Before my eyes a congregation was formed. Each evening a synagogue was created in the wilderness as we made our way from hamlet to hamlet along the caravan's trail.

He would tell the ancient story of our people. Attending as well, although remaining at the periphery of the assembly, were Gentiles of all kinds. Many knew the Jews were "people of the book", the only people they knew as such, and that was a mystery to them as they had in their ignorance no contact with the written word. It is likely, it occurred to me, they never before heard it sounded out in their presence.

I would stand with them at times, curious as to their thoughts, and listen to their comments to each other about what they were hearing. "They were slaves in Egypt and their God led them out of servitude," one said, "but even their God cannot stand up to the Romans." And another, "But the Romans can't force them to desert Him. They don't dare insult their God, especially in Jerusalem. I know some soldiers and they tell me Caesar himself orders their protection."

Jeshua would read to them of the words of Moses, how God requires them to care for one another, to deal justly with the poor and with servants. That they should open their hands and hearts to the weak, even the foolish among them. When the seventh year will come "let there be no poor in the land for God will bless you then."

Whom could he be speaking to, I wondered, when he admonished them not to store up wealth and impoverish the needy; this coarse crowd of roughnecks had not even a roof to put over their

heads but still they would murmur assent. Then some would look
furtively for the presence of their masters; such talk often aroused
anger and fear in them. I, too, felt that uneasy gaze since my position was known to all.

For the Jews present, however, these were not strange words or
ideas. They had heard them in their childhood and even now they
are disputed in the larger towns and cities where interminable
arguments divide whole sections of the population into sects and
creeds holding one view or another. And these divisions in the
population mirrored the division in my mind.

His words, delivered like the roaming preachers who visited
my boyhood, transported me to that earlier time and I recalled the
reality of his words in the destitution of my neighbors. Later, I was
to learn, Jeshua's father, too, was a victim of these transgressions,
reducing him to a tenant on Jonah's farm.

But he spoke also of other things: how our Holy Law must be
obeyed in its other respects. The importance of following the rituals: saying the "Hear O Israel" reminding us that the Lord, our
God, is One, how He had made covenant with us. The Law of our
great teacher, Moses, deserves obedience for did he not intervene
with God when we forsook Him in the desert, and then secure His
promise of love and protection, as our Torah teaches us?

Over and over in our history, he told them, our people rose up
to God's will and prospered. Then, in the flush of His favor, they
forgot the source of their prosperity and sought approval in His
gifts, turning their backs on the Giver. We are in such a time now
and this is the true cause of our misery. As he spoke, the people
looked to each other, ashamed, as they knew in their hearts that
they were guilty of these sins.

And then they drifted away, many not wanting to hear these
words of condemnation. Some would stay and speak to him, asking how they could change their lives, how they could live better
as Jews in their poverty, now separated from family, no longer a
part of their village, no elders, no teachers, no synagogue.

And then he spoke the words of Moses, as Moses himself spoke to the gathering of Israel in the desert at a time of despair such as now. As he spoke Moses' words he appeared, I truly believe, as our first prophet must have appeared and sounded.

For this law that I enjoin on you today is not beyond your strength or beyond your reach. It is not in heaven, so that you need to wonder, 'Who will go up to heaven for us and bring it down to us, so that we may hear it and keep it?' Nor is it beyond the seas, so that you need to wonder, 'Who will cross the seas for us and bring it back to us, so that we may hear it and keep it?' No, the Word is very near to you, it is in your mouth and in your heart for your observance.

I do not know what more he said to them, those who still lagged behind for a private word. But when they left him they showed a lessened strain of the burden of their lives, some in their faces and others in their bearing. For me there was a stirring, of what I cannot say, but that flickered long enough to mark itself. I thought once, it is good just to gaze on him. But then, as later, I could not find it in myself to fully submit to this recognition. I sensed it would require an obligation beyond my ability or desire to accept.

At one of the meetings, a person whom I noticed coming each evening waited a while for the last of the people to leave, then quietly made his way to the Rabbi (yes, this is how I too have come to think of him!). He was not a Jew but a holy man from the East whom I was able to recognize from some contact with others like him in Jerusalem.

Though I was some distance from them, and they were in the evening shadows, I could see the foreign sage greet Jeshua with hands folded in their manner of greeting. I was surprised to see Jeshua respond in kind and with a verbal greeting I could not hear. They stayed close to each other in a way that suggested some familiarity but I could not imagine how they could have had knowledge of each other before this time. They may have had words, but of that I could not be sure. Nevertheless, as they parted my sense was of two friends taking leave of each other.

I knew little of these people but knew they had a teaching the

Greeks found interesting and compatible with some of their own. And we Jews have our own savants, delving into mysteries they claim to be part of our scriptures, who speak of this alien creed with respect and understanding.

But this knowledge and interest is found in the salons and schools of Jerusalem with its scholars of all kinds, not here in the wilderness. How odd, I thought, are these meetings in this place, among these crudest of onlookers who are held rapt by the elevated holy words of our Book.

And now discourse with an alien sage? Who, indeed, is this Galilean village workingman? I thought then, he remains in the center of his own world which follows and forms about him as he occupies this personal space, a world of its own which the outside cannot disturb, but which sends out parts of itself as people enter and leave it.

Soon I noticed he spent special time with some of those who sought him out, whom, I thought, fell under a spell of sorts, if it could be called that. And I saw, with my own eyes, how the roaming sages of our people, perhaps other peoples as well, gathered disciples, followers, servants of their teaching. And, indeed, some of these dispossessed, homeless men talked of following him to the desert community that was his destination, though how they were to do that I could not know.

Of these was a servant of Marcus, a wagon driver for us, a Samaritan named Tomas. He asked permission of me to leave his service in Damascus. His original agreement was for him to return from there to Jerusalem with new goods entrusted to him by Marcus' associates in that city. But he no longer had an interest in pursuing this course. "I want to join my Rabbi in his new community," he told me. "He bade me come with him and I cannot refuse. There is no peace in my life without him."

My first thought was and I expressed it as it arose, "But you are not a Jew, in what way do you follow this Rabbi?"

"I am a Samaritan," he said, "and we think of ourselves as Jews even if the Judeans deny us. Were we not in this land when they returned from exile? Did we not have our own Temple? Are we not circumcised according to the covenant? Besides, it matters not to my Rabbi, it was he who sought my service."

It would be beneath me to enter into a discussion with this man, though I surely would dispute his account of our people's story. This Samaritan deserves his Galilean master, I thought, but at the thought I realized my arrogance and felt a glimmer of fear at my irreverence. Nonsense, I said to myself, the desert heat and stillness is addling my head.

How easily these ignorant workingmen and peasants can be affected by words without considering their meaning, and by a posturing needing no words. I was reminded of the Greek plays that I saw in Rome when I marveled at the power of the actors to move their audiences.

But in any case, I could not give him permission. At best, I told him, I would convey his request to his masters, who are also mine, in Damascus and they would decide. I would hope he would not want to steal away and leave us without service. That would go very badly for him if he did so. "No, master," he said firmly, "I will honor my agreement and my Rabbi bade me to do so. But he assured me I will be allowed to serve him and I know that will be so."

The matter rested there, or so I thought. As I busied myself with my formal duties, I became aware that more of my thoughts and interests revolved around the Rabbi and his doings than they did my own. I looked for him when he was not in sight and took notice of him when he was; and I marked his unusual interchange with others.

He could be alone, his appearance was one of a deep silence, and a person would accost him. At times he would greet that person, though I could not hear how, and then they would part, hardly time for any words to pass between them, and the man would nod an expression of gratitude, as if a blessing had been received.

On some occasions he and the eastern monachos, or monk as we would say and as I then knew him to be, would find each other.

I knew them to be of like nature. One a Jew at one with our God, the other believing I know not what, but they had a similar connection to the world, or lack of connection. The monk, I learned, lived in a community, isolated from the world, without women, eating simple foods, enjoying no possessions or bodily pleasures and sharing that emptiness with his fellows.

He was now returning to that life, if living it could be called, after a missionary sojourn. And the other was now readying himself to enter a similar world, seeking it from childhood, leaving his family and society behind.

And yet it is to the Rabbi that men are drawn like iron to the lodestone, and at that thought I reflected there is the same sense of magic to it. What could he offer them? Whence his power? Indeed, observing Jeshua and the monk together revealed nothing untoward. They seemed to speak little to each other, coming together and walking silently, then parting, content it seemed just to be in each other's company.

At last we approached Damascus, the city where I would be most busy. Marcus' trading partners would have to be located and identified, the merchandise separated, cataloged and properly transshipped. I would have a busy three or four days in the city helping them prepare for the return shipment to Jerusalem, seeing to the wagons and animals and, the thought came, finding a replacement for the man, Tomas, who planned to leave us. At this, I thought of the Rabbi and was not pleased at the extra problem this caused; could a trustworthy person be found to replace him? What would the Damascus people think?

We made camp that evening, a day's journey from the city at a huge caravansary, almost an outlying town, established by custom for the trading caravans passing this way. Here the caravaneers prepared their cargoes for delivery to the city proper or for transport to more distant places. It was a place to replenish travel stores and vent the pent-up desires accumulated by large groups of unattached men after a long, boring trek.

Raw, strong wine and large meals of meat and coarse grains

after the long days of meager desert fare were sought after. As well, of course, the mobile brothels with their slave whores, large covered vans that would move from place to place servicing the men.

A scheme of the agents was to pay their free servants — there were actually few slaves on these caravans — their wages at this time knowing most of them would be destitute again by morning and so be dependent on them for future service. Some traders, thus, had experienced servants bound in servitude for many years until they could no longer carry on. We had none of this nature in our group as Marcus hired wisely, mostly Jews it is true, but he also held himself bound by Jewish practice in his treatment of his servants, Jews and Gentiles alike.

We finished our preparation for the next morning's activities and gathered together to take our evening meal. Because of Jeshua's presence we were in the habit of evening prayers which he would often lead when he was present. Without him, I must confess, neither the others nor I would have followed this practice, so easy is it to fall away. This evening, however, he was not to be seen. I only missed him now, and then I realized I had not seen him that day.

Rather than eat without praying, Tomas, whom we all now knew by his closeness to his Rabbi, took it upon himself to lead the prayers. To my surprise, as he chanted the prayer, I had no thought he was not a Jew. I sensed a strong presence in him. Again I noticed how the most ordinary people were changed by contact with the Galilean, and I spent much wasted time trying to understand it.

As Tomas finished and before we had time to start our meal, a man approached, a rough-looking character, obviously a caravaneer, and addressed me, speaking in the rebellious Galilean manner. "You know that Rabbi traveling with you, do you?" And answering his question as he asked it, he said, with a malicious chuckle, "Well, he has a present for you, but what anyone can do with this present I'd like to know."

Thereupon he told us the following story: "I was with a group of men amusing ourselves with the women brought from Damascus. Of a sudden there was a commotion in back of one of the vans, screaming, then the sounds of whipping and men yelling and such. We rushed to the place and joined some others watching a servant beating a woman according to his master's orders. I would have said she was dead then; she would no longer move to a blow. Even the servant thought so as he looked to his master to end his work.

"He prepared another blow seeing no order to stop when your man pushed his way into the group, elbowing me out of the way so I was ready to give him a what for. Before I could open my mouth I heard him speak, but so low I didn't think anyone else could have heard him. He just said, 'wait' and, believe me, everything stopped; the servant looked up at him confused and his master likewise."

At this point, before he continued, the man's eyes took on a strange look as though he was now seeing the thing as it was happening.

"Your Rabbi looked straight at the master and told him to stop this, that he was killing this child. The Syrian, for that's what he was, laughed at him and said that was his intention. 'She is a useless piece of shit and worth no more than food for the desert dogs, which is where she is going.'

"You could not hear a sound from the watching men. The Rabbi just looked at the master, saying nothing. If it were me I would have told the servant to finish her off, dead or not, and be done with it. I truly thought he was going to do that and your Rabbi could have gotten it to boot. The Syrian, though, seemed like he didn't know what to do; then, and I swear this is so, he started to explain:

"'I bought her three months ago, in good faith, from her father. She was to do cooking and cleaning and wait on the women and she did that at first. But one day a customer spotted her and wanted her and no other, and what was I to do? But the little bitch would have none of it. She fought and bit and no beating would tame her. There are some men who want just this so I thought she could pay her way with them. But that didn't help either; she would work one night and not be able to lift a finger for days after.

"'Can you not see what I was up against? Tonight a customer came to me and said he heard about this little twit and wanted only her. When I told him about her he only wanted her more and I thought, so be it, I suffered her enough. The man came and entered the enclosure where our women work, we are not like other places where they fuck in plain sight like animals, and before long the usual shouts and blows were heard.

"'But then came a great scream from the man. The little bitch bit off half his cock and blood spouted from it like a fountain. Some people rushed in to help him but from the looks of it he will not last long. I'll have to pay his family heavily for this.'

"The Rabbi kneeled down and was seeing to the girl," the roughneck continued, "paying the master no mind, not seeming even to listen to what he was saying and I was not sure what he was doing. Then he covered her with what scraps of clothing she had left and looked up to her master."

"'Give her to me,' he said, 'she still breathes and if she stops I will tend to her.'"

"'Give her to you, did you not hear what she cost me?'"

"'I will pay for her then, find me your cost.'"

"'You'll pay! How can you pay? Look at you, your sandals are gone, your tunic in rags. How can you pay?'"

What now, I thought, am I to pay for this? No, there is a time to say no. I am the master here not the servant to a fevered religious fanatic. But my heart dropped despite my defiant thoughts and I knew that resolve would also fade away.

My informant continued his story: "'I will pay,' your man said, 'tally your costs and come to me at the place of Jacob, the Jewish agent in the Caravan.' Then he just picked up the girl. He paid no mind to the Syrian who looked befuddled, or to any of the other onlookers. No one stopped him . . . "

He interrupted himself then and again spoke as if he were

speaking his thoughts out loud but to himself. "What manner of man is he?" Then to me, he spoke chidingly, "Are you Jacob, his master? Your servant goes his own way. You are a strange master and this Rabbi is a strange servant."

I disliked his manner — we are too far from proper discipline, I thought — and was about to put him in his place when one of our men whispered to me that "the Rabbi" was coming and carrying what looked like a bundle of rags. As Jeshua approached, Tomas ran to him to see to his needs. Jeshua ignored me though I was directly in his sight and went to one of the wagons.

The others held back, looking to me for a sign indicating what they should do. I hesitated, not knowing how I would deal with this situation, feeling all manners of eyes on me. But again, as always with this man, events move as he orders them and I found myself reacting to his decisions.

The men, noticing my hesitation, looked to Tomas for instruction and he had them clear a place in the back of one of the wagons to allow Jeshua to lay down his burden. Curious despite myself, I edged closer, the men making room, to see what new "burden" my Rabbi contrived to find for me. One look at the creature lying there, dead or alive could not be told, except it was clear she was a girl, not a woman, for her tattered covering scarcely clothed her frail body. How she could have fought her assailant as described by our informant is a mystery.

The men finished their preparations seeing to her comfort and, but for me, Jeshua asked all to leave. He carefully removed the strips of cloth, gently pulling some away from the bloody welts caused by the whip. She made not a sound, not a whimper, as one would expect even from a hurt animal. He managed, I do not know how, to arrange her limbs in a way that indicated no strain. I would guess now she would be older than I first thought, but no more than twelve years I am sure. From some secret place — his whole life is a secret from me — he produced a balm that eased the removal of these pieces and calmed the wounds. At no time during his efforts did the child regain consciousness. Indeed, I saw no sign of life. I said nothing, nor did he, but I confess, I wondered if God, too, obeys this man.

After a time he found a robe to cover her and moistened her lips with a dampened cloth. He stood over her quietly for a while then said to me, "Jacob, I have a place to bring her tomorrow where she will be comforted. But I will have to leave her in Damascus. I will bring you to that place so you will know it. On your way back from the East you will return here, fetch the child and bring her to Jonah's house. Tell Sara I ask she care for her."

My mind raced with a thousand thoughts. I did not want to do this. To what place can he bring her, whom does he know here? And what of all my work? Already I have neglected my planned meetings with the camel drivers arranging their further travel. And tomorrow I meet with my masters, Marcus' partners. Can I tell them I must see first to a mostly dead slave girl and a desert holy man? But I was helpless in his presence.

Knowing my thoughts, he said, "Calm your mind, Jacob, you will not be unduly burdened as I promised you. I will ask no more of your kindness and after this service I will leave you and go on with others to my destination."

Before I had a chance to contemplate his last words, to rejoice at the thought of his leaving me, or, as later happened, to sorrow that he was no longer around to mystify me, another marvel occurred. One of the women servants of the Syrian came into our area. As she approached, the men moved away from her and she tightened the covering around her as she felt that disapproval. But she spied the Rabbi standing near the wagon where the child was lying face up, covered to her neck. I had moved some feet away but close enough to hear what transpired.

She went directly to him and he remained motionless as she approached. To my utter consternation he greeted her as he would have greeted a fine woman. "Peace to you, lady." She could not respond she was so flustered. After some moments of silence, looking down as befit her position, she responded in a bastard, almost unintelligible Greek.

"My master sends this cloth to you, it belongs to the girl you bought." Then, looking down at the child, she stared for a time and asked, "Is she dead, master, she looks so peaceful." Awkwardly, not waiting for an answer, she continued, "He says also, you need not pay for her. He knows you are poor and he wants you to think kindly of him."

Had I not heard this with my own ears, from the woman's own mouth, I would not have believed it. But what happened next was even more bizarre.

The Rabbi, reaching out to her, put his hand under her chin, and raised her eyes to his. How could he touch her, unclean as she was? "Do you think kindly of him, lady?" he asked, "does he treat you so?"

"I have never known him to be kind, sir. Why do you call me 'lady,' you know what I am. Do you mock me?"

As was his way, he did not answer her query. He simply looked into her eyes holding her face up to his and then let down his hand. For a moment, her face remained in that position and then slowly she looked away.

Then he told her, "Tell your master, now that he will beat no more, I think of him kindly. Go in peace and remember me."

The woman left, but not as she came. Once again I saw that expression on her face, the subtle change in bearing, that so marked the others who chanced to meet and converse with the Rabbi. And what can explain the deeds of the brutal Syrian? What is it that they feel from this contact? Why do I not sense what they do? I think on it and think on it and bring to bear all my education and training but yet an uneducated clod like Tomas or slave whore sees what I cannot.

From that first meeting in his Galilean village to now, not yet two weeks, he became a sage before my eyes. No, that cannot be so. It must be that I am only now seeing what was always there. To think how I resented his relationship with Sara, whatever it was. Does Sara, does Jonah, do the others from his boyhood know him as I am beginning to know him now?

But now the practical needs of the world again emerged. It was a time of rest for the next day's business. The raucous carousing diminished throughout the area and a thankful quiet descended. There were some blessed souls who slept without care, but others, I among them, lay without sleep, my mind filled with thoughts of the previous hours. The Rabbi sat quietly near the girl, neither asleep nor awake as far as I could tell.

Day broke and a great stirring took place in the encampment. I must have found some sleep for I needed a moment to regain my normal state of alertness. I noticed Jeshua and Tomas had fashioned a hammock of sorts for his ward so she could lay suspended in air, protected from the jolting of the wagon. I felt a pang of resentment as he simply attended to his needs, instructing my servants without a nod to my position.

I walked to the wagon to see what displacement they made to my other goods to find a place for her. She was still covered but for her face and when I looked into it her eyes opened for an instant. That instant was enough. What I saw was life and for life to have been restored to that body was an act of God.

Miraculously, too, there seemed to be no pain. I had planned a litany of remonstrance, I'm sure the last time I did this useless exercise, to explain to this "Rabbi" why I could no longer satisfy his fortuitous plans at my expense and that of my master's to boot. But that one moment of contact with those eyes drove these complaints from my mind and I found myself aiding in the comfort of the child, my contrary thoughts fading away in this effort.

It was, as it always is when following the Rabbi's way, simpler than my fears led me to believe it would be. We traveled into the city as planned and at one point Jeshua bid me stop and wait. He went off by himself for a short time, leaving me perplexed as I had no thought that he knew the city. Then he returned with the woman of whom he had spoken earlier and brought her directly to the girl. The woman looked at the child for a moment, perhaps touched her, I could not tell, and then they came to me. "This is my master, Jacob," he told her, "a good man. Look well on him so as to recognize him when you next see him." To me he said as follows, "This is Hannah, a woman who will make this child well. We will call her Anna as no name has been given to us for her. She seems not to remember the time before her beating."

He continued then with the most amazing instructions, but they were strange to me only when I thought about them later. At the time I listened carefully, not to miss a word, and, as usual I had not thought or ability to desist.

"Together we will convey Anna to her nurse's home. This is necessary so you will know it again when you return here. If you forget the location go to the synagogue and ask for Hannah, the woman who heals. By then little Anna should be well enough to accompany you."

Then he grabbed my arm and turned me toward him and held my eyes to his. I remember thinking of the strength of his clasp, but nothing matched the strength of his gaze.

"Promise me, Jacob, you will do this for me."

It would have been easier for me to stop the sun in its path than to have said no to this man. And as time went by, despite temptation and reason, I became so bound to this promise that not fulfilling it would have been impossible, though God knows how I tried.

After those bewildering hours, he left, not to be seen for many years, but forever after part of my life. He made his own arrangements to travel on without my protection or support, little as it had been, and how he did that I was not to know.

In all this time I have never seen him with either money or clothing except for what he wore. Yet when one would think his rags would fall from his back, somehow he found something else that would cover him once more. He ate little and always what was offered, yet when I saw him last for his final instructions to me he appeared fit, covered and shod.

My tasks in the city went smoothly enough. Only one other event occurred in connection with Jeshua, ordinary on the face of it, but extraordinary when one reflects on all happenings in the

Rabbi's presence. As we planned the return trip to Jerusalem, discussing the state of the wagons, the present nature of the check points to be encountered and the servants to be needed, my associate informed me we had one man too many, one would have to be discharged.

It was then that I remembered Tomas' desire to go on with his Rabbi. In the rush of things I had completely forgotten about him. I told my associate we had a man who wanted to leave our service and he wanted to be free of his agreement with us. This was a perfect solution and solved our problem without bringing any disapproval on us. Neither Marcus nor his partners would deal improperly with their servants. Indeed, so pleased was the partner that he would make Tomas' wages available to him for the part of his service he had already fulfilled.

When I found Tomas to bring him this news I saw he was already prepared to leave. "Were you going to leave without permission?" I asked, surprised and a little nettled for I spoke highly of him. "No, no, master, but I knew it would go well as my Master (I did not miss the new appellation) said it would be so."

And I could see this simple man spoke without guile. And then I asked him, "Tell me Tomas, what do you see in this man that makes you trust him so? He is a man after all, is he not?" For a moment Tomas said nothing. I could see he was wondering too at the question. Then, slowly, not sure of his answer, he said, "I think, master, it is because with him I am without fear."

JACOB III

My next days were busy and frantic. Free of Jeshua — only now did I realize how the least of my charges required so much of my attention — I finished all my arrangements with Marcus' partners and I was preparing to see to my Arab carriers and our transport to the East. This was no simple matter and one made more complicated because I had little experience with dealing with either man or beast in this enterprise. But again, Marcus' understanding of his business made it possible for me to do best what I could do and not concern myself needlessly with matters of which I had little knowledge.

Rather than own and maintain troublesome camels and hire drivers, notoriously the most untrustworthy, besotted and lowly of all the Palestinian dispossessed, he contracted with certain nomadic Arab tribes who owned their beasts, traveled with their families and knew the far stretches of the empty wilderness.

Once their trust could be assured through formal and traditional alliances, safe passage for our goods could be maintained even outside the protection of Roman forces. I was responsible for all contact with various authorities and proper delivery at the final destination.

Now that my work in Damascus was completed and all my attention could be put on this other area, I learned in short order the wisdom of Marcus' decision, though at first I thought his use of these Arab families was more expensive than necessary. In the ignorance of my sophistication, I believed driving these animals was a simple matter, not much different than controlling a donkey or a horse, animals with which I had had some experience. Once more I was disabused of a false understanding and fortunately, before I was permitted to make a fool of myself.

Only these large beasts, the two-humped camel native to the eastern land to which we were going, could traverse the almost five month journey so heavily laden. They are, in fact, the only means of transport through the shifting desert sands and the sparse wilderness of the higher areas of this land.

They need little food and can eat anything that can be found in the countryside. Indeed, I have been warned to keep well clear of these animals; sensing a meal, their sharp teeth have been known to strip the clothing off more than one unwary traveler. I have been told they can smell water a day's distance and in my time with them I could see nothing that would make me disbelieve these stories. Besides that, they provide rich milk and meat for sustenance. Their hair is spun and woven for all kinds of fabric needs and their skins prepared as well for leather goods. And even their droppings are not wasted as they burn well for fuel.

For these reasons they are counted as wealth by their owners as a city merchant would count his gold, but they are difficult animals to handle, requiring the skill, understanding and patience one acquires only when raised with them as these nomadic people were. And it almost seems they understand their value as they often protest without provocation. They will bite and kick and spit, and at times during mating season they will become savage animals, threatening anyone who comes near them. Clearly, however, they are part of the lives of these desert people whose existence could not continue without them.

One cannot say that their drivers are kind to them, often pushing them beyond what seems a normal limit of load or distance. Although not a problem with Marcus' people, it would be most true of those drivers in the employ of traders and who do not own their animals and care little for them. Consequently, more than a few animals would refuse to go any further and simply kneel by the side of the road and no amount of beating could move them.

In this case, the driver would try to redistribute the load or seek to pay for a less burdened animal to transport some of his goods. When I would pass one or another in this situation, stalled helplessly on the road, I would give a silent nod of thanks to Marcus for his wisdom. Never once did I have to give thought to this problem as my carriers were well compensated and could be depended upon completely to fulfill all agreed-upon work. Indeed, they seemed to treat this venture with the same concern that we did.

Thus it was the desert men left Damascus two days earlier than I, after dropping off and picking up a mix of merchandise going to different destinations. They left early to join a large caravan preparing to leave before I was ready. This train, stretching miles into the desert when fully underway, was easy enough for me to overtake as we encountered our first oasis and last custom stop, a stop only intermittently manned now and again by Roman soldiers. Then we entered what seasoned travelers called the "Silk Road", established centuries ago by Chinese armies and subsequently deserted by them.

This road, made possible by a string of oases separated in such a way as to allow caravans to progress for months at a time through the deserted wilderness, connected the Western world to the East. Because of it, a huge trading network spanning the world linked Chinese, Romans, Greeks, Egyptians, Persians, Indians and other peoples, either conquered or influenced by them.

I did not yet understand the enormity of it all as it did not occur to me then that with this great movement of goods and men so too moved their thoughts and ideas. But this understanding came, as it was bound to come given my mind's inclination to think on thoughts until no more can be squeezed out of them, not satisfied ever until their meaning is revealed.

But more than that, this leg of my journey was one of quiet and ease, thanks to the competence of Marcus' servants. And also, now out of Roman control, Parthians, who were interested in maintaining secure passage for the caravans, ruled the area. Their interests lay in harmonious accord between all peoples and traffic passing through their land because of the significant revenues they produced. So as I plodded along, sometimes on a small riding camel, but more often on foot, the slow steady gait would allow my mind to consider the events of the past months.

Over and over it would be drawn to the extraordinary nature of the Rabbi, this Jeshua, who determined my future though I did not then realize the extent of his influence on my life. He was often a burden I thought, causing me and others to perform unwanted tasks with cost and no gain, one who now I was pleased to have seen the end of. And when I thought of those times I felt relieved that he was no longer with me, and then, immediately, I felt a sense of loss in his absence.

It was odd. These feelings about him mirrored the discontent I have suffered so long. The reasons, in fact, that I have undertaken this adventure in the first place. In the press of this new life that discontent was overshadowed, but now with the chance to reflect and the influence of the tranquil nature of the desert, that disquiet again came to the surface of my mind. But now it arose with a new force, clothed as it was with the flesh and blood of a living person.

I no longer concerned myself with the relationship between Jeshua and Sara. It crept into my consciousness without the spur of reason that the Rabbi is one of those men whose life will be lived without women. I do not know why but I could not think of him otherwise.

In this I felt an insight about him I was not sure either Sara or her father recognized, judging from their interaction with him as I remembered it. But my thoughts of Sara were still tinged with uneasiness; it would be almost a year, if not more, that I would be away and likely I will have long been out of her thoughts, if, indeed, I ever had a place in them.

Now, putting Sara aside, my mind echoed the question of the perplexed lout who told us the story of the Rabbi's dealing with the child, Anna, and her Syrian master in Damascus. "What manner of man is he?" he asked, and looking for the answer to that question would occupy the next weeks and months of my waking life.

It is said the things one learns in childhood never vanish from memory and the truth of that observation came home to me as the stories I heard in my boyhood village came to life in the person of this Rabbi. Jewish prophets who talked to God and to whom God talked, wise men, women too, who did miraculous deeds and healings, were part of that boyhood and made a deeper impression than I wanted to acknowledge.

Also in my youth, and later in adulthood to be sure, I heard the new promise of a prophet/hero who would be sent by God to restore our former glory and bring new glory to all the world's children. God is only waiting a sign that we deserve His messenger and he will appear. To this end many pious Jews took themselves into secluded areas where they could live pure lives based on God's laws.

Others, though believing with them, lived in villages and cities, taking wives and raising children but by the example of their lives they stood apart. Part of me was drawn to these stories and in my childhood fancies I often thought of myself as this prophet/hero leading armies of Jews against Rome.

My subsequent education in Rome, my associations with Greek scholars and knowledge and, no less, my introduction into the beauty and pleasures of Greek and Roman life displaced these early thoughts and whimsies. I saw them as village superstitions and resisted my heart's attempts to keep them in my mind.

But now that veneer of sophistication and its intellectual arrogance was shattered. I could not deny the reality of the Rabbi's existence nor the power he exhibited. Nor can I describe it except to say when he was present he was a presence and in that presence my heart swelled.

Finally we reached our destination but for one full day. That evening, before making camp, my headman informed me that we were on the outskirts of our city and would arrive there the following afternoon. So bemused was I with the content of my thoughts and the soporific quality of the desert, that the notice of our arrival came as an awakening shock.

Once again I was thrown into the feverish activities of the

world and my mind filled with the needs of the moment displacing the dreamlike quality of the previous weeks. I cannot now describe the myriad impressions I received the next day as we slowly made our way to the large staging area to where the agents of merchants and traders would come looking for their contracted goods. Marketers came also intent on buying material for sale in the several markets in the inner city.

As I was to learn, this city, Bactra, was the central city of the former Persian province of Bactria. It futilely resisted Greek rule and after a heroic resistance was crushed and then took on Greek culture. The city and country enjoyed one more brief period of independence and power expanding north into China's Turkomen outpost and also deep into India before it was finally subdued by the formerly nomadic horse people of the northern grass-covered lands.

Now, caravans traveling as far as my native land in the West and from the Ganges valley of India or the great river valleys of China could always expect a favorable welcome in Bactra and men of widely differing understandings rubbed shoulders and traded thoughts. The walls surrounding the inner city spoke of the time when defense from marauding armies was necessary just as the sprawling, undefended outer city spoke of the present period of tranquillity. Conquest and power, I mused, are powerful movers of men, but peace and peaceful trade bring more wealth, satisfaction and pleasure.

I appreciated, too, the civilizing influence of Greek culture, especially after the harsh months in the desert. Bactra was a wealthy city in which one could find all the amenities afforded by wealth anywhere, not only in the Roman countries. Natan, Marcus' partner, was one of the more prosperous of the merchants and bankers. The value of this was soon apparent when his able and prepared servants came to find us in the caravan area.

With great efficiency they identified our group, unloaded and inventoried the merchandise against our documents, arranged the transporting of our goods to his storehouses in the city with only the most minimal help needed from me. It was not until then that I felt the fatigue of my journey, when I was able to give these tasks over to someone else.

I was now free, temporarily at least, of any responsibility. That the transport was accomplished without problems, all the material arrived intact, and the expense of the journey was well within its allocated budget, were all attributed to my good offices. And, indeed, when I had opportunity to hear of the experiences other agents suffered with stolen or lost and damaged property, of the exorbitant fees charged en route, of the delays and harassment suffered, I only then appreciated the relative effortlessness of my work.

If I bore difficulties on this trip, I had thought, they were those created by the Rabbi: only those caused me consternation, only those caused me unease. And of course those were nonexistent events to my appreciative masters who knew nothing of them.

I was escorted to the large Roman style home of my host who understood the hardships for me of the past half year. Servants were available to minister to my body and its coverings. My clothes were cleaned and well laid out, and I was treated to the luxury of hot baths equal to the fantasies I had while in the dry and dusty desert. The shock of the change in my circumstances was almost disbelief and I fought with myself to stay awake and savor the caressing of my senses.

Later, sitting down at table, waited on by servants, speaking again in high Greek, I was transported back to my time in Rome and then later Jerusalem that provoked a strange disorientation. But this was not the land of Roman conquest and this Jewish family, part of a large and wealthy community, was not the captive of an occupying tyrant with brutal forces at his command.

Though they looked to the "Holy City" and were closely attuned to the world of Jerusalem and the Temple, their Jewish lives for centuries took place outside its orbit of power. Natan's manner was annoyingly didactic, especially to one like myself whose tone I fear is much the same. From him I heard a different story of my people's travails than that which I had until then known.

The rulers of this country appreciated the presence of these people, his people, he told me, because of the wealth and commerce they were responsible for generating. In addition, they had an easy tolerance for all beliefs and since the Jews kept to themselves in this regard they were the best of all possible subjects.

Natan explained, as I had early learned, his ancestors came to this country when driven out of Jerusalem some six hundred years ago by Nebuchadnezzar, and although they came as captives they did not come as slaves. Even in those disastrous times they were allowed to farm the land and work their crafts as they had in Judah. Natan's family was one of those that were attracted to the city where they were permitted to enter all sorts of commerce and, indeed, government service.

In time, they became wealthy and powerful and it was no wonder that so many refused to return to desolate Judah to rebuild the Temple when permitted, indeed urged, by the new conqueror Cyrus. I noticed now an apologetic tone creeping into Natan's discourse. "Though we are more independent of the Temple than you Judeans are," he said, "we are Jews nonetheless. We preserve the words of the prophets, and if the sacred Torah is now written in Greek, it is still the guide to our lives. Our sons are circumcised, the Sabbath is obeyed and though I know we do not suffer for our God as do others, you know it is written 'suffering need not be the path to heaven.'"

Where that was written I was never to learn, but I could not let go my host's self-serving opinions. "Yes, Natan," I said, "you have done well for yourselves and that is easy to see. Why God smiles on your good fortune is one with all his mysterious ways. But you know the story where the Tempter suggests how easy it is to love God when he provides only good things to the lover." I noticed his disapproving expression and I feared I had offended him. I am sure the story of Job was not unknown to him.

In order to soften the tenor of my remarks, I thought to divert his attention by speaking of the Rabbi, for some reason brought to mind in the context of our discussion. "Natan," I asked, "did you hear of a Rabbi coming through this country recently, a Galilean, to lead a community in this area?"

"A Galilean Rabbi," he laughed, "a Rabbi from Galilee is not likely to be anywhere, least of all in this country," he chided, making me feel he wanted me to know he was aware of the nature of my country. "But seriously, Jacob, I would know of no one like that. We have our own synagogue and Rabbi, and though some find him less than desirable I cannot imagine him replaced by a Galilean."

"No, no," I interjected, "I did not mean he was to replace your Rabbi. But is there a desert community here such as we have in Palestine where Jews who call themselves the pious ones gather? These are Jews who live according to the ancient tradition as God ordered so as to urge Him to send a new messenger for our liberation. Surely you know of our need and desire for this."

As I said this, I realized that in my effort to placate Natan for my previous ill-advised comments I succeeded only in making things worse. I had only to look around me to see he would have little use for "liberation". His was not only a bountiful wealth, but also a secure one. It was long well-established as were he and his family and protected by friendly rule as much beholden to him as he to them.

In this country, away from my own, I could see more clearly the interest the priesthood and wealthy aristocracy of Jerusalem would have in quieting talk of a "Messiah", an anointed one, who would stir and lead the people to revolt and change. They believe, and in this I now think they are correct, such an act would bring mutual destruction on their heads. Surely Natan understood the nature of this danger as well as they.

I saw by the expression on his face that I had correctly sensed his thoughts and I hastened to make amends; I did not want to offend my generous host, but as well I was truly contrite. "Pardon me, Natan, it is so difficult to leave the tribulations of my country behind me, occupied as it is by a tyrannical foreign power," I apologized.

"There is terrible suffering in our land and it is no wonder that the people look to God for guidance and sustenance. When one arises who seems to have God's ear and by words and deeds convinces people of this fact they grab onto this hope. The Rabbi of Galilee, of whom I ask, spent much time with me these past months, and I must confess to you he made his mark on me."

My tone softened somewhat as it always does when I speak of the Rabbi, and this expression of humility, subtle as it must have been, was felt by my host. "Jacob," he said with a friendly chuckle, "you have spent too much time in the desert and not enough resting among our pleasures." Before we could talk further, a servant came to us and Natan was called away. His parting words to me were friendly and reassuring relieving me of my fear that I created some resentment toward myself.

"I am not unaware of your strange 'prophets' who strive to imitate the prophets of our earlier days. We know of them here and, as you will learn, we have our share of 'holy' men who are not Jews but live and speak as does your Rabbi. This is a country full of them with their begging bowls and strange dress. Please mark me well, Jacob, I know fully of what you speak and I share more of your issues than you may now think."

Later I was informed Natan planned a dinner reception for me. The servant who gave me this news informed me, I thought at his master's suggestion, that his master was impressed by my understanding of the concerns that stirred him and his associates. He would be pleased if we could continue our discussion in their presence so that they could benefit from my knowledge of present-day Jerusalem.

Although distant from Rome and not in fact ruled by it, they were, I realized, not sheltered from the effects of events taking place there. Especially true, of course, was the relationship of their co-religionists to Roman rule; in many ways their fortunes were tied to the fate and position of the Temple, the destiny of which, they feared, was more in the Emperor's hands than God's.

Natan's standing in the city and his contacts with its rulers involved friendships and dealings with all kinds of people. One time, shortly before leaving for my return journey, I was permitted, through Natan's favor, to attend, as a minor guest, a large gathering of the city's elite. There I could observe the regard in which he was held and the influence he exerted. It was shocking contrast to me to remember similar gatherings in Jerusalem where the Jews, even the wealthiest and most powerful among them, were on their guard for every word or gesture, fearful of their Roman masters and the dangerous ease with which they could be offended.

But this dinner was not one of those. Attending were Natan's and Marcus' associates who formed part of a world trading network which had arisen after the armies and conquerors from civilized lands and untamed wilderness had spent centuries sweeping back and forth across the world. Victorious by turns, now exhausted, temporarily perhaps, from the effort and loss of blood, they made it possible to open markets in the most distant land.

These urbane men questioned me carefully about life in Jerusalem. I was astonished at their knowledge of the conflicting interests and rivalries tearing at the city. Information I had thought of as trivial, the small talk of gossip, such as the replacement of Roman functionaries representing the procurator to the Temple authorities.

Or who of Marcus' circle, which was theirs as well, was called to Herod's court when he last visited his palace in the city. This was the stuff of intrigue and importance to them, impacting on the fortunes of their enterprises. And they sought all sorts of information regarding these activities.

In addition, they had an uncommon interest in the doings and thinking of the common people. In Jerusalem one took for granted the ebb and flow of sects and groups around the teachings of our Law. It was not unusual for the students of various rabbinical schools to battle in the streets over disputed points in the Torah.

Temple guards would often have to maintain order, fearful

that large-scale civil disorder would draw in the Roman troops stationed at the Antonia fort; this always resulted in great losses of blood as the people would then turn on the soldiers. That which was for us, therefore, a normal state of affairs, from this distance made the city seem a tinder box only waiting for the right spark. This volatility was harmful to their business and these foreign merchants appreciated the rule of law and order the Roman Empire represented. For them, I realized, their business was godly.

It was in this conversation, also, that I perceived the hidden tentacles supporting this power and wealth. It was like the roots of an ancient tree, unseen, branching out in all directions, drawing and accepting sustenance from wherever offered. Although far from Jerusalem and even more distant from the power centers of Rome, or, in fact, the teeming Ganges valley in India, not to speak of the river civilizations of China, these merchants and bankers had contacts and wielded influence. In later years this knowledge and understanding would prove of great use to me.

After dinner, when the special guests left and members of Natan's family retired to their various pursuits, servants enclosed our table behind movable partitions to provide a quiet private area where we could continue our discussion. Joining us in this place was a man who did not dine with us but whom I noticed was present within hearing distance of our conversation. A man who listened intently at everything that was said, but himself said very little, then only a whisper to Natan or a nod at what one of the others offered.

I knew by his dress and deportment, and of course by his very physical position, he was not on the level of Natan's guests. I guessed he was a servant, possibly a slave if Natan kept them, but one of rare ability whose trusted and valuable position was the reward of that ability. His name was Jason and later, when the others had gone, Natan brought him together with me in a strange intimacy I would not have thought possible with those of so unequal rank. We stayed together to finish the evening with a remarkable conversation exploring the subject that had so dominated my life the past several months: the nature of the Rabbi from Galilee.

Natan began, "I was impressed by the effect this Rabbi you speak of had on you. I know, Jacob, I may have been dismissive at first, but the idea of inspired, possessed Jews is a contentious one in this country. We are not unmindful of the conditions of life of our fellow Jews, those in particular now sinking deeper and deeper into despair under Roman rule.

"We know, too, that at times such as these our people search for and would find one who, selected by God they are prone to believe, will enable them to throw off this Roman yoke, believing that by doing so they will restore a former glory. Am I correct, Jacob, in this assessment? What is your sense of the situation?"

"Largely correct as far as you go, Natan, but, with your permission, I think there are aspects of this situation that are difficult to understand from this distance." I started tentatively for I knew how delicate these questions could be.

"Jacob, please," Natan said, reading my thoughts, "these things are too important to fear confronting. Speak freely to me and bear in mind my servant Jason is equal to any I know in understanding these matters."

Jason's understanding, indeed. I came to learn the depth of this extraordinary man's knowledge and found no one in my later life that exceeded it. He came into Natan's service as a tutor for his children. This was primarily for Natan's son as his two daughters were left into the hands of their mother; in any case, neither girl showed any inclination for worldly knowledge.

The children's religious education was separately arranged, but since language and secular knowledge taught in the Greek tradition were much admired by wealthy Jews outside Judea as well as within, the need of a tutor was essential. It has now been many years since this service was required of him. The son is now grown and an agent of his father's business in a large Roman city, and the two daughters are long married, tending to their own families.

His special abilities with language made him of immeasurable value to a man of Natan's needs. He knew fluently all the official languages of the region: Greek, his mother tongue, Latin, his second language, and Aramaic, the common speech, and learned later, after being brought to this country, many of the local, ancient dialects. And for this alone Natan would have retained him in his service.

But he had a greater genius. One that only Natan, of Jason's other masters, had the discernment, or the permission, to see. He was able to peer behind the mysterious veil that hid the world that the Jewish prophets of old professed to enter. And now, also here in this country, he saw it with the native holy seers who glimpsed this same mystery albeit in their own tradition. All this and much more I had yet to learn of this man as I responded to Natan's inquiry.

"You are right, Natan, in your understanding of the plight of our people. I will not belabor the wrongs of the Romans. But our lot is made even worse by the collaboration with them by the priests of the Temple and members of that party who align themselves with the authorities. Is it a coincidence, Natan, these are chiefly the wealthy who grow fatter on the impoverishment of the people? Is it a wonder the people see evil in their works and throw up zealots who accuse them of hiding their greed behind our holy religion?"

I felt my passions rise as my sense of injustice rekindled with the pictures that my words had evoked in my mind. I saw the outrage and agitation in the streets of Jerusalem whipped up by orators damning the latest of ever-increasing demands on the people. Aimless fanatics driven to their wits' end threatening chaos, but Rabbis too, with their reasoned arguments threatening God's wrath. I caught myself, but not in time, realizing it was Natan's friends, associates, indeed the mirror of his own position against which my tirade was directed.

"Excuse me, Natan," I started, "I am carried away with my feelings and I may . . . "

"Nay, Jacob," he interrupted, "all of what you tell me we here have also conjectured. Like you, we see the danger in this. We fear it could end in catastrophe."

At that Jason began to speak. He spoke quietly and immediately my agitation subsided. His manner reminded me of someone's and his first words brought that person to mind.

"Tell me, Jacob, did the Rabbi of Galilee of whom you speak join in this condemnation? How did he speak, sit, and conduct himself with others? Will you tell us of him?"

His questions, perhaps his way of stating them, released my pent-up desires to talk about the Rabbi. And I knew now that all the discussion this evening was prologue to what I had to say, in a way providing context to it. I spoke for the next period of time without pause or interruption, encouraged by my audience's rapt attention.

I spoke of my meeting Jeshua in Galilee, my first impressions and the assessment of him by Jonah. That I was asked to convey him to this country to head a community here of Jews similar to those scattered throughout Palestine. I mentioned Sara, my feelings about her, and my concern over their relationship. I told of my bewilderment about his ability to discern my thoughts, and only now in the telling did I become aware of its extent.

I described his ways on the journey, how he would appear and disappear at the oddest times, coming into camp from the desert and only then was it noticed he was gone. Other times one saw him walking alone deep in thought, and then when again looking in his direction, found him gone.

I described how when he prayed, people would gather around him and then it would become a teaching. It was then they began to call him "Rabbi", though we know that he is not truly one. How people would later seek him out for counsel and I knew not what would have been said, but when they left him they were somehow different; a counsel that provided solace? True, he called the people to obey Moses' teaching about caring for one another, succoring the poor and dispossessed, using wealth wisely and for good purposes, but it was not in his nature, as I now recall it, to condemn its owners.

But then I spoke to them of how he saved the child from her

Syrian master. How the Syrian later asked for his blessing through the office of one of his whores. I spoke of his treatment of her, her response to him. I thought as I recounted this episode, what a strange way for a "holy" man to express holiness.

This story evoked a deepening of attention, if a greater deepening was possible. It was only here that Jason would ask for a detail or an elaboration. "What did the Rabbi say? How was his manner?" He was especially interested in the care of the child after the Rabbi carried her to our camp. And then, when I described the woman in Damascus in whose care the child was left, Natan asked for a more detailed description of the woman.

Finally, I mentioned his unusual friendship with the foreign monk and how the Rabbi left me in Damascus to complete his journey with him. I felt a great burden lifting when I finished my discourse and knew my sense of wonder at the mysterious nature of the Rabbi was shared by these two auspicious men. I hinted as much.

"Tell me," I asked, looking at them both, "am I making too much of this? Did the desert air and its loneliness do to my head what it sometimes does to one's vision? Even for me, as I tell you these things I saw, their reality is tinged by doubts."

Natan answered. "What you say, Jacob, is real enough. Our problem is not with what you say and the authenticity of your Rabbi. No, the problem is what it means, what he means, who he is. In your country he would be dismissed as a messianic imitator, an insane one at that. Traveling in rags, blessing whores and whore masters, teaching care for the poor and dispossessed, healings of slaves better left to die, what work is this for the messiah of Israel?"

"Messiah," I almost shouted. "What are you saying Natan? You are right, what work is this for the promised one? How can we speak of my Rabbi, remarkable as he may be, in this way? I was happy, Natan, you accepted my story with the forbearance you did, knowing how implausible it could have sounded. Now I am more bewildered than before with this talk of 'messiah'. "

"Patience, Jacob," Jason quietly interjected. "We have been

awake many hours this day and it is not good to worry about some things when we are so tired. I suggest we retire for the night and deal with these questions tomorrow when we are fresher."

"Yes, but not for me," Natan replied. "My business and personal things will occupy my attention for the next several days. But Jacob, you are free for the next weeks at least as your return plans are yet to be arranged. Jason will be your companion and escort for as long as you remain here. My interest, however, is that you and he explore these questions as deeply as possible. Do not be surprised to hear things you have never considered. Jason is, I assure you, as learned in these matters as anyone.

"But our city offers more than food for the mind Jacob. You will find places that cater to the needs of the body as well and Jason is also knowledgeable in this area. I am sure you are familiar with these entertainments so I am not afraid of offending your Jewish sensibilities, especially after spending a half-year on the road."

This last was said with a jocular tone but I must confess I was not unhappy with the prospects it held out for me. Truly I was spent, and I knew well the nature of the "entertainments" he so generously proposed as I did, indeed, remember my youthful Roman days. I was brought to my room and despite the agitation of my mind, my general fatigue soon put me to sleep.

JACOB IV

I awoke the next day with the same thoughts, questions really, that had faded in the shadowy onset of the previous night's sleep. Who is Jason? Who, what, is the Galilean Rabbi? The answer to the first was simple; Jason himself provided it as our friendship progressed in the days ahead. But the answer to the second remains hidden from my understanding.

As I surmised, Jason was born a slave. The nature of the heavens at his time of birth, as his later understanding assured him, overcame those humble beginnings in his tiny Greek village. He was brought as a servant to the household of a middling Athenian scholar who earned a moderate livelihood tutoring copying and translating books. The master enjoyed as well a minor teaching position in one of the many philosophical schools of the city.

His master held to the ancient Athenian teachings of the venerable Plato and was called upon at times to defend his philosophy in the often contentious debates forever roiling the city's intellect. I recalled echoes of those debates in Jerusalem in the houses of Jews like my friend and employer, Marcus, who were educated in the Greek style. Jason was brought into this environment as a prepubescent boy at the time when languages and learning came easily and, because it was a small household, his master immediately discerned his abilities. In short order he moved from servant to student and in his young manhood, a favorite assistant.

At the death of his master he was still a young man and, through the grace of his benefactor, an accomplished student and a free citizen, although now penniless. It was the custom for modern Roman families, in that enlightened Augustan age, to arrange to bring such students into their households to provide the advanced education the public schools for Roman citizens could not, limited as they were to the elementary education of young children. Perforce, he put his fate into the hands of an agent located in his city who provided such service and found, as his stars decreed, a place in the house of a contemporary Roman-Jewish family where the next stage of his life would unfold.

In this household, also, lived a Rabbinical student, brought from Jerusalem for the same purpose, the education of the master's children, but of course, in his case, to make of them Jews. Interesting, Jason mused, at this point in his story, the tenacity with which these people clung to their God; is their God's commitment to them as strong, he wondered? No matter, his master wanted for his children what all Jewish parents in this alien land wanted for them, to be Jews and Romans both. Could that be? Did only Jews think they could teach birds to swim and fish to fly yet have them remain birds and fish? He challenged his Jewish friend with that question: "Yes," replied the student, "they can become both, but only by becoming neither."

Because of these thoughts, he and this Jew became fast friends exploring the ideas of their two worlds while sharing a common third, the hidden world revealed by Greek thought and the invisible God of the Jews. Jason found himself first intrigued but then captured by Yahweh who over millennia became the still unfathomable Lord of the universe. When hearing the "Hear O Israel" in the quiet evening, he felt it resonate in his very being. And little by little he slipped into this mysterious world. Though it was difficult to find a Hebrew bible in this Greek-speaking Jewish world, he nevertheless learned to read Hebrew to know Moses' instructions directly, and he became known and respected for his learning.

By and by he began to observe the Jewish ways. He obeyed the dietary laws, the Sabbath, and the ritual washings and prayers. He received permission to celebrate the Seder in its time of the year and the High Holy Days and began to wear some distinguishing clothing of the Jews, although only in the confines of the compound.

At first this was to the bemusement of his master who looked fondly upon him and respected his desires. To many of the servants, however, this was a source of amusement and gossip. When Jason began to talk of accepting the covenant of Abraham in circumcision and formally converting to Judaism, his master recognized in this there was danger.

The Romans were tolerant of other religions but demanded recognition by these others of the divine status of their Emperor. Only the Jews were exempt from this requirement because of a decree of the state for their past service to Caesar. They were acutely aware that this "favor" could easily be disavowed and in that case their community faced destruction since no Jew could accord divinity to any but God. In ancient times such idolatry was proffered once by them and the punishment for it was never forgotten. Conversion to this Judaism, then, meant in fact that the person relinquished his allegiance to Augustus, which meant Rome, and that would be treason punishable by death.

Inevitably, the gossip of the servants reached the ears of other Jewish families who expressed their alarm to Jason's master. The crisis point was reached when a minor Roman functionary suggested he knew of the situation and the potential for a serious scandal was clear. Jason's sole desire was to live as a Jew and it was clear that would not be possible in Rome, nor as he soon realized, in the Empire anywhere, without hiding a secret life.

It was providential then that a personal friend of Natan was in Rome opening new business contacts and learned of this problem. He knew of Natan's desire for a person of exactly Jason's abilities and realized it provided the perfect solution. In Natan's service, Jason could pursue this aspect of his life in freedom and Jason's Roman master, sharing the sadness of his family in this matter, understood that releasing Jason from his service was the only course of action.

I heard this story from Jason during the several days we spent exploring Bactra and exchanging details of our lives. My time in Rome was long after his but I knew of the family he was in service to. Unfortunately, I could tell him little of their present fortunes though they remained intact, the children he tutored were surely now the masters.

As he ended his tale I teasingly asked him how "much" a Jew did he remain. Was he, indeed, circumcised? There were Jews in Jerusalem who would deny even Natan's "Jewishness", calling such people outside Judea "fake Jews" though the Temple authorities never refused their generous tributes. Would they accept Jason, circumcised or not? Jason lived in the household as a Jew so far as I could see. But in the Jewish households here, even more than in Rome I observed, Jews and Gentiles alike lived largely according to Jewish custom and Gentile servants were so often more rigid in this than were Jewish servants that I was at a loss to distinguish them.

He looked at me studiously for a moment and replied with that manner of one who is not sure he would be properly understood: "Jacob, I was not circumcised and as to my Jewishness, I promise to explain fully. But the explanation demands you know things about this country, and the thought and teaching that dominate it, which few foreigners are aware of. I do not flatter you, Jacob, when I say because of your nature and intelligence you will not find my discourse boring, but do not be startled if you find dimensions uncovered of your Galilean Rabbi that you could not imagine."

Even the mention of the Rabbi in this context was enough to catch my attention for what could he have to do with all this? I thought again, who is that man who demands such notice from these intelligent, worldly and wealthy people. In appearance he is a common wandering preacher ministering to a destitute population. But Jason caught my hand and pulled me to a secluded place in a city garden where we would be little noticed and undisturbed. The thought that it was a place suitable for lovers flashed through my mind, and then I wondered at the need for this quiet and intimacy.

"Your Rabbi," he began, "is not of a type unknown in this

country, although at first hearing that sounds incredible. A Galilean Jew, a mendicant preacher, able to captivate and charm even the lowest of beings and to subdue and quiet the most brutal. How can such be found elsewhere but in Jewish Palestine among half-starving God-crazed zealots? But often, Jacob, the essence of a thing — you know that Greek thought, Jacob — can be most clearly seen when looking away from it. Such is the case with the Galilean.

"Some five hundred years ago, from the account I received, there was born in the foothills of the great India mountains, into the family of a wealthy chief of a warrior tribe, a man given to the world as a gift. We would say a gift of God though these people do not speak of such. And this must be so, Jacob, because despite his boyhood spent in luxury, his every wish granted, with all manner of suffering hidden from him, with nothing less than our original Garden surpassing his own paradise, he cast it all aside, defying his father's kingly ambitions for him.

"How compassion and love arises in such a one, Jacob, cannot be understood. We can only stand in awe at its presence and mystery. For this Gautama, as was his family name, gave up all, family, wife and child, to find a way to end human suffering. For many years, his disciples teach us, he searched all paths trekked by the ancient sages, almost dying in the grip of terrible austerities, until in frustration and despair he cast himself into a motionless silence, determined not to arise until death or knowledge came to him."

Jason now took on the look of a person in reverie more than one engaged in discourse. I was loath to break into his mood but I felt compelled to. "Jason," I said gently, "you are right, I am not bored, but entranced really, but what has this to do with the Galilean? Are you finding comparisons between them? I cannot see how."

"Patience, Jacob, you will see as I did, I am sure." Then he continued more forthrightly and I was somewhat relieved that I did break into his strange state of mind.

"It was in this silence, finally, that enlightenment came, buddhi they call it in their language, and he saw the way. But now the question arose, could the path be taught? And then he realized that was the wrong question. Could the path be learned? That was more to the point. As the Buddha, the enlightened one, his was a call to teach. Let those who were ready, those who had ears to hear, let them come to him to hear; to teach, that was his work.

"At the beginning he brought his teaching into the world to his fellow monks who themselves had flocked to different masters. He was thirty-five years old, hardly the sage they were accustomed to, and his first sermon to them taught a middle way between the rejection of depraved and ignoble bodily pleasures and the pursuit of bodily hardships and sacrifices: the two paths followed by the worldly and by monks. In their place he gave to them what they came to call the noble truths revealed to him in his experience of enlightenment.

"As he taught, disciples gathered around him and as his noble truths elevated them to this buddhi state they went out to the people with his message. They came to be known as the compassionate ones; Guatama especially, whose goodness and love, it was said, surrounded him like a mantle. In his presence there was a peace and calmness and disturbance quieted as he approached it.

"His teaching was embraced by the people as he called on them to care for each other, comfort the sick and succor the poor, the children and the elderly. Great wealth, in gold or the misguided sense of personal importance, and great poverty, in material things or the misguided sense of self-worthlessness, both have the same source and result in the same suffering and destruction."

I could hardly contain my rising excitement at these words. "Jason, Jason," I cried, grasping his arm to stay his words, "you are describing the Galilean. How can that be? The Rabbi speaks out of the teaching of the holy Torah, the same words I heard from the Rabbis and street preachers in Jerusalem. Do you not see the similarities? But more than that, you draw a picture of my Rabbi from your image of the other, you should know how alike they are shown by your words. From what teaching did this wisdom come?"

"You can see now, Jacob, why we must talk of the Galilean,

who he is and why he is here so far from his home. You have only
sensed the power of the Buddha, one man, and man he really was,
to change his world. But you need to hear more of his efforts and
then you will know something of the Rabbi that even he may not
yet understand."

His last words unnerved me even more than his first and I
appreciated the isolation of our little alcove, for my agitation was
noticeable and I was forced to pace a moment to regain my composure. "Why is he here Jason?" Then I answered my own rhetori-
cal question: "He is here to head a community of Jews who are
living the prescribed life of their sect: that was made clear to me at
the outset of our journey. This is why he came with me and why
he was sent by his people. And who he is? Jason, my head is spin-
ning and I cannot think clearly; what more do you have to tell
me?"

"Buddha's wisdom," he continued, "came from the stillness he
was able to enter and when he came back into the world he taught
that wisdom that was revealed to him. He saw people so long
mired in terrible suffering that it seemed normal, even to those
whose appearance denied the misery. The suffering sprung from
desires, those unfulfilled as well as those fulfilled, for even fulfilled
desires begin to die once achieved; desires, however, he recognized
could be overcome through right living and above all by the people
themselves learning how to enter that stillness within."

My mind flashed back to the words of Moses in that quiet
desert sermon when Jeshua read to the assembly — a more motley
crew could not be found for such teaching I thought then. "Jason," I interrupted, "I heard the Rabbi say similar words from our
Torah. It was the Law Giver who said, I am sure I remember, 'the
word is very near to you, it is in your mouth and in your heart.'
Could this not be an equivalent instruction?"

"Judge for yourself, Jacob," he replied, "but you are racing
ahead of me. Hear me out first. I really believe we can understand
the Rabbi's present life and read his future in the Buddha's past."

Jason explained how, at first, Gautama spoke to his few dis-

ciples living in a closed community, but then they began to circulate among the people at large. People gathered to them, entranced
by their words but also by their presence. They taught in the
language of the streets and asked only to be heard. They demanded
no tribute as did the Brahmins who continued to espouse the
established ancient rules and rituals, such as to bind the people to
their service. And this class of which Gautama once was part, despised, resisted and persecuted him and his people.

Nevertheless, he persevered and because his teachings spoke
so eloquently to the minds of the educated and to the hearts of the
masses, they kept the teachings alive and sustained its teachers.
Although in the early years the large mass of the population was
not able to hear or, for those who did hear, to follow these teachings, he planted seeds in many parts of the land and founded
centers of learning and teaching. Before he died, then, this new
wisdom was deeply planted into the soil of India, waiting only for
the proper time to burst forth in full bloom.

After his death, his closest disciples debated and enlarged upon
his teachings and new forms of understanding emerged to allow
different followers to find the best way for themselves. But the
essential core of his teaching remained for all: Find yourself! Find
yourself! Go deep within, realize your higher nature and live your
life in accord with this nature and by your life and word you will
be a lamp to other beings.

"Now," Jason continued, "some two hundred years ago, a great
Indian king, Ashoka by name, expanded his grandfather's conquests to all of India. But because he was so appalled by the blood
spilled and the suffering of the population this required, he for-
swore war as a means of statecraft. He embraced the Buddha's
peace and looked to spiritual means for governance. He encouraged the spread of this teaching throughout India and sent mis-
sionaries to neighboring lands. The monk that partly accompanied you on your way here may have been part of that tradition.

"King Ashoka issued a series of edicts describing the teaching,
or dharma, of his new religion and commanded the people to fol-

low them: kindness, truthfulness, purity, the tolerance of other beliefs and mutual respect were among some of these edicts. Other rules ended the practice of killing animals through hunting and ritual sacrifice. These edicts were carved in rocks and on stone pillars. Jacob, you will see them yet in this country.

"Ashoka died and his kingdom fell prey to the ambitions of other rulers and the weakness of his sons. This great spiritual country served, however, to show what life could be like when ruled by philosopher/kings as was observed by my Plato. Alas, decrees demanding spiritual obedience without the willful surrendering of the people cannot be enforced by truncheon and spear as secular law can be. In your country, Jacob, the rise and fall of kingdoms obey the dictates of our invisible God, but here, the sages say, the heavenly stars control the nature of the age, and they are not now in propitious alignment.

"Still, the teachings of the Buddha took firm hold among large sections of the people. And those able to enter the inner realm he described, lay people and monks, understood and escaped the suffering of the ignorant and in whatever way they could they tried to bring them out of that ignorance and this became their mission in life. What do you think, Jacob, the people would say about this man if I told this story on the streets of the lower quarters of your holy city?"

"If you are asking me, Jason," I replied, "if I think they would say he is the awaited Messiah, our liberator, I would say not. They are looking for a Prince, sure enough, but a Prince of heaven, one that would come among them and rally the people with great words and powerful deeds and then lead Jewish legions against Rome and re-establish the kingdom of David.

"Indeed, the sect the Galilean was raised in, if I understand rightly, thinks this too. But I must agree with you, Jason, in many ways my Rabbi is more like your Buddha than like King David. And neither could be the one the Jews of Palestine await. Besides, what would the Jewish Messiah be doing here, in this country?"

"True, Jacob, but the one the Jews await will not come. We are convinced here that if the Jews follow a man who will lead them to confront Rome with arms they will follow a false savior, be themselves destroyed and the city itself put to the torch. But to your question of what the Galilean is doing here: I told you of Gautama's early days, his days of searching for guidance, searching for himself in truth; and I told how, finally, he ceased searching and gave himself up to silence.

"I believe your Rabbi is now in that situation. He exhibits great powers and shows those qualities we have come to recognize in great sages. But he does not yet know who he is or what he is, but somehow he knows finding these answers is the first of his needs."

"I will grant all this, Jason," I replied, for now ignoring the new question Jason's words raised in my mind: that is, who is Jason? "I am sure of these powers, as you call them, I cannot deny what my eyes have seen and my ears have heard. But why leave his home, his country? Why come to the place of another Jewish community when he could have easily found one closer?"

"Can one find peace and silence in present-day Palestine, Jacob?" He spoke now with a new passion. "The very air of that country is alive with tumult. The countryside cries with despair and misery by your own account, and you, in the favored position you are in, even you can see how it presses on the lives of the people, and how it offends you.

"I cannot answer your questions now but the answers will come for I truly believe, and the belief gives me much solace, that the anointed one of God that the Jews have foretold has come in the person of the Rabbi of Galilee. It is said here that that there will be one who will come in the footsteps of the Buddha. This one will exalt the life of the Buddha and that he will bring this teaching to the peoples of the West as the Buddha has brought it to the people of the East."

Now it was my passion that was struck. "Who are you, Jason?" I cried, "that you speak of the Buddha as one with them? And if so, why this interest in the Galilean, in Palestine? You push me one way and pull in another. I feel I am riding an ass with a head on each end."

"I know, Jacob." Now his words took on a soft kindness. "But I am as perplexed as you are with these mysteries. I went to Rome with a Greek head; I came here with a Jewish soul and I speak to you today out of a Buddhist heart. I look at you and see the past of this country just as you listen to me and hear the future of your own. Is this not strange?

"I am not a prophet but I am sure of the words I speak: the Galilean will somehow find a place in this land and not leave it until he ascends a Mt. Sinai through his spirit as Moses did in flesh. Then he will return to his country and people with new words of God. He will be hailed and then vanish in flesh as is the nature of these messengers, but before that end he will have planted the seeds of this new word; those seeds will find fertile soil and in time their fruit will cover the land. Emperors will heed them and the people will wonder how the world could have been without them."

As he spoke a fear grew in me. He took on the manner and form of the prophet he denied he was. I felt I was face to face with revelation and I could not fathom the source of his message nor could I dispute its truth. And then an eerie sense of standing apart from my body came upon me and I found myself watching two forms, one of which I knew to be my own, occupying an adjacent space. Abruptly, I felt "Myself" being drawn back into my body and as that realization arose it was as if I returned from another world; I was startled to find the familiar, warm, aromatic garden spot that had ceased to exist for me only moments before.

I looked at Jason and was relieved to see the ordinary man I knew him to be, though I never again thought of him as "ordinary". He saw my discomfort, my confusion, and reached for my arm to reassure me. "Do not fear, Jacob. This knowledge and contact with these words have great power because they give you understanding and certainty, and with that comes freedom." I did not know then what he meant but what he said calmed my fears; indeed, his words provoked a strong feeling of well-being.

Much time had elapsed and we noticed the deepening shadows, although it seemed no time had passed at all. "Come, Jacob, we must go and prepare for our evening meal. Natan insists we all spend this part of the day together." As we walked off I was acutely aware of our surroundings: the heightened colors of the foliage, the sounds and smells of the city. They all demanded attention from my consciousness and the time spent in that garden bower began to fade such as a dream would as the sleeper became more and more awake.

The next day began as the previous evening ended, with a feeling of ease and contentment. The time spent with Jason was still sharp in my mind, but even so, seemingly distant in time. These were new and unfamiliar experiences and I thought of them as a separate part of my life.

Jason sent word to meet him in the morning dining area and as we enjoyed the normally light breakfast common to this country he suggested we enjoy the civilized pleasures of which this city boasted. Bactra was indeed a wealthy city long under Greek influence if no longer under its rule. And, as is common in the Greek world, there was as much homage paid to the excellence and care of the body as to the mind and spirit. If yesterday Jason's concern was to the latter, today it was my body of which he was most solicitous. Later, I realized, Jason's earthly needs were as intense as my own.

The private baths this city offered, judging, that is, from the one to which Jason brought me, were equal to many in the larger cities of the Roman lands, if not to their most famous. The interiors were lavish in comfort and decorated in such a way as to tantalize the senses. The images adorning the walls were not unfamiliar to me, for in my formative years as a young man in Rome, I and my Jewish schoolmate companions would steal to the Roman houses where these same paintings appeared. I knew bathing was not the only purpose of this place.

Jason earlier sounded out my Jewish sensibilities in these matters. He was not reticent in the matter knowing I was not an innocent as he knew the households of my early Roman days well. These were establishments only the wealthy could afford and, as is always the case, essential for business purposes. Natan's sponsorship was generous for this reason and Jason's was a familiar face here.

But in fact, Natan himself did not indulge these pleasures. Like the Jews in Judea, by and large the Jews in Gentile countries held to the laws against looking upon graven images and to the laws regarding Greek bodily esteem, harlotry and other forbidden carnal activities. But unlike those in the Holy Land they could not proscribe these activities in lands not their own.

They were also more forgiving and less judgmental than their counterparts in Jerusalem; it was difficult, in a country that celebrated and encouraged these practices, to be otherwise. Therefore it was neither uncommon nor frowned upon for those like myself, already accustomed to this world, to participate in it.

Thus it was I found myself alone in one of the large private bathing areas. Jason led me to it then went off, presumably to his own area. I entered through an opening into a small hallway leading to the bath proper. The wall of the hallway shielded the room and when inside, the atmosphere generated a feeling of privacy and isolation. The ample light of the room's oil lamps was augmented by a skylight rising toward the ceiling and combined they offered a subdued and soothing atmosphere. The stone walls were misted over and dripping from the rising steam in the large stone well into which one stepped from the porch fronting the bath itself.

The floor of the porch was covered with a bunting of some kind providing comfort to the feet and off to the end was a stall for a cleansing shower one used before entering the bath proper. There were two benches strategically located, one against the wall for seating and another more centrally placed that I recognized as used for the bodily massages favored by these people.

As I was standing on the porch deciding how to proceed, I sensed company entering the hallway and realized two people had joined me even as I was turning around. A boy and a woman I saw, and in the softest of voices the woman said, "I am here to serve you master; my name is Daphne."

"Daphne," I laughed, "and I am not Apollo so you'll not run from me?" And after a good look at her, I added, "Were I that god I surely would also chase you."

At my words she smiled appreciatively and then said, "You are not from this country, master, I know by your speech. Where then?"

As she spoke, with practiced hand she began removing my clothing and handing them to the boy beside her. In short order I found myself undressed and the boy left with my garments for cleaning. All was so matter-of-fact I felt no discomfit, more a sense of anticipation. I tried to tell her where I was from but she had little knowledge of that part of the world nor could she understand its location. She nodded when I explained it was where the sun fell into the sea but she could not, I am sure, envision the sea.

"Ah, you have come a long way through the desert, master; let us remove the dirt and sand from your body." And with those words she led me to the shower area and directly a warm cascade of water flowed over me from a container overhead. It was so cleverly contrived I could not see where it was placed. I do not know how much sand and dirt was washed from my body but at that point I must confess I gave little thought to cleanliness as I was then led to the broad bench and placed on it for the massage the Greek healers are famous for.

I could no longer resist the desires now arising, nor had I the intention to do so, but until this time I did not realize how much fatigue had entered every layer of my being. When I felt the warm, scented oil finding its way into the folds and curves of my body, soothing the taut muscles into an ease they seldom experienced, I fell into a blissful state of near-consciousness and the world disappeared. Perhaps not disappeared, rather, its concerns were overwhelmed by the intensity of a blissful, ecstatic temper in which the breath ceased and bodily functions were suspended.

I was content to lie there in what must have appeared to the woman a sleep-like torpor, though in my mind there was a clear awareness of the deliciousness of the moment. In time I realized I was alone although I have no recollection of my servant leaving the room and I had no care that she did so. Nor did I care that her purposes in serving me were not achieved. I felt actually a satisfaction in that, as it occurred to me that the release accompanied by that kind of service always resulted in a despair that destroyed the pleasure of the moment.

How much time elapsed in that state I cannot say. I have no memory of leaving that pallet and entering the warm bath, but only entering a more conscious condition sitting on a stone stool in the pool basin, enjoying a contentment and satisfaction never before felt and to remain unique in my life.

Daphne entered then, softly crossing the porch to where I was sitting. She had laid my clean and scented clothing on the bench and held out a large drying sheet for me to climb into. "Your friend waits for you in the anteroom," she said. "There are refreshments for you. Are you well, master?" she asked, a little nervously. "I wanted to please you."

"Daphne, you are truly Aphrodite's daughter. You are a pleasure to gaze on, believe me. And you did please me but in ways neither of us could have known. Please do not fret about this." My feelings for her were generous and later I asked Jason, who held Natan's purse, to be sure to give her an extra gratuity.

As we left the bathhouse, Jason asked what I thought of the establishment and how it compared with others I had visited. I noticed he too was wearing newly laundered clothing but I was sure his experience was not the same as mine. Before I had a chance to answer his question, however, he added, looking closely at me, "You look different, Jacob, you are less drawn, more at ease, less strained, really, in this short time. Most of us do not leave the baths replenished, should we say, but rather spent."

I felt as he described me. Then I told him that the condition of dissipation after such a visit is usually the case with me also. I felt now the confidence with Jason that I had had with Alexander and I confided my history of malaise that grew from my dissolute life in Jerusalem, which included the type of house we just left. Then I described the experience here and how the apex of desire was reached but not expended and then settled into an euphoria that is present yet. This is what Jason must detect.

"It just happened, Jason. I remember most this overwhelming feeling of fatigue and then that serenity I did not want to disturb. Is it this country? Why did the thought of the Galilean come to mind when it occurred? Can you explain this, Jason?"

Jason looked at me thoughtfully. "Each time I feel I plumbed some depth in you, Jacob, you reveal another level. I cannot throw much light on what happened to you at the baths. I know, however, of a teaching in India, from the Brahmin tradition, that conditions the body to reach such heights as you describe and then to go beyond it to some mystical realm. We Jews have among us some who pray with such fervor they claim they are 'transported', as you describe." He laughed then and added, "I would not want to describe to them, Jacob, your method of praying."

"We Jews." I mimicked his expression. "Is it my method of praying that reminds you of your Jewish soul?" As I was teasing him and enjoying this banter and new friendship, I was struck by the sight of a man who looked familiar. How can that be, I thought, in this city? But then I realized whom I saw and a shock of excitement caught my breath.

"Tomas, Tomas," I shouted as I grabbed Jason's arm and pulled him in the direction of the man I called. Tomas, and it was surely he, heard my voice and turned to me. He was more kempt than I remembered and with respectable clothing, but it was no doubt Tomas. And, as was my memory of him, he was leading an ass pulling a wagon loaded with provisions. His first expression was one of puzzlement as he caught my eye, but then I saw the mark of recognition.

"Why master," he declared, "peace be with you . . . how is it with you?"

I lost my composure upon hearing his words and voice. I felt a deep affection for him at that moment and I knew it was because of his association with the Galilean that moved me so. Impulsively I threw my arms around him and in that hug, kissed his neck. As I felt his resistance to my behavior I regained a sense of propriety; this unseemly behavior to my former servant must have discomfited him as it embarrassed me.

"To you peace, Tomas." To reduce my chagrin, I pulled Jason toward me and though speaking to him, with a nod toward Tomas, I explained that Tomas was a companion and "disciple" of the Galilean of whom I so often spoke. Then speaking directly to Tomas, I asked, "Tell us Tomas, where is the Rabbi now? Is he in this country? Can we see him? Jason is a wise and important person in this city and he would like to meet with him."

At that Tomas looked closely at Jason and then to me. I saw now not the servant I knew when he left Jerusalem with us as an abject wagon driver. The change I noticed developing in those last days near Damascus, when he informed me of his intention to leave our service, had more fully matured in the recent months. He looked steadily at us and then spoke in a firm voice.

"He is not with us, Jacob," he started and he called me by my name without any sense of arrogance. For my part his address seemed so natural I felt no affront. "We arrived here together and found the community he came to lead. Master and I prepared that evening for our rest and sometime that night I noticed he was missing from our shelter. I remained awake, awaiting his return, fearful for him in that unknown wilderness, though I knew of his habit of spending these nights alone. He had his very special way of prayer.

"Shortly before sunrise he returned and came to me and pulled me aside from the others. 'Tomas,' he said, 'I must leave, I am called away.' Leave to where, Master? How called? I asked. To leave me, Master, who will care for you in this strange country?' It was then that he told me what I should do, how I should live, to always remember him, and wait for his return.

"There were other words he gave me that are locked in my

heart and when these words entered that secret place, Jacob, my fear left me. With that he left without so much of a nod to the others, but he is with me yet in spirit and I know he will return in his flesh."

I was moved and astounded at the simple eloquence of this unlettered servant's speech. I saw that Jason, too, was visibly shaken by what he heard. Only yesterday in that garden hideaway he was prophesying just this event and I saw the effect the reality of that prophecy was having on him. Where did the Rabbi go? How could he enter this country with such confidence and fearlessness? He seemed equally at home in the wilderness as in community, if not more so. But I knew then, with a certainty equal to Tomas' conviction — upon whom I now looked with different eyes — that the Rabbi would return for him. But return for me, of that I was not sure.

Tomas then told us of his own situation. Even before they reached this destination, he confessed, he felt the Rabbi had other thoughts but because of fear he would not consider them. "I had a dream," Tomas told us, "that he would leave me and I told him of this fear in my heart. 'Remember me, Tomas, and I will never leave you' he said to me, but I learned with Master that his words at times hide his meaning and some of that fear remained."

At this Jason spoke for the first time. "What are your thoughts for your Master, Tomas? What does he teach you that binds you to him so?" Jason's tone pleased me. He asked Tomas' feelings with a respect not called for by the clear differences in their stations. He spoke in his own way as a man with a trained elocution, but there was no trace of condescension in his manner.

Tomas was slow in answering but he did not seem unsettled by Jason's questions, nor his manner. "Pardon, sir, but as you can see I am unschooled. I can only say this: When I am with my Rabbi I am at peace and without fear. When I am not with him, as now, and I call on him when beset in some way, I am eased.

"As to his teaching, I can say little. He says always our Father wants what is good for us and we seek him by looking within. He

asks us to care for each other, to help the poor, to see to the hungry. He says to love one another but I am not sure of that word. He
says not to do to another person what we do not want another
person to do to us. Is that a teaching, master?"

I looked at Jason and for a moment I thought I saw the same
remote expression I noticed the other day. Then he said quietly,
"That is a teaching, Tomas. Remember those few words, Tomas,
and you know all the teaching there is. You have done me a great
service today. The Rabbi of Galilee is truly a holy presence. By
your contact with him and his love for you, you are blessed. And
because you brought this knowledge of him to me, a burden of
fear has been lifted from me. I want to thank you for this."

"No! No! Thanks to you, sir." He could hardly speak the words
and I saw his eyes brim: when last that happened only God knows.
"I know your heart, sir, I know your heart. This day will stay with
me." And they remained looking at each other, drawing inquisi-
tive glances from passers-by whose presence heretofore had gone
unnoticed. Before the mood dissolved I again wondered at the
power of the Rabbi, who, when only simply thought of, could
join these two so dissimilar people in this bond of love.

And what is this fear they seem to understand in each other
but do not speak out? I feel no fear, especially here in this country
without the Roman sword in our faces, or Temple guards searching for signs of blasphemy, nor a capricious ruler with his onerous
needs. But they speak of fear. I thought I would ask Jason about
this in time but I knew I would not; I sensed somehow that words
could not address this question, that it was part of the Rabbi's
mystery.

I realized how much even I was caught up in the total absorp-
tion of the moment, when the sounds of the city and the movement in the streets shattered my attention. Again, the eerie feeling
of suspended time entered my awareness and I wondered at this
strange sensation. But instantly I was in the world once more and
I heard Tomas preparing to break away from us.

"I must leave," he was saying, looking at me. "I am presently

in service with a large family and I drive their marketing wagon. I
have no plans, just to await Master's return and in that I am content."

But Jason was not content to let it go at that. "Tomas," he
said, "I am in the city in the house of Natan. If you have need I
want you to see me for it. Further, you will do me a great service if
you contact me when your Rabbi returns or if you otherwise hear
from him. Will you do that?" Then, with a nod, Tomas left, not to
be seen or heard of again for many years.

JACOB V

Time and place have taken on an alien quality since I entered this land. Although my presence in this city could be measured by hours and days, its impact on my spirit was far greater than can be accounted for by these few short cosmic cycles. This awareness came into sharp focus as Natan and his business needs intruded on the mysterious world I entered into with Jason, or as he would insist later, I led him into.

Natan had spent these several days selecting from the goods I brought from Jerusalem and Damascus his needs for local use and choosing what was to be transshipped further east. Between barter and purchase he acquired the rare spices and exotic herbs treasured in the West. In addition, he bargained for that silk cloth that is only produced by a still unknown means, kept secret by the far-eastern people whose monopoly made it very expensive and especially valued. They said it was made by a worm, if that could be believed, and it was worth one's life to try to smuggle that creature from its land.

He now brought me into this process so my time of ease and preoccupation with less worldly activities ended. The happenings of the last few days were pushed to the back of my mind but not to be forgotten. They would gestate there, I knew, carrying on a life of their own until, when earthly demands quieted, they would emerge as feelings of joy or sadness, clarity or confusion, or whatever mood was evoked by thoughts of the Galilean.

The day had been fixed for the leaving of the next westward-bound caravan. Bactra was the connecting link of this major route between the civilizations of the East and West. It was here that caravans going in each direction were outfitted and replenished with men and animals and commercial transactions finalized. Natan was one of that consortium of merchants who controlled this traffic. Their business, not to mention their very lives, depended on the stable, protected and orderly transport of goods, credits, and documentation.

The six-month trek across this wasteland required the planning and discipline of the longest sea voyage. An appointed caravan leader paid by the merchant group but approved by the regional satrap was the undisputed law all independent segments of the caravan had to acknowledge. Each individual merchant, even a small trader with only one animal, needed official permission to travel with the caravan. For this he paid a fee to the government minister overseeing this activity. He was issued a document attesting to his protected status and only with this could he join the caravan.

The caravan organized its own security force to protect it from the small groups of marauding bandits infesting the countryside. This could be a formidable force insofar as a typical caravan consisted of as many as a thousand of the large two-humped camels. The government, for its part, had established a tribute treaty with the large nomadic tribes in the northern steppes who were capable of destroying the largest caravan and were otherwise impossible to subdue. This treaty had held for many years and was periodically re-established, a testament to the beneficial function of benign and intelligent statecraft.

Thus the seemingly simple matter of the transport itself represented a substantial investment by Natan and the other large merchants. It was important that this group would select the caravan leader and the security force captain; indeed, they were in fact the group's servants. I was brought into this planning meeting with merchant representatives such as myself to receive instructions from the caravan leader and the security captain as to our responsibilities on the journey. As servants of the controlling merchants, we were part of the disciplinary force maintaining order.

Before my inclusion by Natan into the inner organization of

this enterprise, I had no inkling of the hidden relationships among merchants, city and country rulers, local tribal chiefs and assorted desert sheiks. In the Roman lands all commerce and trade were closely regulated. Law was proclaimed and law was obeyed and it was unthinkable that tribute and tax would be negotiated.

In this more indulgent country, then, the most exquisite tact was required to maintain harmony among such a disparate and enterprising gathering. Jason's value to Natan and the others was that of master of the art of managing their conflicting interests. He showed a remarkable understanding of the needs, the desires and the ambitions of each party. After witnessing an example of his skill in settling a dispute in the area of authority, and in the way of a compliment, I suggested he open a school near every army barracks and put the soldiers out of work.

He answered with more seriousness than my remark intended, but what he said remained with me as the explanation of the constant upheavals in my own country.

"Jacob," he began, "I told you once that I speak out of a Buddhist heart. That is more natural, in this country, than you may think. The teachings of the Buddha have now entered the hearts and minds of so many in this land that it is part of the air we breathe. It calms the fires in men and permits reason to flourish which, as our Greek teachers taught, is man's first need. Shortly you will go back to your own country and there you will see the truth of my words."

This conversation occurred as final preparations for my westward trip took place. I received my instructions and papers from Natan for the people in Damascus and Jerusalem. Natan pleased me with his affection and his expression of confidence in me. Previously, he was so intent on business with little interest in the other affairs of my life and my stay in Bactra, I had no idea how satisfactory he considered my service.

But my parting from Jason was surprisingly difficult. True, we had spent, all told, not that many days together, but I revealed more of myself and learned more of his spirit than with others with whom I had spent years. He responded to this thought as if I had spoken it aloud. "Jacob, I must say something to you. Our Plato has his master saying, 'that we do not know or learn anew, but recollect from previous lives.' It is when I am with you that these words have meaning for me. I feel I have known you always."

I did not answer, I had no need to. I felt toward him more than affection as I grasped his hand and threw my arms around him in a farewell embrace. I would say I loved him but I could not yet use that word. It truly must be the quality of the air in this country. I thought when Jason was describing Buddhist teachings, and when Tomas was speaking of his Master, that these were womanly things. And now I felt in me an unfamiliar disturbance as if these same "womanly" things were rising in my breast.

It was a tribute to the organizing skills and wisdom of these men that such a hazardous and difficult undertaking could be accomplished with apparent ease. All contingencies were prepared for and even the testing of the gods, theirs and ours, was met with skill. One unnerving sand storm, frightening for me in its intensity, was met with confidence and calmness by the experienced caravaneers who took the shelter provided by their animals. These beasts were well-able to contend with the worst of these desert terrors because of the natural protective qualities of their heads, faces and skin.

I had two experienced servants to care for my personal needs, cooking our meager meals and setting up the evening shelter. My services, besides looking to the security of our merchandise, included various administrative tasks. Because of Natan's status, I, as his man, was included in the settling of the numerous minor conflicts among members of the caravan. Always, questions of authority and placement in line and other matters of dispute arose to be settled by a committee of which I was a part.

And at one point I was asked to accompany the captain of security to deal with a local tribal chieftain who was not satisfied with the tribute promised him to permit us to cross "his land". I was impressed that the issue was settled peaceably by the captain.

I asked him how it was that this was their land since they drifted from here to there with no borders, guards or stable villages.

"They think they own the territory they travel through," he told me, "and resist even other tribes' encroachment."

"Do you agree with that, Captain? I think a Roman centurion would not hesitate a moment to put them to the sword and flight, their families as well."

"My lord would not permit my doing that," he replied. "He would say, 'those who live by the sword as their first thrust fail as men, they die by the sword, for there is one forever pointed at them, and who can live without sleep?' Rome rules an empire of its enemies, no less internal than external. They say there is peace because there is no war; but there is no peace in Rome. The war is in the hearts of the people who hate the conquerors, hate their neighbors and hate themselves. In this hate there is death."

I had to remind myself this was a soldier speaking. And I remembered my remark to Jason: Put a school of reconciliation outside each army barracks and we would no longer need soldiers. "You do not talk like a soldier . . . " I started. "Not a Roman soldier," he interrupted, "but I am a soldier of my lord."

"Jason," I continued, "you know Jason, Natan's man?" and as he nodded, I went on, "suggested to me that the beliefs in your country more than your arms make for this peace. Do you think this is so?"

"I do not argue with Jason, his wisdom is well known. I can only say my lord shares many of these beliefs and encourages their teaching to the people. His advisors include masters of this wisdom and I know he heeds their counsel. But he knows men and the world. He knows the greed and ambitions that drive them. His aim is to govern so as not to allow enemies to arise, for that is the only true way to peace, but if one does he will not offer his unprotected neck. Nor will I."

He left me with those thoughts, so reasonable to my trained mind, but which fed my doubt and confusion. How would the Galilean answer? "You must not kill" is God's commandment and

I could not imagine the Rabbi disobeying it. Nor could I imagine who would find him a threat. But can one live in this world by that command? Certainly even the children of our God do not.

Thus I spent the days, weeks and months of this expedition. When his time permitted, the captain often came to look to my needs and visit to talk. I learned much of his country and he much of mine in those visits. His ancestors were Greeks, followers of the Macedonian army and, by Alexander's design, were settled here in their conquering footsteps. They were valued as soldiers by local and regional satraps and were bred to this profession. In time, of course, this new land became their own.

Finally our parting time arrived and the Captain had to see to his future assignment. Again I felt the sadness of leaving a good friend. Two days hence we were to reach the first outpost into Roman country. I was never to learn how that demarcation point was determined, but it was the same small village post we entered when we first came from the West.

Once again I was caught up in the administrative tasks of dealing with Roman functionaries, shepherding my own goods through the check points and working with the caravan leader aiding others, sometimes with language, sometimes with documentation. The leader was a good man and intent on bringing all who were part of his charge safely to their destination.

Because of these duties, I had little time to think of my state of mind. It took a full four days to move our entire train through this isolated watering place. This was a speedy accomplishment I was told because we were the only company of travelers in the area at the time; it was not unusual to wait two weeks or more before a large company like ours could go on its way. In time we were once again into the slow-moving pace demanded by the country and the burdened beasts.

It was then I became aware of that familiar sense of oppression and unease that I had always accepted as a natural part of my existence. Strangely, I did not notice its absence during my period outside Roman lands. But now, as it forced its way into my ken,

Jason's words came back to me: "The thinking and ideals of the people infuse the air we breathe and feed our minds as good or bad food feeds our bodies." We were in Rome now and the pernicious Roman air came with the territory.

And though I felt this discomfit, my freedom from it, even for the short time I experienced that freedom, changed my understanding and thinking of the world. There were times, I must admit, in the coming years, when my memory of this country and its promise faded close to oblivion. But never did it disappear entirely and I was able to recognize in the words of our teachers the promise of the hope of a life in peace in the midst of oppression.

As we approached Damascus my thoughts turned to the days, close to a year ago now, when I neared that city from another direction. It occurred to me how different that person was from the one now returning. And I knew, though I understood later more than I did then, that the change I detected was inside me, in my heart and soul and mind and in this there was both joy and bitterness. Joy for the vision that was opened to my sight but bitterness at my inability to surrender to that seeing.

Damascus was as I left it: a maelstrom of activity, unbearable noise and an impossible stench, which sucked the weary traveler out of the order and quietness of the desert into the chaos of urban frenzy. Fortunately, I needed to make no judgments. My master's servants met me at the caravan encampment, as they did before, and treated me with a kindly concern for my comfort.

While I was not supplied the appointments with which I was met in Bactra, all matters of caravan business were taken from my hands except for the documents and the communications entrusted to me in Bactra. From a world of myriad responsibilities, my concerns were reduced to the simple care of only myself.

And it was in this circumstance that the new challenges of my life, those shunted aside by the other demands of the times, now came to the forefront. I never forgot my promise to the Rabbi to convey the child he rescued to Sara. But it was not prominent in my mind and I now realized that that lapse was more by design than by accident.

Remembering that time, I now looked upon that promise as a burden. The image in my mind of a broken and half-dead girl — nay more dead than alive if the truth be said — being given into my charge for days at a time under the conditions of travel we faced, made me think the best for all would have been if she had not survived.

Indeed, I had almost convinced myself that she was most likely dead and I knew were I to keep silent about this matter it could never otherwise be revealed. Who would know? Further, in the unlikely event she was alive, the woman — did he call her Hannah? — would be best fit to care for her. So I persuaded myself, and I was satisfied until the time of decision arrived and my masters gave me the departure date for my return to Jerusalem.

Alas, I could not deny my promise to the Galilean, and I knew I could not rest until I learned the fate of his charge. Again that recurrent question: whence his power? Would I ever again see him in this life? Yet, in some deep recess of my mind, I could not face that prospect, no matter how remote, with no answer to his question: "Jacob, where is the child?"

Among my employers there was one in whom I believed I could confide my thoughts. This class of people, perforce, included those about whom it was said, with admiration or scorn as the case may be, "he has a Roman head" meaning by this a person who was accomplished in the ways of the world and the needs of the marketplace. All questions were answered with those needs in mind and the proof of the value of this lay in the worldly success of the individual.

Jesse, though not much older than the others, and it is usually in age that wisdom blooms, appeared to me as one who could understand my needs in other than these mundane terms. Quiet in manner, he seemed a steadying influence in this confusing and often tumultuous city. It was to him the others turned when faced with difficult decisions. Thus it seemed natural for me to ask him for some private time, a request he readily agreed to.

Where to begin? In my mind any part of this story reflected my lack of judgment. It was clearly an unneeded responsibility, uncalled for, to what end; all these questions were those any reasonable person would ask. I felt trapped now by my own stupidity and in this temper I blurted out: "I am charged with taking a sick child to Galilee and I need permission to convey her with one of our wagons."

I do not remember the reaction I expected, but in the most matter-of-fact tone, Jesse replied: "Really, Jacob, how interesting, how charged? Who is the child?"

His attitude instantly calmed my fears and with a sense of relief I poured out my story of her condition and rescue, describing in this context the actions of Jeshua whom, unthinkingly, I referred to as "Rabbi".

"Rabbi? Rabbi? Is he indeed a Rabbi?" Jesse asked.

"No, not really," I said, a little flustered, "but he seemed so learned in the Law he was called that by all. It became easy to think of him as such. But despite his learning he had the look and dress of the Galilean workman that I knew him to be. I know his family and I know his village. It is so peculiar, Jesse, to be caught up in this matter and to bring it you."

I continued then, telling him more of the Galilean's nature. How he talked and what he said as I remembered his words. His manner and his lonely ways, seeming apart from others even when conversing with them. But most of all his effect on them, how they responded to him and his expectation — I did not realize I thought this — that he be obeyed. Simply that, that he be obeyed.

At this point I felt as if a burden was lifted from my spirit. Why I do not know but I sensed I surrendered this problem. But surrendered to whom? To Jesse? He gave no such indication of concern. An eerie feeling stole over me as I contemplated that this sense of relief occurred whenever I spoke of the Rabbi. He comes to life in me and yet this is so despite myself, I do not seek him as others seem to do, yet I cannot reject him.

Jesse's expression was one of deep thought, almost as if he were

far away. My mind went to Jason and I wondered how much more
of this Jesse would want to hear. I had spoken nothing of the events
in Bactra. Discomfited by the silence and Jesse's lack of response,
and with the thought of Jason in my mind, I broke the quietness
impulsively and with an almost deferential tone: "Jason said he is
a special holy man, perhaps our Messiah."

For the first time I saw a sharp reaction in the man. He pulled
himself up straight in his chair and looking directly at me, he said,
"Jason? Natan's Jason? You have spoken with Jason about this man
as you have spoken to me? You must tell me everything, Jacob, of
your time with him."

Never was I listened to more intently. But it was for Jason this
attention was given. Those who knew him, Jesse made me understand, revered him for his wisdom and I recalled my own reaction
to this man when I too glimpsed the depth of his knowledge. Now
every word, every sentence I spoke to Jesse was heard, questioned,
repeated and questioned again.

He had to know what Jason asked me over and over again. I
was forced to recount our conversations in the garden, how Jason
described the nature of the Rabbi as a Buddha, and what Tomas
said about his master. But it was when I told him how Tomas and
Jason parted that day in the dusty Bactran street that I saw a different Jesse. I described the coming together of the illiterate donkey driver and the learned counselor for the city's elite and how
their exchange of spirit, not less than the exchange of words, was
revealed in that remarkable public embrace.

Into the face of this man, as worldly as he was learned, valued
for his position and wealth, there crept the same expression I witnessed in the faces of the most humble and despised of our people.
What to call it: tranquillity? composure? peace? No matter, I came
to think of it as the Mark of the Galilean.

Unable, or unwilling, to speak, Jesse sat staring at me, I think
without seeing me, for in a moment I had the sense of a return of
recognition from him, perhaps, in fact, a return to this time. In
this period I lost the perception of our relationship.

We were not servant and master but two inquiring minds and I was free to ask him in what manner he was so affected by this Rabbi of whom he knew nothing but my stories. Of course, in asking my question, I revealed my own lack of comprehension.

He looked at me again in that studious way of his and said, almost wistfully, "Jacob, I cannot tell you more than Jason, or what you learned from Tomas, or what you have seen of this man with your own eyes. It is not for me to say who is more blessed; those who are content in this world and question not the spirit of God, or those who in the poverty of their own souls are compelled to forever search for Him. But I say to you that when that search is ended then peace will reign in the seeker's heart."

We sat there, both withdrawn in our own thoughts, I reflecting again on the nature of the peace to which these people refer. *These people*, I realized I thought. Is Jesse now one of these? And who am I? Spreading a word and a doctrine to people who seemingly understand more of what I am saying than I do myself.

Breaking the silence and the otherworldly mood of the moment, Jesse said, "Well, Jacob, what of the child? You are blessed, Jacob, to do this deed for him. Do you not feel so?"

I felt a surge of dejection and confusion as I realized I came into this meeting to find an excuse for not doing this thing for which Jesse calls me blessed.

"Just a stray child, Jesse? What need did he have to carry her away from her destiny. Who knows, a worse one may await her yet. Do you know how many such children litter the streets of Jerusalem?"

"Of Jerusalem, Jacob? Of Damascus, of every Roman city and hamlet. Indeed, I know. God's tears are ample for another flood if He did not promise to hold that fate from us. Surely we deserve it for our treatment of each other. It is as good in God's eyes to save one child as it is to save one million, for in reality it is the same thing. It means the darkness is not complete and that one spark keeps His Word alive. Thank you, Jacob, for bringing me this story and allowing me to bring out from myself a hidden knowledge that has festered and troubled me for a long time."

He then rose and called a servant, a young man, Rufus, whom I recognized as one who helped me when I first returned to Damascus. We nodded in mutual recognition as Jesse told me Rufus would locate the child: Hannah's presence was not unknown to them. Jesse would make arrangements for me to fetch her if she was alive and able to leave. Then after giving Rufus some private instruction, and, I noticed, a purse as well, he dismissed him. Turning to me, he said, "Rufus will make the necessary inquiry and preparation and will find you when it is done. Peace be with you, Jacob, go with God."

This was the last I was to see of this man. Once again I experienced a sense of loss; loss of a teacher, as it were, who came into my life, uncovered a layer of understanding, then disappeared, leaving me with more questions and less certainty than before.

Thus it has been ever since I first laid eyes on the Galilean. Why could I not simply submit as I imagined these others do, quiet the thoughts and doubts, not fight the demands? From my awareness emerged the same feelings that I recalled from my Jerusalem days that led me into this journey. But submit to what? Instantly, Jesse's words flashed through my mind. A festering and hidden knowledge had been revealed to him. Did he know of my discontent? Did they have the same roots? God! God! Could I ever have peace?

Thankfully, Rufus came and informed me the child was ready to leave. In truth, he told me, it was necessary for her to leave and I was to see why when we went to her. Our master, Jesse, had made available to us a wagon and animal suitable for our trip to the South. Arrangements were made that I transport the child directly to her destination carrying the vital documents, letters of credit, and the easily carried valuables that could be only entrusted to one like myself, one with the protected status of a Roman citizen.

It was surely a sign, I thought with some surprise, that Jesse felt so strongly about the Galilean that he made such an effort to see that this wish of his be satisfied. I could not yet believe all this trouble was being taken on behalf of this ragamuffin. A wagon and driver were made available to join a small fast-moving wagon train conveyed by a Roman guard heading toward Jerusalem. I was to bring the child to her destination and then wait for the larger transport to catch up to me and then I would proceed to Jerusalem with it. Jesse may have done this for the Galilean, but, in truth, the effect it had on my life, not to say the life of this homeless one, was incalculable.

Rufus and I set out in the latter part of the afternoon period of rest when there were few people in the streets. So, as we turned into the street where Hannah's house was located, I did not question its deserted appearance. But I was soon to learn the time of day was not the reason. Hannah's house was a haven for the unclean, lepers and others whose scars and disfigurements gave them an even more hideous appearance.

The house was entered by one large doorway placed in an otherwise unbroken wall facing the street. This door led into an open courtyard that looked upon living quarters in the other three sides. I recoiled at the sight of the few dwellers I was able to discern in the growing shadows. It was very quiet and one felt compelled to speak softly. But in that quietness it was possible to hear sounds coming from some of the openings in the walls, which appeared as separate cubicles. I could only believe they were the sounds of despair as the atmosphere of the place was one of the deepest anguish.

In a moment I noticed two figures coming toward us. One was clearly a child and I shortly recognized Hannah, the woman I met that day so long ago. The small figure was covered from neck to foot in a dark, oversized cape. She wore a cowl type head covering but with her face exposed. At first she appeared unsteady on her feet but then I saw that it was because she could not straighten her back. Even in the growing shadows I saw the disfiguring scars on her face and I thought what her body must be like.

Why, I wondered yet again, did the Galilean rescue this one? Is she not better off dead? Jesse's words came back to me. Does

God look on this and smile? As if she read my mind, Hannah said, "Your Master charged you to see to this child. As you see, she cannot remain in this place."

"My master? You mean the man who brought me to you with her? He is not my master though I admit I promised him to take her from you. But is she well? Can she travel without care?"

"Your promise, sir," she said almost inaudibly, "was to the Master of us all." And then she added, with more force, "Accept him now or later, he cannot be refused."

Then, turning and speaking to the child, she said, using the common vernacular, "Tell us, Anna, can you travel without care?"

For the first time I looked into her eyes as she looked up to me for an instant. There was no blemish there but an intelligence that belied my first impression of her. Because of that, it was less of a surprise to hear her speak. Although in the manner and cadence of the streets, and with the heavy accents of an uneducated person, she said firmly, "I care for myself, master. I live, for God did not want me to die." I knew, remembering the condition of her abuse that this could only be the truth, and with those words it was done.

CYPRUS IV

I do not know how long Aaron's body, motionless, seemingly breathless, remained in its quiescent state. He opened his eyes, then closed them, and then opened them again, staring at what I could not say though I could imagine. He looked at me and I saw recognition in that look.

"When you touched me, Master [he uses this form of address now and I do not dissuade him; in this I know my work with him is over] I felt myself as a point in a universe without end. I could see everywhere, behind, in front, past and future. Is this how God sees the world? And then the spot itself expanded, I expanded, and the universe collapsed into a world of things and there was Jacob — I knew it was Jacob, just knew it.

"His image was so clear in my mind I knew the hair on his head, the look in his eye and the thought in his mind. Then clouds covered the image and I saw Sara come from the mist, and she too became the clearest of images as Jacob faded, and then Sara came again. Faster and faster they changed, making me dizzy until I could not separate them, and I knew that their days apart were over."

"In some ways yes, in some ways no," I said to Aaron. "But the ending of this account is my burden. Are you sure you have all Jacob and Sara can give you?" I asked him.

"I need only close my eyes, Master, as you have shown me, all doubt of this has flown from me."

With this he closed his eyes so as to reassure me and I looked closely at him and saw it was so — I knew he saw the last days of Sara's and Jacob's separation.

SARA AND JACOB

When father told me he had just received word that Jacob was a day's journey away, that he planned to stop at our village and he had need of my attention, my mind was beset with a flood of thoughts. The memories of those days so long ago when Jacob first came here and then left with Jeshua flooded into my mind. I then had no knowledge of Jeshua's influence on him or of the events of his journey. Nor could I fathom what possible need Jacob could have of me.

The next day he arrived with the girl, Anna, poor soul, still so deeply scarred. We needed to bring Alexander here for her care. We did not know how Jacob was charged to bring her into my personal custody and, though not so charged, to bring greetings to Jeshua's family who still lived under father's shelter. He planned first to return immediately to Jerusalem as required by the merchants there for whom he was in service. That is, as soon as his regular transport caught up to him.

It needed another three, perhaps four days for that to come about. Could he again stay under father's roof he asked. It was not thought odd that he would do so for it was well-known we were kin to Marcus who was his friend and master. Nevertheless, it had escaped no one that he showed me more than usual attention the last time he was here. His interest, it must be said, was almost offensive to our custom but he was otherwise so agreeable that it was excused as ignorance.

We knew Jacob had spent many intimate hours with Jeshua and I could not conceal my desire to hear about them. I was not surprised to learn he recognized the special qualities of this companion: the deep learning which compelled other travelers, in time, to refer to him as "Rabbi." He spoke of the quiet assurance Jeshua showed in all his dealings; and he mentioned also that in his presence, somehow, the tumult and rancor that curse those tiring caravans would diminish. And yet Jacob's heart could not follow his mind and he still could not accept him as a guide and teacher.

I will never know how the story arose that Jeshua was going to this far off place to head a community of Jews of our sect. But I knew it was not the truth. When he took his leave of me that final evening, an evening never to be erased, he told me of his need for a solitude he could not find here. From his earliest boyhood the special qualities of his mind and the different way of his being were known.

It was for this that his father was so conflicted: the joyous recognition in him of the mark of God's beneficence on one side and the painful realization that Jeshua was *his* gift to God, but a gift he feared to make. In this fear he thought to mold the son into a householder's life through betrothal and family and thereby keep him with him.

When Jeshua's father approached mine to arrange our betrothal he did so knowing of Jeshua's resistance to this effort. But his father persisted even after my more perceptive parent warned his tenant that he would lose his son altogether. Father, nevertheless, agreed to the arrangement and when he came to me with the news he also warned me that it was doubtful that it would come to fruition. If Jeshua's father was confounded by fear, I was blinded by love and I asked God for this to come about, but even in this sinful prayer I feared it would not.

From my earliest contact with Jeshua it was his kindness, his quietness, his thoughtful manner that captured my heart for they were a balm to my emotions. There was a softness and understanding in him that I did not know men possessed until, after he revealed it in himself, I searched it out and found it in others. But unlike him they denied and hid these qualities, seemingly ashamed of them. So, alas, in my own childishness I did not permit myself to see the futility of this dream.

My love for him was seeded that day when his whisper cut

through the frightening confusion of my first healing experience with the comforting words, "Did the world stop for you, Sara?" Of all beings then in my world only he understood, as did I, that this event of transport was a visit from God and not the evil one as others may have thought.

This seed sprouted in my days and years in Jerusalem when he would come to mind as a guide in my troubling periods of confusion and growth. And it reached full flower when, upon my return home after mother's passing, I again spied his now mature person, and his presence bore into my soul.

Could Jacob's arrival be an augury of a new direction in my life, somehow guided by Jeshua's spirit? I seized upon this prospect, and it gave me solace from the turmoil into which I was heading. Father was in the process of finding a husband for me and he was determined upon this course. For several years I had been able to resist his efforts in this because of his need for me to minister to his household. I had believed also his affection for me led him to consider my desires in this matter, a belief I now realized was false for when I demurred at his decision he made it clear his will in this matter would not be thwarted.

In addition, he pained me with accusations of unseemly, not lawful, behavior, behavior he thought a husband would be able to correct. In supervising the household, he complained, I had forgotten that I, too, was a servant. He told me how he regretted encouraging my unwomanly intelligence, my skills with animals, my arrogance with the men servants, complaints he only now expressed.

I could not defend myself against these charges for I knew some of them were true. And when, in frustration and anger, I pointed out the countless times he confided in me regarding the stupidity of our village leaders and wished they had my "Greek" head, he shocked me with his response: "Careful, daughter, women like you are not looked upon kindly."

I was desolate at the change in our relationship but I should not have been surprised. Father, himself, was preparing to take a new wife, a young widow close to my age, from a nearby village whose husband had been taken by fever before any children were born to her. None of her late husband's brothers would take her and her village was not short of eligible maidens. I did not think at first, when he told me of this arrangement, that his new wife would displace my position in the household but it did not take me long to recognize that foolishness.

Father understood rightly that no house could abide two mistresses. He feared my willful nature would not allow me to accept his new wife as my mistress and this would prove nothing but trouble for him. I knew I could not hope to vie with her for a dominant position in the household. I am worldly enough to understand men's weaknesses; these are not matters that are resolved only in the head but other places as well which a wife but never a daughter could occupy. I prayed nightly for direction.

Now, for the moment at least, the matter of Jacob's arrival allowed me to leave these disquieting thoughts. I remembered well Jacob's earlier visit with us despite my distress with Jeshua and I must admit his appearance made a mark on me. As well, it did not escape me that he more than once paid me heed in that manner of the men I had observed in Jerusalem.

Unlike these village men who look at us women as they look at farm animals, trying to judge how well we can work and breed, those others look to satisfy different needs and desires. In this there is a sinful power for women to use if they are not fearful of God's wrath. I thanked God more than once for Jeshua's strength in saving me from that trap.

Jacob arrived in mid-afternoon of the day following his message. It was a busy time and a perplexing one for father and me. He came, as I said, only to deliver this strange child into my care and we could not understand then the import of that. He asked leave then to await the arrival of his merchandise transport at which time he would relieve us of the burden of his presence.

Father, of course, made him welcome and assured him he was at Jacob's disposal, noting Jacob's service to Marcus, our kinsman.

Because they just finished a difficult journey, especially harsh for the clearly ailing child, we postponed our questioning of these untoward circumstances for a later time when he was cleansed, rested and refreshed.

I left the others to my father and with the aid of a maidservant I took the child, whom I learned was called Anna, aside for care. It was not until we managed to remove her old and clinging covering and submerged her poor body into a hot bath that we were able to see the results of the beating she had suffered. Of this she remembered nothing and it was later from Jacob that we learned of her story.

It was clear a miracle had occurred to save her life. My servant gasped and I, myself, could hardly suppress a cry when we saw the extent of the damage to this frail body. Hardly a part of her had not been exposed to the work of the flail and her skin was pulled into tight formations as new growth replaced the original that had been torn from her body.

But healing was no less a miracle. The wounds had closed and were clean and mending, the bruise marks were fading and the skeleton and muscles functioned more loosely than should have been expected. Food and some rest should allow this healing to continue but I thought I would bring Alexander from Jerusalem to see to her, forgetting I would soon be the mistress of this house no longer.

I left her in the care of the servant who was instructed to see to a broth for her and put her into a quiet area for a comfortable sleep. I then went to arrange for the evening meal. Jacob's arrival would not require a greater effort but I knew that later in the evening other guests would be on hand to hear of the traveler's report of the strange circumstances of his visit. Jeshua's family especially would be anxious of any news of their son and brother. I arranged for wine and sweet bread for their comfort.

At table we learned of the reason for Anna's condition, the story of her rescue, of the promise Jeshua exacted from Jacob to bring her to me, and of the guidance and support Jacob received in carrying out this promise. He spoke of his reluctance to accept this burden, and when he said he could not believe she would survive that first night, I remembered the marks on her face and body and knew the truth of his words.

And father asked, almost to himself, and with a faraway look in his eyes: "Tell me, Jacob, why would he do this? A useless slave, discarded by her master, deformed, surely ignorant. Why send her here to Sara, who cannot accept this chore? I think she would have been best left to her fate. Did he give you any reason? Just demand this promise?"

"I asked that selfsame question, Jonah," Jacob replied, "of my master who arranged that I bring her here directly."

"And he said what?"

Now Jacob's voice took on an odd quality, as if he himself did not view his next words seriously: "To make God smile." He paused for a moment, then repeated those words, "To make God smile."

"I do not understand, Jacob," father, now flustered, said, "what does that mean? 'To make God smile.' Do not blaspheme here, Jacob. We do not speak so lightly of God." And then he made his little prayer to show his obedience to the Almighty.

Jacob did not respond right away and when he did he did not answer father's question; perhaps in a way he did answer but it would be long afterward that one could see it as such.

"Jonah, you yourself told me when we first spoke of Jeshua, how apart from us your tenant's son is. I do not think that is quite true. Better put, I think we should say not that he is apart from us but that he shows us a part of ourselves that we do not know. Torah tells us God made us in His image. When we look at each other, hear our words, see our acts, do we see His image?"

And then his voice took on a rising tone and I noticed in him a manner that I would see again and again when he would speak of Jeshua. He seized father's hand in both of his and in an imploring voice asked: "What do you see in this man, Jonah? What do you see?"

Before father could answer, the first of the evening guests arrived. The small congregation was seated in our central living area on benches we arranged so there could be a large oil lamp in the center of our circular group. Shortly thereafter, Jeshua's parents joined us. His mother, the only woman attending, put herself in my care. She took a discreet place with me in the shadowy recesses of the room with those of our servants permitted to observe the gathering, although I knew that others in the household had found their hidden places.

After greetings were exchanged, Jacob began to tell of his odyssey. Almost immediately he passed over its details and entered into a description of Jeshua's deeds and words. From what I observed, judging from the rapt attention of his listeners, he could not have done otherwise. Jacob was speaking of a man they knew from boyhood and his description was of the person they knew. He spoke little of their personal conversations, just to mention how he, Jacob, gradually became aware of what he had been told by father of the special qualities of his companion.

His audience was not surprised at this early witness because this was the Jeshua of their knowledge. But when he told of the later events they, as well as I, caught a sense of how Jeshua appeared to those who knew him not. How the people would surround him for services in the evening; how some would speak to him later for guidance; how he acted with such familiarity with the coarse Jewish and Gentile roughnecks who served these caravans. But when Jacob reported that the people started to refer to him as "Rabbi" with no sign of Jeshua's disapproval, a small commotion erupted among the group. I, too, was taken aback as I thought it would be so unlike him to allow this.

"Hold on, sir," one man interrupted, "can you be speaking of one we do not know? Jeshua from our village is no Rabbi and he would not pose as one, learned though he is for one so young."

And then this man's son spoke, a boyhood friend of Jeshua's that I knew from our village and I remembered him as one who had dealings with Jeshua regarding work, or so I had thought. One now only a few months married. "I do not want to gainsay my father," he said while looking directly at him, "but this could be our Jeshua."

Then he said words I thought were only in my heart. "There is about him a nature he learned early to conceal but from a few of his companions. He found from many elders a fear of him and some, I must say, are in this room tonight. But there were others, some also here . . . " this with a glance in my direction, unnoticed by the group I prayed, but searing me with its import, "who were aware of an unearthly presence in our friend. More than once, I confess now with a joy in my heart, I was moved to call him 'Rabbi', he who was, is, a youth like me. I do not doubt this man is he."

The man's father looked at his son with bewilderment. And there was a murmuring among the others at this outburst. I looked at Jacob and I saw that same expression, that mark, when he spoke of Jeshua that I noted before. (And I never ceased to wonder in all our future time together, how this man, this good and deserving man, could resist the light he saw so clearly.) And he said to the son: "I cannot speak of your friend anywhere without bringing forth in one or another the sentiments that move you so." To the group he added, "There is no mistake. This is the son of your village."

It was then I saw the answers to my prayers. If God would arrange it I would not refuse this Jacob my hand. As soon as that thought entered my mind it left as Jacob continued with his tale. He told again of Anna's rescue and revival and again the reason for this escaped them. Only the son who had spoken sat with a beatific look on his face.

Then Jacob reported on the events in the eastern country. They were astounded when they heard he did not stay with the Jewish community of their sect. Where was he then? Where could he be? Jacob told of Tomas. "A disciple?" they asked in wonder, "he, just a boy." He spoke of Jason, the important counselor to the wealthy Natan, who embraced the servant in the name of the "Galilean", and they marveled at this strange expression. But when he mentioned the talk of the Messiah and the suggestions that he may be the One, there was a dazed silence.

Finally, our village Rabbi, who had sat through this recitation with his typical reserve, spoke up and, directly to father, he said, "Jonah, this madness should not be permitted in your house. Jeshua, this son of your tenant, our Messiah? I will not hear this blasphemy another moment. You have fallen far, my dear friend. I warned you of your disobedience when you continued to teach your daughter the language and laws of our Torah, but this is an even greater sin."

My mind went to the time these two friends fell out with each other when my father could not resist my insistent demands to study our traditions. It was not seemly, perhaps sinful as it was said, for girls to do this but my ability and quickness so entranced him he could not refuse.

Without another word the elder rose from his seat and pulling his cloak around him, needing the help of one of his students as his old arms could not reach the edge of it behind him, he took his leave. The others followed, some with an open expression of support for the old man, but a few with a sense of bewilderment. As the young friend of Jeshua passed Jacob, he managed to whisper, "I wish leave to speak to you again."

Jeshua's parents did not leave with the others. In truth, they were not given much attention despite the discussion around their son. In our village as in the rest of Palestine, their landless status determined their servitude, even, as in their case, this condition was not always so. Making and repairing wheels and carts was not a full step above driving a donkey or camel, the lowest of our occupations. So it was not thought odd that they lagged behind.

During the period of Jacob's chronicle, Jeshua's mother was holding my arm and only then did I feel the pressure of her hand as the assembly was breaking up. She pulled me toward her while watching her husband approach Jacob and in that subdued whisper which was her mark, she asked me to inquire of Jacob how her son was when he last saw him. Did he appear to have eaten; was he shod; was his cloak in repair?

I did so shortly afterward and was pleased to send her word

that he was well and, Jacob believed, favored of God. For his part, Jeshua's father now accepted the fact that his son was gone to him. Even were he to return, he realized his son's life would take its own course. It was the talk of his holiness that most disturbed him. True, he knew of his special nature, remembering how he encouraged him and took pride in Jeshua's early learning and the praises heaped on them both.

"Am I being punished for my pride?" he lamented "I lost my land but I thanked God for my son, through whom, in my ignorance, I thought I would be redeemed. But now he is gone and, as our Rabbi says, this talk of his great holiness is madness. My son, the Messiah? How can this be? There is terrible danger in this, for him and for us all." I felt the despair in their bearing as they left our house that evening for the short walk to their own.

But my distress was equal to their fear. Jeshua our Messiah? From childhood I had heard of this One coming to our rescue, leading the armies of righteousness against the dark world. How could our townsman, my Jeshua, whom I loved with my body as well as my soul, be this One? It truly must be madness. But when Jacob described him as he did I knew it was our Jeshua of whom he spoke.

Is it possible we knew him too well to have seen his true nature? We saw him as a man, a mirror of ourselves and because of our poor spirits we could not attribute this holiness to one we knew so well. But my heart filled with wonder as my head did with confusion. For, like so many of the others, I had seen a different light in him, lasting no longer than the twinkle of a star but long enough to embed itself in my soul forever.

I greeted the next morning with relief, as it ended the agitation caused by the previous night's events. I started the household on its daily routine and went to look to my new charge. To my surprise I found Anna already about and helping one of the young maidservants bring water into the house for the morning meal. I came upon them unnoticed and heard my servant laughing loudly at something the new girl was saying. I did not realize then she was laughing at how Anna was speaking, since she could not understand a word she said.

It was then I learned this waif saved by Jeshua had an additional handicap: her speech was almost unintelligible, the common language surely, but so few words for expression and such a terrible speaking manner, one I never heard before. I, too, could barely understand her. The common thought crossed my mind, "of what use can she be, why was she saved?" I felt an anguish at my own sinfulness. I, who so tenderly cared for animals, could I have left this child to her fate? As my eyes met hers I was held spellbound when I heard her say, "God wants me to live, lady, God, He does truly." I knew I had not spoken my thoughts aloud, how could she know my mind?

In time I teased her story from her. She had lived in a tiny isolated village, the kind that dotted the countryside far north of Galilee. We knew of those places from the stories told of our people who fled there to escape the wars and persecutions so rampant the past centuries. But there is no hiding from destiny and what they may have escaped in the past they would have to face up to in time.

Her helpless village was declining in numbers even in the space of her small memory as bandits and marauding soldiers would raid it for slaves for sale in the Damascus market. Others, the young, were so hopeless they would leave, deserting their parents and siblings. She had no recollection of her father working though he once said he was a farmer. When her mother died giving birth to her last sibling, brother or sister she knew not, her father then took her to the master in Damascus who destroyed her body.

She thought she was a Jew though she had little notion of what that was. She knew of no reading nor of any book but knew of the talk of our invisible God. And if, when walking with her father, they would spy an earthen form on the side of the road, he would cover her eyes as she knew the Jews did, but she did not know why. Of people like this I heard it said, "Jews without Torah, they are the living dead." But Jeshua sent her to me. And I knew in my heart that someday he would return. And if he asked, "Where is the girl?" what would I say? But I knew also, Jeshua or no, I could not do otherwise but care for her.

It was she, herself, who made me know that. Her being bespoke life, an acceptance of life, and that very day I realized that when I made my visit to the barren woman in our village who had taken in a castoff child of her own. This was a girl found in the wilderness and left to languish, perhaps by a desperate father it was thought.

She was found by a Bedouin family who sometimes took these discards and brought them up in their service, almost dead they said. Otherwise, such creatures succumbed to the elements or the wild beasts. After keeping her a number of years, the Arabs decided to sell her to a village that would take her for a reasonable sum and this childless woman accepted her on the urging of father who paid for her.

But the child was a difficult one. Likely the same age as Anna, neither one yet into their monthly cycles. When she first came among us she acted like a terrified animal that must have undergone brutal treatment. She would not leave the sight of the woman who kept her, would not eat without the most gentle coaxing, and at slightest expression of disfavor she would hide in a corner with a frightful keening. Only after a number of weeks of the gentlest care, would she spend some time alone or help others with their chores outside the protection of her new mother.

My visits were important to her for it was in my arms that she had her first sense of safety and comfort. It is my secret joy that I have this gift for healing and giving ease. No one save Jeshua knew of the exaltation of my being when I was graced by God's love and other hurting souls could feel His presence in me and draw comfort from that. Again Jeshua's words came to mind about this power and presence. If this were a gift I prayed it came not from an evil source. But no matter, I neither asked for it nor could I deny it. When this little girl saw me coming she flew to me with an unbounded delight that brought smiles to the faces of all those around us.

My Anna — my Anna, is this how I already thought of her? — must not have suffered any less than this one. Yet she was full of life, indeed, childish mischief, as my servants reported. There was no sign of fear in her and when she brought laughter upon herself for her awkwardness in dress or speech she joined in the merriment. Seemingly unaware of her bruises and scars, she made no attempt to hide them. It would not be long before the love that I already felt for her would be shared by all. And with that thought a touch of fear broke that blissful mood. I knew the shadows that faced these two.

Anna's scars would mark her forever as unclean and she would pass her days destined to be unmarried and alone. And the other, this poor other, thought most likely not a Jew: who would have her? And why could she not be a Jew? Who knew by whom she was cast away? It was these thoughts, when they emerged, that destroyed the normally staid mark of my nature.

It was not unknown among our people that Jews, not only Gentiles, exposed infants to the wild or sold children into servitude. Our prophets condemned our kings for wasting the wealth of the people, forcing them into just this disgrace. Was it not for this that Solomon's son was refused the throne of Israel in olden times? How often my father would have me read that story to him. Yet in their obstinacy, these men, whom God put over us, denied Jews, too, did this self-same thing out of their abject oppression, thus damning without appeal this helpless child any hope of a better fortune.

And I would ask God to forgive me in my most sinful thought: that He Whom I loved and feared, Who gladdened my heart with his presence, allowed me to be despised and oppressed because I was a woman. Did he not know the ignorance and stupidity to which I so often submitted? And with those thoughts came dread and exhilaration; and I feared the exhilaration more than I suffered the dread. Was it the evil one who pushed me —I despaired at the thought — to question God's laws? And then, as always, these thoughts retreated to the dark recesses of my mind, never disappearing, just awaiting their next call.

Thus the following days unfolded. Jacob was waiting for his transport to reach us when he would then accompany it to Jerusalem. I noticed he spent much time with father. I remembered he had been raised on a Judean farm and he was at ease on this one. Father told me later he knew the earth and he knew the animals and he spoke of him with favor despite the commotion he caused when telling of Jeshua. I spied them laughing together once — rather, Jacob was laughing as father no longer knew how — at something it seemed Jacob had said.

I had one occasion to spend a moment with Jacob. When our paths crossed I now reflect it was an odd occurrence. I had Anna in tow and he stopped to inquire after the child. He expressed satisfaction that she looked content and lively after only a short time with us.

"You do well with her, Sara," and looking at her he said, "God surely favors you, child."

I was startled that he would so openly accost me and at his bold use of my name, as if my standing with him was less than as mistress of this household. I was at a loss to respond but Anna saved me from this need. "Yes, master, God favors, He does." My pique was dissolved as we both chuckled at her solemn tone, so peculiar in this little girl.

But he had caught my reaction to his presumption and for the only time I remember I saw him discomfited at his manner. "Excuse me, lady, for my tone. I confess I have been thinking of you lately, though in your father's company. Please believe me, I may have slipped into some familiarity I have no right to claim."

I hope I was successful in my attempt to maintain my composure. I laughed inwardly at his clumsy attempt to mollify my feelings. In the villages of Galilee men like Jacob are scorned with the term "city slicker", but my years of acquaintance with this sort in Jerusalem gave me a different understanding. I did not take personal affront at what would be outrageous behavior of a guest to so openly confront an unrelated woman. But I knew, as innocent as I was of the improper behavior, the gossip would reach father's ears.

But was I truly the innocent? I grasped Anna's hand to take my leave and possessed by that stubbornly bold demon I could not dislodge from my nature, I looked him squarely in the face as I wished him good day, looked long enough to examine his eyes, his mouth, his nose, his ears. God forgive me for my thoughts, and I bless Him that they remained securely locked in my heart, but his appearance pleased me greatly, no more, however, than the sense I had that this was a good man. For the remainder of that day this encounter and that man were all I could think of.

With Jacob's presence the tensions with father had lightened although I was ever-shadowed by his plans to soon marry. When he called me to him that evening I had a premonition it was about these plans. I was right in that and listened intently as he told me of them. But I was stunned at what he said next. "Jacob desires your promise of betrothal and asked me to arrange it. I told him that would be my desire as well. This is what I want you to do."

My heart stopped. Was this not the answer to my prayers? Yet in the fullness of my joy I railed at the circumstances. "Tell me, father, were you not making other arrangements for me? Did you not tell me so? And did you not berate me for my resistance? You know my nature, you who encouraged it so, and now you trifle with me as if I were a bought servant."

Oh God! How I punish myself with my own transgressions. I no sooner have sinful thoughts then they get thrown back into my face. Only this day I was bewailing the wicked stubbornness of these village men and now, when I am given what I prayed for, I cannot let father escape my judgment on him.

But he was better than I was. Looking at him I saw what I had never seen before, an expression of shame in his face. "Be calm, Sara, child, I must confess a sin to you. I did not before make arrangements for your betrothal. I told you I had because of my own anger. I need a wife and saw you as the obstacle to that need and I was at a loss. Believe me, child, the thought of sending you, especially you, off to a stranger's house and bed weighed heavily on me and I am not sure I could have done so."

Addressing me as child as he did in my girlhood opened my heart to him as it had not in many years. I could not resist the need to touch him and though our embrace came hesitantly and he was discomforted at my emotion, I found the comfort in his strong arms that I remembered from my earliest days. I felt my resistance to him melt and I wanted to say words to comfort him but more I wanted to submit to him.

"Father, I am commanded to honor you. But I want you to know I honor and love you without need of our Law. Be pleased that I look upon Jacob with favor but I ask you, when you inform him so, that this was my choice as well as his. I, too, have sinned in my haughtiness toward you, but I am unable to fight this evil in me. Even now I cannot abide the thought that my fate, and forgive me father, the use of my body, is being decided by others. Does Jacob know this of me?"

"Sara, Jacob knows you better than you may think. He came to me first for he could not do otherwise. But he said, 'Jonah, I ask for Sara from you but only if it is her wish as well. Have her think on it. I cannot accept this arrangement unless it is her desire.'

"I must confess," father continued, "I find this strange when betrothal is arranged by the parties. I know this is more frequently done in the cities where men and woman are thrown together in sinful ways and parents lose control of them. But these transgressions are not permitted in our villages and will be less so everywhere when our Messenger returns. It is best when these things are arranged by elders, for families are strengthened and improved by these selected unions, and also because women lose their sense of place if they believe they are special in their husbands' eyes.

"But you, Sara, have always been different. Your mother would warn me, though I needed no warning, that I was making you unsuitable to be a proper woman and wife. But once your eyes and ears were opened to Torah I could not close them again. Even would I, I could not oppose your will. When you returned from Jerusalem at your poor mother's death, young as you were, you so easily put yourself at the head of the household, though most of the servants were ahead of you in age. Somehow you always knew what to do before anyone else could decide.

"Over the years I have had offers for your betrothal and rejected them all for my sake rather than yours. Only with Jeshua would I have agreed and that because I was so taken with his nature. He would have brought a blessing to our house. Certainly it could not have been for the bride price; his father is even poorer than he is. Jacob is a gift as much for me as for you. I was becoming fearful you were not to be wed and I thought it would have been my doing.

"But we cannot question nor fathom God's ways. We simply must pray for deliverance when we suffer and thank Him when we do not. Let us thank Him together, Sara, for bringing Jacob to us in this hour."

I do not know what Jacob thought when he expressed his desires to father, insisting the decision was mine as well. I did not realize until then how far outside from the common ways of our people I was. I remember thinking then how this conceit of mine could have diminished father's authority in his own household and I berated myself for my habitual haughtiness. Nevertheless, I cannot even now curtail this attitude; it is as much a part of me as the air I breathe and water I drink.

Jacob, for his part, entered this union with open eyes. His bride would come to the canopy veiled but not unknown. This Jacob wanted Rachel and Rachel he received. I accepted him for a number of reasons: I could no longer stay in father's house; nor could I much longer refuse marriage to another certainly less worthy man; and I knew in my heart that Jacob was a man for whom a woman could feel true affection.

Our betrothal was announced and celebrated. Jacob left for Jerusalem to fulfill his obligations to his employers and to reveal his intentions and receive his remuneration from his last journey. He would then visit his ancestral home and restore his standing with his family, though he suspected he was no longer part of their material designs. As an omen that this union met with God's favor, Marcus, with the salutations and support of aunt and uncle, gifted us with that Galilean farm that so well nourished us for these many years.

Just so our lives progressed until that day when Joseph came with the news of Jeshua's return.

JACOB AND SARA

My first days on the road to Galilee were measured only by the rising and setting of the sun. The child, Anna, was as she promised, quiet and sufficient unto herself for her personal needs. Indeed, not two words a day passed between us. Jesse's servant, who looked after our wagon and donkey, our small rations and few chores, kept his place and found company at resting periods with others of his position.

My time then was quiet and permitted reflection, too much I fear because now alone with no duties but to deliver this child, the absurdity of the situation closed in on me. Were it not that Jesse, Marcus' associate and my nominal master, arranged for this I would have thought myself out of my mind. I wonder now why I did not more strongly advise against it.

Although the girl was a visible reminder of the fact of Jeshua, the experience of him faded like the memory of a dream. It seems there are times when he is more real than life itself and then, these other times, when I can hardly give credence to what I tell others about him. This is a mystery in me as he is a mystery to me.

But against this was the thought of Sara. Now that my meeting her again was only days away, I wondered once more about her situation and how it might have changed in the full year of my absence. I know I too have changed in this time. I have a faint recollection of the reasons I undertook this journey, of my conversations with Alexander and my life in Jerusalem. It all seems so alien to me now. I know I was Jacob then as I am Jacob now but it is only the essence of Jacob that has continuity, not its garnishments.

We were an odd sight. An ailing, bedraggled child, an obviously skilled servant and myself. The wagon, empty but for some few personal items, was unusual for its waste of valuable space. It required reason and expense to travel a distance and none could be seen for the former and no little could be counted for the latter. We were shielded, however, from gossip and suspicion by my presence. I made my Roman citizenship known early to our military escort and the new clothing furnished by Jesse, along with my bearing, lent me an air of authority. Thus we were escorted without incident or unpleasantness to our destination.

We entered Jonah's farm not too much the worse for wear from the uneventful trip, though the child was clearly indisposed. I was pleased at the welcome we received and happy we had the day before sent on a messenger alerting them to our imminent arrival. They were anticipating our coming and I knew they would be puzzling over my message that I had business with Sara. She was there to meet us and with that meeting the feelings I had when I last saw her returned unabated; they were perhaps enhanced after my long, often solitary, expedition.

It was because of the child and Jeshua's instruction to deliver her into Sara's care that I felt less constrained to speak to her. She was perplexed as I knew she would be, as well was her father, when I told her it was by Jeshua's request I brought this child into her care. But the child's condition, which required immediate attention, and my status as a guest needing refreshment and rest, saved me for the moment from embarrassing questions. I was grateful for this; I do not know how I could have answered but with the truth and no one knew better than I how bizarre that would have sounded.

This thought was confirmed that evening at dinner and then later in the circle of Jonah's fellow villagers where I could no longer supply only bits and pieces of this story in the hope that they would not press for more. Initially, the atmosphere was encouraging as the quiet of the evening and Jonah's wine provided a mood of ease. I started to explain how it was thought to be in the best interest of the child to bring her here as soon as possible as a longer trip would be taxing on her. As this explanation developed I sensed

an unbelieving reaction in my listeners — all this effort for a vagabond child?

I felt somewhat unnerved, for in truth I understood my questioners' disposition in this matter more clearly than my own. De-
fensively, I told them that this was a decision made by my Damascus master, Jesse, who, indeed, provided the transport. And why,
they demanded, would he do such a thing? And into my mind
flashed the same thought with its answer instantly following: it
was for Jeshua that all this was being done.

It was then I found myself compelled to tell of their fellow
townsman in that haunting manner which I cannot help assum-
ing when I speak of him. Nor am I yet used to the varied responses
I receive when I do this telling: some find my tales of no interest at
all, and others find the stories disturbing and threatening.

But there are always those who are galvanized by what I say as
if I put into words and made manifest thoughts and emotions that
were only waiting to be released from some unknown place deep
inside them. Alas, I am not one of any of these types. I cannot
ignore him, I cannot despise or challenge him, and I cannot surrender to him. But neither, and this is my new source of anguish,
can I free myself from him.

I realized early in my report that their greatest attention was
placed on my descriptions of the words and actions of my companion and far less on the details of our journey. They would nod
as I told of him holding services for vagabond Jews in the wilderness and they understood my sketch of his quiet and solitary manner. But when I inadvertently mentioned that some referred to
him as "Rabbi" and he did not deny that calling, there was a loud
expression of disbelief. This should have put me on my guard but
I ignored their murmurs of disapproval.

I have been a Jew among Jews all my life and more than once
I have despaired about how far I am from understanding their
passion and their reason. But I am most perplexed regarding this
idea of our Messiah, a king, God's instrument who will lead the
armies of light against the powers of darkness. A warrior from

David's loins? Or a Moses who after resting for millennia from his former labors now returns with his magic staff?

They pray and plan for him in their desert enclaves, whisper of him in these tiny villages, and scoff at his promise in the salons of the city wealthy, many, albeit, with crossed fingers. And they talk knowingly of signs, the signs that will mark his coming.

But would they know him if he came? He could hardly be missed striding at the head of hordes where God placed him with his angelic multitudes. Or, as some look for him in the country-side, like so many other masters before him, casting out demons, healing the sick, multiplying the fish in the sea and the grain in the earth, thereby enriching the fishers and farmers. Surely, then too, he would be noticed.

But what if he did none of this? What if he did what my Galilean did? Walk the earth with his strange confidence and authority, in communion with God, making sacred the ground he trod and the air he breathed. I saw with my own eyes that in his glance, or with his word, or with a deed for this one or that, the least and the mighty were wrenched from their fate and thrust into a new way.

He could hardly walk the land in any direction without con-fronting despair and poverty, cruelty and oppression. But this Messiah did not take up his cudgels and fling himself at these evils. One would seek him out and after a few words leave him with a little firmer step, perhaps a spark of hope. The most un-clean of persons could gain his attention; or an exalted one would strive to do his bidding; and for little Anna — can there be one less deserving or useful, one already dead — he commands life and these great resources.

Are these not signs! Then my mind threw up the childhood image of my nursemaid beginning her cooking fire. With embers captured from another firehole she added a few dried straws and softly blew them into a flame. "More, more," I cried as the straw caught and flamed. "Wait, little Jacob," she said, "if you blow too hard or add too much you will lose the spark and without the spark there can be no fire."

Is this image a lesson? A teaching? Is it so with salvation, too, that one needs add only what the ember can sustain? Can God's will be so constrained or is it man's poverty that is so weak? My head ached then and aches now with these questions. I search with the light of reason but only the clouds of mystery are lighted, throwing the glare back into my eyes and blinding me.

The evening ended in commotion. I was to see this commotion more and more in connection with Jeshua, whether in rumor, in spirit or in the flesh after his return. I noticed, however, neither Sara nor Jonah was upset by the village elder's outburst against him. She was in the quiet shadows comforting Jeshua's mother as Jeshua's father lamented the loss of their son.

The Rabbi's remarks concerning him confirmed in the father's mind, I suspect, that his son was lost to the frenzy so often induced in those chosen. But in truth, and I would convey this to the mother if I could, I saw no frenzy in Jeshua, but only the quietness and peace that others somehow gained from him.

I awoke the following morning amid the sounds of a farm coming alive and for an exhilarating moment I experienced the joys I had known in my Judean boyhood. When fully awake the thought came of how much I would be at home and at ease were I again dealing with the simple needs of this life. At the thought of pursuing this path, I felt a sense of freedom I had forgotten I had ever known and this new feeling stayed with me and colored my mood for the rest of the day and beyond.

I began spending time with Jonah as he went about his holdings directing the work of his people and I was taken with the sure grasp he had on his calling. I had thought the knowledge gained in my early upbringing was long erased by the learning of my later years but I found now it was only covered over by that sophistication.

In my travels through this part of Palestine I thought I had taken little note of the varied quality of the land and its suitability for farming. Now, however, close to the earth as I am, I realize I did in fact consider these conditions. I remember idly thinking of the fruitfulness of this part of the country as opposed to the more barren, higher ground as I passed through it. And my pondering is fully concerned with these questions.

Indeed, for grains, fruits and olives, as well as animal feed, it struck me how much the earth here is superior to the farms surrounding my home village in lower Judea. Further, Jonah was a good husband to his land, nourishing it as commanded by Law and never taking from it more than it was willing or able to give. I felt moved to express these thoughts to him. And to my delight I was repaid for that impulse with the first signs of affection I had seen from an apparently unbending and dour man.

Once again I observed that tendency in this usually reticent, country man to speak out his thoughts, likely as not in response to my own halting overtures. "You find favor in my eyes, Jacob. I must confess I did not expect this understanding of the earth and God's bounty from it from one so citified. Though I knew of your former life, I thought you had left it behind."

"You are right, Jonah," I replied, "I, too, thought I had left it behind. But now on your farm and watching your care of it and your people, the sense grows strong in me that I would like to return to this life. But I despair that that prospect has much merit. I have few personal resources, but for what I will recover from my present work for my master. My family's holdings in Judea have for many years been duly apportioned outside my presence. At best, there I would have to accept a lesser role if, in fact, one could be found for me."

I felt some sadness in speaking out these concerns because these thoughts, now brought to my mind's surface, assumed a more concrete reality, a reality I was reluctant to face. Jonah listened quietly to my words. He almost appeared preoccupied with something else and I wondered if my exposure of these intimate musings strained our still fragile friendship. But no, rather than a strain it provided an opening for him to air complications in his own life and as he did so, I felt rising in my heart a growing affection for him.

"I am taking another wife, Jacob," he began, "a woman from a village near here. The betrothal has been made and the agreements have been witnessed. The wedding day waits the time I can bring her here to live, and I cannot delay that day much longer, nor do I want to. I have been too long without a woman and I am in need of more sons."

"And why can you not bring her here directly, Jonah?" And as I asked that question I blurted out the thought that had been vexing me since I returned and found Sara unmarried and unbetrothed. "Can it be because of Sara, Jonah?" And I knew from his response that that was surely the case. In a torrent of rising emotion I lost control of my reason and asked him why she was yet unwed.

I told him how she had captured my mind from the time I had first seen her and how seeing her again had only strengthened that feeling. I spoke of my fear of saying these words, for the speaking of them could mean the end of my dreams, but now Jonah's distress, and the reason for it, gave me new hope. And I told him, finally, that as a husband I could bring to Sara little in the way of worldly resources or promise. "But I tell you, Jonah, if a way can be found to accomplish this I would find a way to repay God for this gift because I think of it as His bounty."

He remained silent. But in his silence I sensed in him a struggle to restrain emotions he did not usually encounter. At last, overcome, he reached out and pulled me toward himself in what was almost an embrace. "Jacob, I tell you truly, your words ring in my ears as sent from heaven and they lift a heavy burden from my heart. I will give your message and press your suit with Sara with my blessing and my authority. But I must warn you of the weakness of that authority, as I heed it myself. Our decision is not enough. Sara is not a woman . . . "

"Forgive me, Jonah," I started, raising my hand to stay his next words, "I think you will tell me that Sara's fate is not in our hands, but hers, and I know that without your telling me. I want her to know it is my desire, nay, need, that she accepts my offer freely and with her heart. Please, Jonah, do not delay speaking with her. I confess to you I have been living with irresolution and fear since I came again to your house because of Sara and because of my fear of her rejection, and I am weary of it." And as I uttered these rueful words I wondered what happened to the confident, authoritative and masterly man I had thought myself to be.

But that wonderment faded and the fear disappeared when Jonah announced that night to his household, and then to his village, of the coming fruition of his betrothal and the celebration of Sara's and mine, and asked for us God's blessings and theirs.

The heady days that followed have now collapsed into memory, memories that remain as a sequence of events, but mysteriously undifferentiated by time. Strange, indeed, is the past with its beginnings, its workings and endings unfolding outside of place and interval but only in ephemeral thoughts. Yet these insubstantial tendrils emerging from their shadowy recesses in our minds evoke the same play of emotion that gladdened and saddened the heart as they did when first clothed in flesh and blood.

Once the decision was made, the new course of my life was set and in my happiness I started to believe it was directed through divine intervention. My fear of coming to Sara without future promise began to lift almost immediately following our commitment. Jonah's own joy only augmented his concern for his daughter's well-being and he assured me that though I was called Jacob he was not Laban and I would not need wait seven years for her dowry. And he suggested I would be surprised and content with its nature.

Two days after these events my transport arrived and I took my leave to finish my obligations to my Jerusalem masters. My material future was not decided but I knew it would not include another such adventure. After delivering the transport to Marcus and settling my accounts with him, he and his partners hosted a banquet for me in gratitude for my efforts. I was truly not aware of the large profit they reaped from this venture.

Equally important for them was that this was their first at-

tempt to restore Marcus' family's trading business and they had
excellent reports of my representation of them, both on the caravan road and at the transfer points. I was surprised to hear that my
activities at various custom points easing the way for both merchants and officials were reported back to Marcus' company by
grateful travelers.

Marcus was especially appreciative of the recognition of my
service, which reflected directly on him when it was mentioned
during a business meeting with the procurator's custom and tax
officer. A long-forgotten altercation at a custom point, apparently
serious enough to be reported to Jerusalem, had been diffused by
my presence and the officer congratulated Marcus on the quality
of his servant.

This Roman civil administrator was one of those officials responsible for the stable and remunerative movement of goods
throughout this region of the empire. Equal to Roman peace in
the state's mind was the orderly flow of goods throughout the
Roman world; one meant power, the other wealth. If all merchants
were so well-represented, he told Marcus, his, the officer's, life
would be much easier.

Because of this, Marcus confided in me, he already had an
increase in other merchants' interest in using his house for their
transport service. His warehouses were overflowing and he expected
to arrange two more expeditions this year, one to return to the
eastern country I had just left. I was pleased it was my efforts that
had made this possible.

My final service to him was to counsel his new agent about the
current conditions of the roads, especially the major passage east.
The general situation outside the province of Roman rule was little
known to Jerusalem's merchants at this early time of the restoration of these trading routes. For those chancing this voyage, my
experience and information proved invaluable.

It was at this point, too, I had made it known I was leaving his
service. I told him of my betrothal to Sara, his kinswoman, and of
my plans to settle on the land. I was born to that occupation I told

him and I believed my unhappiness was due to resisting its call. I was pleased at his genuine pleasure for my well-being and his expression of delight when welcoming me into his family. I had little thought of that consequence when pressing Jonah for Sara's hand but I must confess I was much gratified at that reality.

Marcus' family shared his pleasure. They maintained a continuous interest in the welfare of Sara who had spent her maturing years in their household. Marcus felt toward her as a sister as did his sister Ceil, herself now married with two children, as Sara knew.

In due course, I took my leave to visit my home village, the last task before returning to Galilee and my new life. Before I left, however, Marcus hosted a quiet celebratory dinner for me that included close family members and mutual friends from our early Jerusalem days together. The occasion was also used to present me with a generous wedding gift which, on top of my contracted wages and bonus for my service, went far to assuage my fears for my immediate future.

Present at the dinner was my good friend Alexander, whose advice and aid was in a way responsible for this turn of events in my life. Later, he and I found an opportunity for private time. I appreciated this chance, for my respect and affection for him grew rather than lessened in the more than a year's time of our separation. He too was pleased and he embraced me affectionately and then holding me at arms length, looking directly into my eyes, he said: "Jacob, time has been good to you. You are larger than you were."

"Larger how, Alexander? Not in girth, to be sure. After my time in the wilderness I would not be mistaken for a scribe, even by one poor in sight."

"No, no, not in girth, Jacob. Do you not know how you command attention? You speak with an authority you did not assume when we last talked. But for now let that go. Its reason will unfold as we talk and I have much to speak to you about."

He then asked for Sara and by the nature of his questions I felt his was a deeper interest than mere curiosity warranted. I remembered how he would speak of her in those days when we associated as companions exploring the variety of Jerusalem life. He was her tutor then and she not yet a woman. I hesitated in replying for I was not quite sure what he wanted to know of her, but it was not simply after her comfort that he inquired. In that moment of silence he continued: "Jacob, if your Sara is as special a woman as she was a girl, and I am sure that is the case, she is now a person Greek philosophers would call a Gnostic, that is 'one who knows'."

"Knows? Knows what, Alexander? She captured my heart, though I confess I see in her a quality little noticed in other women, or men for that matter, although I would be hard-pressed to describe it. . . ." My voice dropped away as the thought of Jeshua crossed my mind and I said to myself I must speak to Alexander of the Galilean. "But knows what, Alexander?" I asked again.

He was quiet for a while. "Jacob, you know of the sects of our people who live mainly in desert enclaves, small in numbers, perhaps, but located throughout Roman lands, and of their austere practices: eschewing the use of meat, of animal sacrifice, of the prohibition on the spilling of blood. They search for God through fasting and silence, accepting a baptismal initiation and a celibate life. For the Temple authorities this would not be too great of a sin, though if their ideas spread it would mean a drop in Temple revenue.

"They have other practices and teaching, however, that our High Priest finds more troubling. They insist on the Mosaic social laws that demand we care for one another, that we succor the poor, resist suffering and we live in the world without doing harm. By doing good deeds we can end our present sojourn as it now exists on earth and prepare a future life with God for all humanity.

"Finally, they say, this life is but a teaching and by living it as prescribed we can reach a loftier platform. From that level all our words and all our deeds will be naturally right and accomplished with God's help and blessing.

"I have heard these people described as Nazarenes, Jacob, and when one or another rises to the plateau of which they speak they are reported to be able to do extraordinary things. The word Nazarene in our common tongue means what the word Gnostic means to the Greek, 'one who knows the mystery of spirit and the ways of fathoming God's desire.' And it is from these people the Messiah will come, our sages say."

Once again I am reminded of how persistently I am pursued by this specter of our people's ancient lore, no matter how I resist and reject its insubstantial, irrational body of thought. It refuses to stay buried and now, is this what Alexander is saying? That the woman I thought of as my heart's desire, the one with whom my new life is to begin, she, too, conspires to trap me in this web?

"What are you saying, Alexander," I cried, "what has Sara to do with all of this? I know well of what you speak. Perhaps better than you about many things."

And at this I told him of my time with Jeshua, how I came to know him as the "Galilean Rabbi". I spoke of his actions and countenance and I then saw in Alexander, too, the reaction I have now come to expect in all who hear my words about him. I spoke of my conversations with Jason and the nature of the eastern Jews.

I was not surprised he knew of the Buddhist teaching, for he was acquainted with their monks from his student days in his Greek city. It was to my surprise, however, that here in Jerusalem, as well, their religion was known and they, themselves, found the thought of the invisibility of our invisible God an expression of their own wisdom.

But I could not go further until I heard more of what Alexander had to say of this side of Sara, an aspect of her being that stirs within me vague visceral currents and blends fear and longing into a strange discomfort. "Tell me of Sara, dear friend. I came to you with joy in my heart because of her and should it not continue to be so?"

He looked at me steadily and with the most somber of tone he said: "Jacob, were I planning to wed Sara as you are I could not contain my own happiness. But I must add that happiness would be marred by a worry: this is a blessed woman and I would fear being unworthy of her. I will tell you something strange, Jacob, but I know you will not take it amiss. I love Sara and because of that I am content she is to be your wife.

"More and more I sense we are living in otherworldly times, prophetic times, and I will tell you now with a certainty I feel but that I cannot understand, this is your destiny. Resist and struggle as you may, and as you already have, I am sure, it will be to no avail. From your own words it is clear that when you surrender to this fate your way is made smooth and I predict this will continue to be the case. How can one not be happy and free when doing God's will? You will sorrow when you fight it."

"Alexander," I replied, "I am not cheered by your words. I would like nothing better than to be a simple farmer, now a husband and father if God so wills. I know you speak out of friendship and love and I will keep your thoughts in my mind. But I do not seek this destiny you foretell for me. I am stirred and left wanting by the Galilean and I do not know why, but I am also bewildered and feel no little fear because of him. As for Sara, tell me what you will of her but know my feelings as well. We are to be man and wife in all respects and I anticipate the comfort I expect from her."

"Jacob," he began again, "did you know Sara was brought here as a child because there was talk in her village that she entered other worlds, spoke out visions, and did healing by sorcery and commanded the evil one? These were dangerous rumors that reached Temple ears and her father felt it wise to bring her here to her mother's sister for the security and protection her aunt's position offered. She came here when we did, Marcus and I, he to return and I to live here and continue my studies and practice my profession."

"I heard some talk of that," I replied, "but I gave little credence to those old country fears. I was newly educated and proud of my learning. Though I was to Marcus' house a number of times I do not believe I even saw her."

"But I did, Jacob. And I spent much time with her as she grew into womanhood before she left us. I was to be her tutor for formal things — her aunt charged me to teach her proper Greek and smooth the rough country manner of her speech — after which she planned to relieve me of this chore and have her tutored for suitable womanly ways by the servant women. But from the very first meeting with her I knew her to be wise far beyond her years."

His eyes took on a faraway look as he recalled that first meeting. "I entered the library where her lessons were to be held and found her leafing through a bound text of our Law, a text in our holy language of which I then had little knowledge. She was delighted with its form since, as it turned out, she never saw one so made, being acquainted only with the scrolls of her village. I admonished her, fearful she would inadvertently damage this valuable property, not for a moment thinking she could fathom the writing or meaning of the words.

"I was astounded to find that she was as fluent with its form and substance as I was with one of my medical treatises. I was only to learn later how many times she had read it through with her father. But then she was searching for a passage a fellow villager had referenced and I could not believe that this child, and Jacob, in every physical way she was a child, was using these obscure writings from the dawn of our peoples' emergence as a guide to her own life.

"I then became as much the tutored as the tutor though we kept to the plan of 'finishing' her in terms of speech and some few questions of deportment. It was only a short time until she mastered the 'high' Greek and a passable Latin, which she found a comical language. She provided much amusement to her friends and cousins and to the servants also, when she would dress as a lady and speak as a servant, an ability she never lost, or dress in the one peasant garment she saved and speak as a lady.

"At one point her aunt thought to relieve me of my duties toward her and give her to the women for her further education. But I found I could not discharge her. She guided my own learning in the Torah and helped me build on my own elementary knowledge of its original script. We needed care in this for we could not permit her learning to become public knowledge. I kept resisting her aunt's plans until it almost became a scandal. But I know you believe me, Jacob, when I say it was her heart and mind that so captured me and I could not ignore their depth."

I was entranced by his recitation no less than his reflective mood. I am sure this was so since it was my betrothed he was speaking of and I sensed from Alexander's present mien that he had thought often on this matter.

"We have a teaching, as you know, Jacob, that we are made in God's image. But Sara taught me we do not represent that image equally. The great mass of us reflects that perfection poorly as we cover ourselves with the dross of life. But there are a few in every time of need who more clearly mirror God's light and it is for them that He maintains the world. It is through them His light shines for the light must come from those who lead the way.

"There are not many who see this in Sara, Jacob, because she is a woman, and most men feel it beneath them to explore a woman's mind as they also close themselves to her heart. And I confess, my friend, I, too, accepted this foolishness until Sara, young as she was, opened my eyes. You feel this too, Jacob, I know, for you do not take Sara as a wife as other men take wives.

"I do not know of the circumstances of your betrothal but I know she accepted you by choice and not by her father's fiat. This is a great gift to her but an even greater gift to yourself if you can deny the world."

Alexander's last words puzzled me but time did not permit further exploration. I reflected, as I listened to him, how conflicted my life stays. No matter what I do, my joy is tempered with sorrow, my anticipation with foreboding. I cannot accept what I see and hear with a full heart or reject it with a satisfied mind.

I find myself being drawn into a world I resist entering, yet there is no obstacle to my entrance into it. Indeed, the way is made smooth with good cheer and seductive enticements and as I take my leave from this good friend I once again have that sense of how little my own disposition matters in the design of my life.

In due course I visited my boyhood village. I overcame an initial reluctance to return, though I yearned to revisit my long-gone childhood. I was forced now to face the truth of my failure to my people. My first charge from them when I left was to serve as a link with our kin in Rome and to become an instrument for our common well- being.

In this I disobeyed, instead, going off to satisfy the demands of my own adventurous and willful nature after taking advantage of the largess and training of my benefactors. Worse, I gave them little thought and made no attempt to apprise them of my condition. Only now can I understand the worry I must have caused.

Though I had fears of how I would be received, I felt a need to confess these failings and receive my father's blessings, knowing I could not, with contentment, embark on my new life without them. Happily, and with great relief, I was accepted warmly and with joy by both my parents. I renounced all claims to my undeserved inheritance, a moot point as I expected, for in the intervening years of my absence — I left in the earliest days of my manhood and we now reckon ten full years have elapsed — my claims on family property had been diluted such that few had any idea of what they could be.

Later, after he learned I did not expect to remain in Judea, the son next to me in age and my father's chief servant, joined in the warm welcome. It was without strain then, that they greeted my impending marriage. Although this union was arranged outside the traditions of our family my father insisted on paying a bride price to Jonah and arranged to send my brother as my companion to Galilee to represent our family and pay his respects to Sara's father.

I was content, then, with the end of this chapter of my life and I had a strong sense of a new beginning, even then while so close to it. The return trip was a time of reflection and summing up. It is always thus on these marches when one falls into the natural rhythm of nature. I realized then I was living outside the ancient traditions of my family and people. I was soon to take a wife who, too, can say that about herself. As I left the physical boundaries of my ancestral home I sensed I was also leaving the protection and guidance of our time-honored law.

I am surprised I felt no great sadness in this. At last I saw in my yearning for Sara my deep love for her. And of our connection with Jeshua? Is he the instrument for my fate? More than once this thought crossed my mind and along with the fear this provoked in me arose as well an assurance, a fearlessness that made me think, but never dared utter, that God, Himself, has His hand in my fate. And in those times a rapture came over me that filled my soul with bliss and my heart with a mysterious longing. And then that too would fade into my discontent.

CYPRUS V

I opened my eyes and saw the day was almost spent. We yet had some sun in the hills across from my low mountain shelter, which itself began to take on the chill of the oncoming evening. And Aaron's valley village was now hidden in shadow. Aaron, too, showed a stirring from his deep meditation. I stole a glance at his face and my heart filled with love at the serenity I saw in it. I knew the source of that peace and I rejoiced that it remains in our world.

Aaron looked at me and, without preamble, asked, "Master, why was Jacob perplexed and still not content? He received what he most desired and yet I feel a yearning remained in him."

"His wandering was not yet over, Aaron," I told him. "After he and Sara married I came into their lives, and I can tell you the rest of their story as I will tell you the rest of Master's. It is through me that you will have a complete account of those times. You must stay the night for there is no path to your home in this darkness."

How I had changed, I mused. Only a few short days ago I could not abide another's presence. Now I look to Aaron's company with satisfaction, nay, anticipation, as my love for him grows.

The night ended in that time of the morning when there is no movement or sound from a living creature. The trickle of water from my little spring was all that pierced the silence and I lay quietly, feeling the bliss of new life making its sweet way through my body. I no longer slept. How long has it been since I last was in that state of torpor? I find myself safely entombed in God's lap, body at rest but mind alert and clear as the morning itself, now, in a mute infinity, then, in the world of vision and sound.

I heard Aaron arise and listened as he went to the little fountain, washed himself and tasted a drop. I sensed how he positioned himself turning to the rising sun, and I could just hear the whisper of his "Hear, O Israel" as he started his morning prayers. It was now time for mine. How often in this long life had I started my day thanking God for its blessings? How many more will I have? Since Aaron's arrival I know they can be but few.

He came to my side with a little water and some dried fruit we had left from yesterday. "Master, the boy will come later with some food. I do not want to leave you."

"Stay, Aaron, I want you here. There are things you must know, and you are a joy to me."

We positioned ourselves as we had yesterday and I began the final chapters of Master's record.

Jacob's world, and ours, is no more. Destroyed by fire then drowned in tears and blood, it was not a tranquil land even before that catastrophe. But this dissatisfaction did not cast a shadow over the early days of Jacob and Sara. Jacob brought Sara to their new home in my little village and the blessings of their marriage continued to unfold in their lives. God smiled on the fertile country we lived in and the land yielded its bounty to Jacob's expert hand. Neither were we far from the sea which men called Gennesaret with its plenitude of fish.

Besides grain and livestock, Jacob had land for fig and olive trees and vines for grapes. He wisely produced what could be dried, pressed or stored without loss. His cleverness and experience had taught him the art of trade, and our village was finely situated for that enterprise. The new capital of Antipas' tetrarchy, Sepphoris, a half day's journey to the north and west of us, was then being rebuilt in the Greek and Roman style.

Its wealthy and aristocratic population — drawn from all over Galilee by the presence of the Tetrarch — created a demand for the country's produce and services. Likewise, directly to the north lay Magdala and to the south, the independent city of Scythopolis. Although it was founded by the Greeks, it had a large Jewish population and was dependent on the surrounding countryside.

It is strange, Aaron, what a mixed skein of good and bad, evil and virtue, forms the substance of our lives. Jacob's learning and intelligence, his ability to assume a high Roman manner and speech, gave him entry to the merchant world of these cities. There he was able to establish outlets and networks for the produce of his farm and, equally important, a market for the surplus of his fellow villagers to whom he was able to bring an increase for their labor.

He earned the trust and confidence of both classes since each accepted him as one of their own and he played this role with ease and with no small pleasure. And his farm life was lived in accordance with the tenets of Sara's sect, though his convictions were not completely hers.

The cities were mixed in population. The majority of artisans, stone workers, small merchants and such like were Jewish and the people paid heed to our Torah. But their rulers were an amalgam of hellenized, aristocratic Jews —these were important merchants with many servants to care for their households and clerks and scribes for their business needs — and the sizable population of Roman and Syrian administrators caring for the needs of the Empire. And always the contingent of Roman military lest confusion were to arise about whose country this really was.

Because of the needs of commerce and interaction with the non-Jewish population, it was common for the city Jews to fall away from the stricter observances in the countryside. They spoke Greek even when reading the books of Moses. They dressed as Romans and went to the theater and games and met in the bathhouses as did those in the large cities of Rome itself.

They would conduct business in synagogue and desecrate the Sabbath, whereas in the villages no work could be performed on that holy day, and the synagogues were filled with the sounds of our ancient language. No villager would venture more than a few steps from his home or prayer house.

One should not wonder at the hatred these farmers and peasants had for the city folk, for in truth, they believed it was this desecration that brought down on them God's wrath and withheld from them His and their Messiah. Could they, they would cast them out of the house of Israel.

It was both the growing destitution in the countryside and the assault on its piety that raised the multitude of cults, sects and crusades that plagued the land at this time. Some protested in open and peaceable ways, listening to the exhortations of the hundreds of itinerant evangelists walking the roads and speaking in the village prayer houses and squares. And others, in secret and shadowy places, entered into conspiracies to raise the population in anger and revolt against the foreign rulers.

To Antipas Herod — though not the cruel tyrant like his father, Herod the Great — and his Roman overlords, it was all the same. All prophecy, all protests could lead to revolt and the head of more than one such preacher rolled in the sand while he was leading his followers to demand audience or protest sacrilege.

And woe to the armed fighter caught by the Romans! After the soldiers' sport with him he would be nailed or strapped to the tree and left to die and be eaten by the vultures who began sometimes before his last breath was sucked. Nevertheless, uprisings took place at every change of leadership, and even when a new government fiat was proclaimed. There was always turmoil throughout the land.

Jacob was known to these groups and although they themselves were often at odds with each other, he had the ear and confidence of all of them. In many ways his nature brought him close to the ones who looked to active resistance. He supported these groups and individuals who were often forced to take shelter in the barren countryside or in the city's labyrinthine warrens.

His blood rose with his association with these fighters and he had resources to spare for their aid. But clearly this was a dangerous activity. He could not escape notice by the government spies who were everywhere.

In this was his first source of conflict with Sara. It came over time, as Ruth came into the house, then I. Jacob became more and more disappointed with Sara's failure to give him sons. It was then

that he began to spend more time with his trade and city activities. He was often away for days at a time, leaving the day-by-day
operation of the farm to Sara and she in turn leaving the household largely to Anna. I was privy to all their decisions and concerns and there was nothing in connection with the farm of which
I was not aware.

Sara's beliefs were as natural to her as the air she breathed, for she
heard of them from the time of her first cry. She lived with the knowledge that her life was a preparation for the final struggle against the
priestly usurpers of the true teaching of Moses and the foreigners with
whom they collaborated and who protected them in turn. Her sect
had been preparing itself for many generations in desert, countryside,
village and town, teaching the rules of purification and obedience to
make way for the Righteous one to raise all of Israel to his banner.

I remember her fear and frustration with Jacob's activities because she, and I, too, believed that until the time was ripe and the
call went out, the activity of these men only strengthened the
enemy and made him more alert. More than once she remon-
strated with Jacob and reminded him of his earlier promise to live
so as to make himself ready to become one with her people.

Now, it was clear, he was less likely to follow Sara's path. But I
tell you, Aaron, Jacob could not set his will against Sara any more
than could her father.

This was the world Master re-entered, no different than the
one he left. But in neither case did he address the events and conflicts of the times. He searched for no reason for civil disarray or for
personal sorrow, for rancor or hostility. It was as if these elements
in the world had no existence. It was not his way to address these
concerns, to tell the people to do this or to do that; the teachings
of our holy tradition tell them enough of what to do and what not
to do. His path was the one to the place of no sorrow, to taste it,
glimpse it, then see the blemish flee from their lives.

I looked at Aaron. He now sat comfortably a pace away from
my seat, which placed me so that he had to slightly incline his
head to look into my eyes. His were so clear, so alert, so expectant.

·I saw he still gave me his full attention. I was brought back to another time and place, with other comrades, when we would be in this position around Master waiting for him to speak, although not caring as much for his words as for his presence. How beautiful is Aaron's gaze, his trust and his love. Is this what Master saw as he looked at each of us in turn? I know we felt that in him.

At first, when Master returned from the silence of the East we saw naught of him. But because of Joseph, we knew he was once more among us. In short order, it became apparent that Joseph was more than a simple herald of Master's reappearance; rather, he was the instrument of the first unfolding of Master's mission. Because of his work as messenger and guide to the widely dispersed people of his sect, Joseph knew every village, every town, every dark city quarter in which they lived.

These were a communal people, far away from the holy influence of their isolated monastic communities. Joseph had kept the vision of deliverance alive in them so that they remained part of the tens, the hundreds, the thousands, that God's righteous Teacher would lead against Rome and Rome's Temple servants.

Because of their trust and confidence in him, Joseph could bring Master to them and gain their attention. He knew that Master's teaching, albeit one of peace, was also one to bring conflict. Alas, Aaron, all men do not want peace. But Master's power sustained them both; his presence, if not his words, would awaken those souls prepared to enter this new world.

For his part, Master sought these communities first because his father was of this sect and Master had grown to manhood with the words of their teaching seared in his mind. But more important, these were Jews who escaped the despair and the hopelessness of Jewish life in those times. Even outside their communal desert enclaves they obeyed the Laws of brotherhood, sharing with and caring for each other. Master' message: *the kingdom is within, look within for salvation and find there the sustenance for a new living,* was more easily accepted by those who, though having nothing of their own, wanted for nothing.

But, Aaron, this message, powerful as it was, stirring the deepest desires of a righteous people, was overwhelmed by the presence
of the messenger. They looked into his face and saw the living
embodiment of his message. In each place he visited he would
strike a spark in the souls of those of his listeners who could see
and hear beyond image and words, and there were always some so
that his footprint would remain wherever he trod. Later he told us
that, once kindled, those embers never die no matter how often
the soul that shelters them finds for itself a new container.

He told us this after his days of travel had ended. A time came
when he turned his attention inward, living, Joseph would say,
entirely in the kingdom to which he guided the rest of us. He took
his shelter in a small desert enclave, an old ruin some said, left by
an ancient sect of believers, believers of what, none could any longer
say. A group of Master's disciples, leaving their former community
along with Joseph at the time Master returned, settled there after
reclaiming a well sufficient to support their meager needs.

The outer wall was rebuilt, though they needed protection
only from the wilderness animals. The small stone cells they used
for their private needs and sleeping were likewise repaired, though
these needed little attention but for new roofing. There was a large
communal room for eating and meeting together.

Despite the many times I was there I never learned where it
was Master put his head. And as I think of it now, Aaron, the only
function of these disciples and the only purpose of this community was to serve Master's needs and the needs of his message. Did
these men know when they first sought this retreat for themselves,
that in fact it was to satisfy their Master's needs?

No matter. It was located but a day's journey from our village.
That it was in an unsettled part of our country without true roads
was a blessing since it was dangerous for me to travel outside the
area in which I was known. Seldom did I leave the confines of our
farm, and then only when sheltered by a covered cart. So when
Master began to gather his most trusted followers for ever new

teaching and instruction and he sent for me to attend these conclaves, it was possible for me to do so.

It was not unusual for Jacob's servant to be seen heading his wagon in that direction, though none knew its final destination. His was one of the farms that supplied the few provisions that were required by these ascetics.

I was asked to attend for a special reason. I cannot describe my emotions when Master pulled me aside and in his quiet way opened my mind to his words as my heart was already opened to his being. "There are things you cannot do, Jonathan, but, likewise, there are things only you can do."

These words caught my attention as would be natural in this situation. But they were the words of one man to another in the manner of giving or receiving information. And then his words would change as would his manner and I would see and hear what the others would see and hear, what only a true Master, a true Messenger could say, and I felt the presence and sanctity of our ancient prophets.

"I bring no new teaching. What I bring was before I was and will live after I no longer am. I am because of this teaching, it is not because of me. In days past men knew this and lived their lives accordingly. Their suffering now is because it was lost in the inexorable movement of the ages. It is now time for its restoration.

"This teaching is eternal, was never born, can never die, but only takes life through men. In some ages there will be few who will have earned its presence and they will be as seeds. And in other ages these seeds will sprout into multitudes and cover the earth. But in all times it is there for those who can move toward me.

"You will listen and watch and learn. First, to you will come many who will come to me so you will know the things of this time. You will keep this knowledge intact as you, yourself, will remain intact and await the time to pass it on."

I could not gainsay him. But I was filled with foreboding because of this task.

"Master, how can this be? I cannot be among men. Who will

pay me heed? You fill my mind and heart with confusion for this weak mind and poor heart can never contain the whole of you. How can I be entrusted with this mission? How can I be as you?"

We were sitting together, Aaron, as we two are now. I can tell you even now how the shadows of the day painted the walls of our small stone cell. How its cool interior smelled, how silent it was but for the sounds of the desert insects. I can tell you also, the shaking of my hands and the fear in my heart.

Master leaned over and took my hands in his. This was the first time we ever touched, never before, only once again. He pulled me toward him and looked into my eyes and said:

"Jonathan, I love you. I would never put upon you a burden you could not bear, nor ask you to suffer for my sake. Cast away your fear, accept what you hear and see with comfort, with ease, and believe me when I say you are a container that can carry it all. You will meet my faith in you with full measure."

Need I tell you, Aaron, that in that moment I was healed? Never again in my life was I troubled by fear, anguish or misgiving. I hear men talk of the freedom of a blessed life, but what they speak of is like a candle to the sun compared to what Master gave to me that day. And, Aaron, what I felt in myself in that moment I saw in Master and knew it in all its glory for the first time.

I no longer wonder at his prescience. I sound, I know, as if he is still among us. But in truth he has never been apart from me since that day he grasped my hands. The tiny sanctuary, which became his permanent abode, was impossible to find without guidance. Even those who had been there before could not again find this place alone. Therefore, when Master summoned those souls doing his work, they would be told only to go to our village near the sea in Galilee and seek Jacob's farm.

Arriving there, they would come upon me. Often it would be a single traveler, though sometimes it was in pairs, after weeks, even months in wearying transit. By this time, most of Master's followers knew of me, for scattered as we were there was contact, gossip and rumor, as is always the case with brotherhoods. So they and I were spared the shock that often accompanies an initial encounter.

Sara's hospitality, or Anna's, as the case would be, as she was by then totally under Sara's guidance, would ease their weariness and it was left to me to ease their spiritual concerns. I questioned them about their activities and learned the effects of Master's work and the knowledge of his presence throughout the land. All had news of the work they were doing. And in this way, I became, as Master knew I would, a repository of the lore, the nature and the deeds of his most trusted disciples.

I absorbed this learning, Aaron, as sponge absorbs water and with it came a growth in confidence and authority. In the short time they stayed with us, until they were ready to move on to Master's presence, I served to prepare them for that meeting. Their minds needed comforting, all of them believing they were falling short of Master's needs and expectations, and I found I could provide a balm to these feelings out of the experience of my own relationship with him.

Master knew their hearts, I told them, for why else would he call them. He needs and expects only that they turn their faces toward him. I repeated what Master told me in my own state of doubt: "I will not burden you with more than you can bear, nor ask you to suffer for my sake."

These were good and simple men who first responded to Master's call. Farmers, tradesmen, workmen they were, most of them with families. Likely they had been adherents to one or another of the sects and brotherhoods that had hearkened to the ancient Mosaic call. It was when Master visited their village or town or city communities that his presence alone transformed their lives. They knew then that their seeking was a true effort, and in him they saw it was accomplished.

But there were others too, Aaron, and Joseph spoke to me of these with wonder, these who would come upon Master by chance. They were the ones cast out by the world without homes, family, or work to keep a piece of leather on their feet or cloth enough to cover their backs. They would find shelter with the animals in the villages or towns and in the city they would glean its leavings in its dung heaps.

"I never saw a tear drop from Master's eye," Joseph once told me, "but when we would come across one, a few, a group of these souls, I would swear the sea could not hold more than what I saw well up in his eyes."

He would stop, Joseph said, and simply look at them. At first they would entreat him as beggars do an ordinary traveler, but Master would stand still, silent, and look at each in turn. Gradually their chattering would stop, and around the group, with Master in the center, it would appear that an invisible shield had descended isolating them from the world.

Passersby would find a way by them; few Joseph said, would pay them any mind. Time passed thus until Master stirred, took a step forward and as he did so, those in his path parted to make way for him to continue. None would try to stay his leaving.

After one such encounter, as they continued on their way, Master turned to Joseph and said: "You see, Joseph, the power of my poverty. It permits me entrance to the sheol of the living, but you see also the poverty of my power; until one comes to me I cannot go to him. There is ease in the torment this gives me for I know that this is our Father's will. As I know I would not leave them to their fate I know He, too, will not desert them."

It must be true, Joseph said, that Master cannot utter a sigh that is not heard in heaven. One day, in a small village in southern Judea, near the wilderness of Idumaea, Master was permitted to lead the services in the village synagogue. Joseph was not unknown there and because of him Master was accepted in his usual role as an itinerant preacher. After the prayers ending the service, a group milled about, caught up in his fervor. As usual, there were those who would not leave without some private words. These he would direct to Joseph or one or another of his local disciples.

A man, clearly destitute, hung back from the crowd, knowing his place, but keeping Master in sight. Later, Joseph found Master's attention was caught as well by this man's presence. In time, the press of people thinned and the outcast found his way to approach Master. As he did so, some moved away muttering, "unclean, unclean."

Boldly, the man approached and in a firm voice that belied his appearance he said: "Rabbi of Galilee, I know of this kingdom of which you speak, but I cannot enter it."

At this some onlookers laughed. One made a circular motion at the side of his head. Another motioned to shoo him away. But Master paid them no heed. Instead he addressed the man with the full attention he would to any.

"What is your name, brother, who are you?"

"I was once called Andrew, Rabbi, but I am no longer called, so I have no need of a name."

A man in the growing group now surrounding the two, guffawed, "so he did have a name once did he, but he is right, he needs no name now."

All eyes went to Master but he made no sign he heard the barb. His glance remained fixed on his questioner. "Tell me, Andrew, what do you know of our kingdom?"

"At night, Rabbi, after I sleep a time, I think I come awake, but then I have a vision where I come upon a country and it appears as in a dream but still I am awake in that dream. It is a beautiful country, Rabbi, which I cannot see into though I know its beauty nevertheless. I decide to enter it, and when the thought to do that arises, a peace surrounds me that penetrates every chamber of my body driving out all care, all fear, all confusion.

"I am drawn to the gateway of this country and as I take my step to enter, it vanishes. Then sounds of the world are heard once more, the day begins and I return to the turmoil and suffering of my life. Teach me how to enter this country, Master, for I look at you and I know you have its key."

When Joseph told us this story, Aaron, his face took on that glow that is sometimes seen in those whose heart is captured for the instant by the sense of Master's presence. He told us how a silence descended on the crowd. The man who had earlier derided Andrew turned to Master with fear on his face.

"These are God's words, Rabbi, how can they come from a mouth so covered with sores and filth?" And then the answer to his own question dawned in his eyes as if a shade had lifted. He turned to Andrew and said: "Forgive me, brother, it was the filth covering my own vision that allowed me to see only filth. As God's words cleansed me I will take you to me and cleanse you."

Master said nothing. But to both of them he raised his hands in the way he has so even one who has never seen this expression before knows it was a blessing. It was clear the two understood it as such for they looked into Master's face and eyes as thirsty men look at an offering of drink. Andrew's head lifted and his back straightened and Master nodded his acknowledgment to them both. Finally, as he made ready to leave them, he said quietly, "Remember me. The way is broad and clear and easy. You, yourselves, have the key."

This place in fact, was the end of their voyage. It is the farthest outpost of Jewish Palestine, close by the home country of its non-Jewish rulers, the scions of Herod the Great. They took shelter that last evening in a tiny farm shed, ate their poor supper, said their evening prayers and made ready to pass the night.

Master slept sparsely. Indeed, he seemed to spend little time on his pallet. Often, Joseph would awaken in the night and find Master's place unoccupied. In the morning, just as dawn was breaking, he would return and begin his morning meditations, joined by Joseph. No word would pass between them until Master would indicate the start and thrust of the day's activity.

Never would Joseph see Master rise and leave his place, though one time he tried to stay awake all night to catch this but he failed. He said he looked away from Master's sleeping shadow for a moment and when he looked again it was gone. Had he dozed in that moment? He could not say.

When in the morning he would see the figure of Master returning, he felt a surge of relief. Until then, he had not realized he had been harboring a fear that Master would not return. And each time Master would vanish and return that same feeling would arise though, Joseph said, one would think in time he would lose that worry. He never felt this trepidation when he was away from Master, doing his bidding. Then, he always felt him close and protective. Joseph once asked me, Aaron, what did I think of this, is it a premonition?

I always thought Joseph blessed: Master's need of him and love for him were so evident, and his life was an extension of Master's own. But even here, I mused, a shadow is cast over this perfection, and whence comes that shadow? Surely not from Joseph's present life. I told him my thoughts on this.

"I feel always Master's closeness and protection, Joseph, and you know how little I am in his presence. And see his disciples, how they hew to him in far distant places and few are with him in the flesh.

"Master's power is in his spirit; his body is the form of his teaching, but the teaching is the substance. Yes, Joseph, I think it is a premonition, but not one of foreboding. Master wants us to know that someday we will lose the flesh. This will be hard, but we can never lose the substance, nor can the world."

That last day began when Master broke the morning silence. "Joseph, our work here is finished. The earth has been turned, the seeds planted and covered, God will send the rain and in the time it takes us to return to our home, strong sprouts will cover the land."

So it was. Master found his place and Joseph continued his work, guiding and nurturing the increasing fruit from that first planting. In his travels he found followers content in their devotion, at peace with themselves and a source of tranquillity for their families and neighbors, tiny, fragile islands in a sea of turmoil. But his practiced eye, blessed with Master's inner sight, saw in this completion a new seedlet making its way to sunlight. To them he would whisper, "Master calls, find your way to Jacob's farm and tell Jonathan, Master called."

When first chosen, few knew how this could be accomplished.

Farmers had their farms, workers their work, most their families to be left behind. Many would face a long and dangerous trek in perilous times. Aaron, you know how a worm bores into the heart of a plant and thrives there until the plant is no more and the worm is all. Joseph's whisper was like that worm and once it found its burrow it could no longer be removed.

Inevitably then, sooner or later, plans would be made to seek Master's presence, and few could voice to others the purpose or need of such an adventure — the heart speaks only to the heart — so to the hardships of travel were added the fears of and for the ones left behind. But once set upon this path, all would state, obstacles were overcome, fears came to naught, and their destination was achieved.

Master's grace fell also on the least of men and these were not left behind though in some ways their shackles were even tighter. I learned of this mystery when one such of Master's disciples told me that he believed he had been bereft of even a speck of the world's bounty until he had decided to leave his place of destitution.

It was then that he realized he had this comrade who would be hard- pressed without him, and he, himself, had that companion who knew the ways of the servants of wealthy people so that a crumb or two could fall their way. He had a place for his head at night, a covering for his cold body, a friendly voice in the dark, and leaving even this poverty filled him with trepidation.

But then Joseph's whisper — how he found him is another mystery — filled his heart and banished the fear. He had never forgotten that day when he first saw Master's face, nor his mind's image of that face which would arise at the worst of his times, and though he did not know it to speak of it, the grace he was given was silently working its way through his life.

When his initial fear passed and he found himself ready to leave the security of his misery, he found a double freedom: one from the internal poverty caused by his ignorance of Master's favor, and the other from his external poverty, caused by his surrender to it.

By ones and twos they would retreat into the place of silence, a place where nothing was to be done, but where so much was to be accomplished. I would accompany them and stay and observe, as Master wanted me to. At their arrival, they would be greeted by a resident monk who would show them to their isolated cells and then provide them with a slight repast and leave them to their solitary meditations or much-needed rest, as the case would be.

On the selected day, the new arrivals would be brought into the large meeting room for their first sitting with Master. It would be his practice to sit in front of them as they do in our village synagogue so as to form a half circle in such a way that each had a direct view of Master and he of them.

One man told me that when he looked into Master's eyes and felt his gaze returned "the world disappeared; my body was as if made of air, one puff and it could be blown away; but the spirit lived and saw, and saw only Master. And then I thought I must have died, that this is how our death is, and with this thought my senses returned. I saw Master looking at another and I knew I had died, and I was reborn, and all fear left me."

As they entered more and more deeply into the silence of the kingdom, as Master told them they would, he was able to reveal more of his nature, and their nature that would be. In themselves they found powers they feared and questioned. Master would calm their fears and as their capacity increased he would teach them new things, and gradually they saw the loosening of the tentacles of old habits and the encrusted dross accumulated over immemorial ages. None knew how much weariness they carried with them to this place until they began to shed it.

I knew the time was approaching when Master would be ready to send them out into their world again, for it was then he would give them a vision of a man who enters the kingdom and makes it his home. What is the mark of such a man? What could be said of him?

You will have nothing, but you will want for nothing. You will know this and be without fear.

You will hate no man — hate is man's greatest burden — for there

is no hate in you. And if it comes out of the terror of the times, remember
me and it will be gone.

Your eyes will look upon a world in chaos, tumult, suffering, but
they look from a place of tranquillity into which no sorrow can enter.
Be of good cheer and know that only you can dispel that darkness in
men. Witness that calmness within.

Do not speak of the kingdom you have seen these days to those who
have not entered it; for then, in confusion and despair they will vainly
search their lives away looking for it where it is not.

Rather, lead them to this country by your own being as I have led
you and teach them as I have taught you, more to those who can see
more, less to those who see less; leave the others to our Father who will
find them in His good time.

And know, we live in an age that seeks out and destroys all light.
When yours flickers weakly and you see the creeping edges of darkness,
remember me and see my light within.

As I prepared them to come here, I also prepared their departure. They left in small numbers as they came and I spoke to each
at the time of their leaving. I cautioned them to reveal nothing
about this place or Master's special teaching and they understood
well. They heard teachings and witnessed practices and they themselves did things that the world could only condemn.

I saw them when they came, Aaron, and I saw them when
they left and I tell you they were not the same. They went back to
their villages and towns and city communities and Master's spirit
went with them and where he had been only one, he was now
many hundreds and where his feet had rested in one place they
were now throughout the land.

"Please, Master, my head is whirling."

My reverie burst at Aaron's call. And he said: "The vision you
conjure up with the words and deeds and the very being of your
Master leads me to the deepest recesses of my soul. It is first a
place of infinite silence and then a place of unending motion, of
sounds and things vying with each other for ascendancy, then fading into each other out of submission.

One comes and brings into life its opposite as it itself dies in the coming. In this way I see the world unfolding, I see all the worlds unfolding, and though I know nothing, I know I can know all. Master, where do these words and feelings come from? I am no longer the boy I was."

I looked at Aaron. I had thought I could no longer be astonished. And in fact, there is nothing new in the world of things for one like me. But in the world of the spirit each day is new as we move to greater fulfillment. And in Aaron's face was that sign I saw in the faces of those men so many years ago as they took their leave from me after weeks and months in the Presence.

How powerful this man, and man he was, how powerful this message, how hungry are men for it that it casts its light down the generations, an eternal, bobbing, lighted candle in a violent sea, ever finding new tapers. Now Aaron is the lamp.

"My Master is your Master, Aaron," I heard myself telling him. "I know the purpose of my life now and I know the meaning of each word Master spoke to me because I see the words take form in you. I pass the burden of transmission to you, Aaron, but do not fear, you are not alone, and you will find like souls everywhere, for now lit, that lamp can no longer be extinguished."

We looked at each other in the silence of my mountain retreat, two persons but united in our Master, needing no words to communicate the substance of our lives to one another. For with access to our own interior worlds we enjoy access to all interior worlds. But all men do not, all men are not as we, so Aaron needs to know more of Master's time with us to give to them the spur to seek his teaching. He knew my thought as I did.

TOMAS THE CHRISTIAN

Then Tomas came. It was just past midday and we were taking our shelter from the sun. We had long forgotten Jacob's mention of his name. He walked into our yard and was almost to the large entranceway to our communal room when Anna spied him and alerted me.

She could not have known who he was but I saw he wore the garb of a foreign holy man, not entirely rare to us, but he did not have the countenance of one from the east. Jacob was not to be home until that evening and Sara was taking her rest in another part of the house, so bold Anna took it upon herself to greet him.

He waited a few yards from the house for someone to notice him and I saw his face light when Anna came to the door. "Peace to you, lady," I heard him say and I was confounded by his manner of speech, so much like the Samaritan people just to the south of us. "I come seeking Jacob, I am told this is his farm."

Anna returned his greeting. "This is Jacob's farm, sir, but my master is not here until this evening and my mistress cannot attend you now. Please, sir, come in out of the day's sun." She then took him into the common room and sent a maidservant for a cool drink and found him a place in which he could rest himself. I then came into the room to greet him, sensing that no hostility could be in him; even so, Anna moved to my side in the protective way she reserved for me whenever I encountered new people. As I knew, she had no need to fear this visitor. There was not one sign of surprise from him at my appearance as he folded his hands with the greeting common to these Easterners.

Looking directly at me he said, "My name is Tomas and I was a servant of Jacob. In that time of my service I found my true

Master and I am ever thankful to Jacob for permitting me to join him. Now my Master calls me to spend time with him and in that call I was told to come to the farm of Jacob, the very same Jacob I knew. I found my way here with another of Jacob's associates, Jason, who became a follower of my Master through my work in Jason's country."

I greeted him as he did me. It would take no more than a moment or two and I would know if one were a true disciple, a gift of insight from Master. None but whom he would see would be brought to his place and soon I knew Tomas was surely one of these.

Sara came upon us as Tomas was telling me his name and purpose and likely she remembered a mention of him during a time of Jacob's retelling. But no matter, I am sure she saw in his face the same aura I did which signaled his interior stillness; Joseph describes it as a window to the soul.

Sara entered, disturbed perhaps by our conversation, and ended our visit knowing, as we should have, the weariness of our guest. She quickly had him settled and secluded. Though he resisted, she had a servant brought to care for his needs. He was used to the harshness of the ascetic's life and he felt uncomfortable amid comfort. Still, she prevailed, saying for this short time he could be generous and give her the gift of service. He settled then in his seclusion to await the arrival of Jacob.

In time, Jacob arrived. How would this meeting be, I wondered, after so many years? We had little idea of their association but for Jacob's sketchy description, now hoary with age. This former servant, truly venerable to the sight, and Jacob, grown more truculent with the passing time. Sara was watching for him and pulled him aside as he returned. "Jacob, Tomas is here. He came to see you and for retreat with Jeshua."

In all the years I knew him, Aaron, I never before saw the expression of bewilderment on his face as I saw then. "Tomas? Tomas!" he began, but before he could say another word, Tomas himself entered the room.

"Peace, Jacob, how is it with you?"

Jacob stared, unbelieving. Though he could not credit his eyes, he knew from his ears that this was indeed Tomas, his former servant. He looked him up and down, at his full head of dark hair, the long beard suitable for an ancient prophet, his monk's dress, and his poorly shod feet. Finally, his senses returned.

"Tomas, it is really you! Why are you here? How are you here? I confess I gave you no thought. When Jeshua returned without you I thought you had been lost in the wilderness. That is a far country in which you were left, a servant without sustenance."

"Yes, Jacob, I was left, but by my own choice. As for being without sustenance, I was as I am now, sustained by my Master and, though I did not need Jason, I had his protection. You remember Jason. He sends you greetings; he is in Jerusalem and he wants to see you."

He then explained that Jason was now in Jerusalem attending to his benefactor's business. "Their seers told them," Tomas began, "that the disquiet in your land cannot be contained much longer and he comes to warn his master's associates so they can take steps to protect their business.

"But he has other reasons to come to this country. He wants and needs to see our Master. He has long accepted him as his spiritual guide since his encounter with me and I have been able to nurture these impulses in him as my own understanding unfolded. He senses, in this call to this land, that he has a service to perform and comes to see Master to find its nature. He credits you, Jacob, as the instrument that ended his search for Truth. He wants to offer to you what you brought to him, though you resisted it for yourself. This is also his mission."

And then I saw the most extraordinary thing. Whether it was Tomas' presence or the mention of Jason's name, I know not. But I saw a strange emotion seize Jacob. He began to sob. I saw the effort he made to control this but it was not possible.

As this happened Tomas raised his arms slightly from his sides, an almost imperceptible motion as if to beckon Jacob to come to him. Jacob moved toward him not able to contain himself any longer. It was then that Sara collected us, the few witnesses, and ushered us from the room. My last glimpse was of Tomas enclosing Jacob into his embrace and comfort.

If we had thought this was a marvelous happening, the erstwhile servant, an ignorant donkey driver, comforting his former master who was still an imposing person of consequence, the thought did not last long. Tomas was too much a man of authority in his own person to be thought of any more as a servant. And as we learned, he was, indeed, such a man upon whose shoulders was placed his Master's mantle, and who served as his Master's voice and presence in that great eastern country.

Over the course of the next few days we heard a remarkable story and witnessed the flowering of grace. During the day, villagers would come and Tomas would speak to them and preach. He could not preach in the synagogue since he was not a Jew, and there was added suspicion thrown on us in town because of that. How strange this world!

In the evening we gathered around Tomas to hear him and he never tired of teaching and speaking Master's words. But I was mindful of my task and charge from Master, to know all of his work, and so I won from a reluctant Tomas the story of how he came to be what he is.

"I left this country," he began, "the servant of Jacob, driving his donkey and doing his bidding. My name was Tomas then as it is now but then it was little used or needed. If one man said 'Tomas' to another, none would know of whom he spoke. I left my new country to return home and now if one there says 'Tomas', a multitude would know of whom he speaks. I left, not able to put one sensible word after another and I return and men wonder at my speech.

"This is the doing of my Master who plucked me from my destitution through his words and being — more his being than his words, as I heard few enough of them in that time. What he saw in me I cannot tell you but I can tell you what I saw in him on that Damascus road that early morning as we were stirring from our rest.

"The night ended early for me for the discomfort of one of my animals called to me before the break of day. As I stood there calming him I idly glanced out into the wilderness toward the place where the sun was casting its first speck of light. It is strange how God lights his world at that time; how the glow in the sky strains to ease the earth's shadows.

"At first I thought the movement in the shifting darkness was a wild creature that caused my donkey's distress. But as I looked further I knew it was a man and then I realized it was the one we called 'Rabbi'. I felt a relief at that. I knew of his habit of going off into the wilderness for communion. The fear of a wild animal or bandit or anything else unknown left me.

"I had long found him agreeable and a source of comfort for me though I did not think he was aware of my feelings. The Jews in the train did not look kindly on Samaritans and I often felt their insults and chidings. But never did I hear an unkind word or a disapproving glance from him. In fact, I was always eager for his presence for then the others did not mistreat me, just his being there somehow gentled their moods.

"I felt that same ease as he emerged from the darkness and came toward me. We were alone in the stillness. I can tell you what happened next because that time never left me and it uplifts me even now as I speak of it. I never saw the world before in its vastness and even so, it was growing larger, and I felt myself expanding with it and Master too and I thought it contained only us two. Then I thought, nay, three, and the feeling surged through me that we were safe in the Lap of our invisible Father Who, though neither seen, nor heard, nor felt, yet lives through the living forms of his creation.

"His eyes caught mine. Only his eyes. I saw naught else. 'Are you my servant, Tomas, will you come with me?' With what ears I heard this I cannot say. I could not speak. I was afraid to speak that my coarse words would not be fitting. But I needed no words knowing he knew he could not be denied.

"An interval passed but of what length it is impossible to say. I felt myself taking a deep breath, the blood stirring, my heart beating as if all had just started anew. I came into a new world and I felt myself a new man. It was as if I were one reborn."

All of us, Aaron, were held in silence by the sheer beauty of Tomas' words. We responded to them and felt their echo in the flesh and spirit of our bodies. I glanced at Sara who was looking at Jacob. Did she see in him what I did, a lighter face less marked by the strain I had come lately to see always in him? His body less tense, no longer coiled to spring like a wilderness cat wary of the slightest movement. If so, she made no sign of it as she looked again at Tomas sitting easily in the odd position these Eastern holy men have.

If we spent our evenings listening to Tomas, and we had yet to hear what more he had to say, Jacob kept to him during the day. For several consecutive days he had stayed on his farm finding reason not to attend his outside business. And he did not tend to farm business as he was wont to do when he remained at home.

Rather, we saw him searching out Tomas who showed his own interest in the workings of the farm animals as he had a special attachment to them. They responded to him in turn in such a way that I only remember they would with Sara. Often Jacob and Tomas would seclude themselves for long periods but neither would reveal the nature of their time together.

In our evening assembly, now attended as well by other household members, I saw the command over them shown by this former servant. One could imagine him sitting in conclave with his followers, they looking to him for the solace and guidance that is the boon to our lives. No one listened with more attentiveness than Jacob, and Tomas was never more compelling than when he spoke of the days of his transformation.

He first began to sense this change in him by his response to the abuse and ridicule from the other caravan servants. He was so full of the sense of Master that their thrusts could not penetrate its shield. In time, as they found their sport no sport, it lessened and finally ended.

As they made their way to Damascus, for some reason, he could not say what, Jacob found more useful work for him and the other servants showed more heed to his words. He felt a new sense of himself. But it was not clear that his encounter with Master that early morning could be held cause for this change, so gradually and innocently did it come. But the time came when no doubt could arise that it was our Master and his work that created in Tomas the conversion . . . but Aaron, nothing can do better than to hear this in Tomas' own words as I remember them to be.

"I know Anna here is the child Master rescued," he began, "that miracle never leaves me. For while watching him minister to this waif who only recently was cast into the dung heap as dead, a sensation crept over me that I thought I had long stamped out in my life.

"I thought of my mother and her tenderness in my childhood and felt the softness in me that that thought always raised. I ever fought that feeling thinking it a danger to my manly needs. But then, watching him care for that child as a mother would, I thought of his sovereign nature, he has no fear of being thought womanly, nay, more than that, his power alone brings that compassion into our world.

"I felt then, I must confess, a fullness in my eyes and I let this softness flow through me, not wanting it to cease, and I savored its presence and strength for the first time. Then I knew, he was more than a man just for me, he was a man for all the world."

That was the time, I believe, of Jacob's surrender though none, not even he, could have realized that just then. But he had been present at the time of Anna's rescue and he accepted the responsibility for bringing Anna to Sara, and he knew of the effect of this tale on others. Now the full dimension of Master's life and mission was unfolding for him and he, too, could not let Tomas be until the last of his story unfolded.

Tomas knew then that Master was planning to continue on his journey east without Jacob. You know how he contrived to leave Jacob's service and go with him. He could not bear the thought of separation. "Though he was my junior in age," Tomas said, "I was as a son to a father, needing his succor and guidance."

"The monk who became Master's guide on this trek secured their passage. He was returning to his home after a mission in our land. In his country he lived a protected life and that protection was extended to Roman lands by agreement. Both Rome and Parthia, Rome's rival to the east, desired stable and peaceful trade and these monks were seen as harmless to them as long as they did not question the Emperor's divinity. That protection was held on the road and extended to us.

"By the measure of all things one can see and hear," Tomas continued, "the voyage was without disturbance. But by the measure of things one cannot see or hear my life was forever changed. What I was shown and what I was taught in those timeless months cannot be told. But it was then I became what I am now."

His days in the eastern country, called Bactria, close to the Brahmin lands, began on that high level though he yet appeared a lowly servant. As he knew would happen, Master soon left, answering his own call. You know how Tomas then found service in the city and then met Jason, another gift from Jacob. Once met, these two were forever joined, if not always in flesh, then always in spirit. And simple as his position was, Tomas found he could not hide the lamp in his heart.

He showed a wisdom that his fellow servants were the first to discern. It was a natural quietness, an unforced kindness, and a softness that was so out of place in that rough quarter it could hardly be unnoticed. He recounted the story of how the most rowdy of the men would cease his aggression when faced with no resistance or anger. Tomas told us this was a gift Master bestowed in the desert — a boon he received unknowingly and never discovered until then. No man need have an enemy if enmity is removed from his heart.

In time the other servants would come to him, some with sorrow and fear, others to find how to be like him, some to know about his teaching. His influence grew and soon the owner and lord of the house heard talk of a "teacher" among his servants. His fear, Tomas learned later, was that there was one sowing discontent among them. This country, too, suffered from that.

One day the overseer came to fetch him to their lord. "Who are you?" his lord asked. "What do you tell people? We are peaceful here and we do not accept disturbance of that peace." Tomas stood before him and for the first time spoke as a disciple of his Master. How the words came he could not say but he felt he, too, was hearing them for the first time.

"Good sir, I am your servant as you see me before you. But I was once in the presence of a great soul who took me from my poverty and kept me with him. He is a Jew from Galilee, a country in Roman Palestine as you know, for your camels go there. He is now in the silence of your country for purification and communion as people here do. To look on me now, I am still that poor servant but I cannot deny the spirit of my Master as it flows through me and enters the lives of those around me."

Now this lord was a Parthian, an ancient native of this country. He was neither Jew nor Buddhist nor Brahmin but a believer of his own native faith. But in the spirit of those days in that land he believed God's garden sustained many flowers. And something about this servant made him think this was a new one.

Tomas then told of his Master, of his nature, of his deeds and of the time spent with him. As he spoke he could see the interest rising in the faces of his listeners. And like all the others, they were bewildered by the story of Anna's rescue. Again, now as ever, the refrain, "why the bother for an almost dead slave girl?" And other questions would be asked and soon Tomas was lost in his joy of speaking of him.

Finally, one of the lord's overseers asked to speak. "Tell me, man, does your Master have any words, what does he teach?"

"Forgive me, sir, but there are some words that do not come easily to my unschooled tongue. But I say to you what I say to all who ask me my Master's teaching.

"When I am with him I am at peace without fear. When not

with him, as now, his presence is still felt within me. I can say little to you learned men about his teaching. His first words are always, 'look within, find there the kingdom of our Father in heaven' and also, never failing to add, he says, 'see your brother as yourself and do him no harm as you should not be harmed.'

"But now I must add something I just came to know because of your questions. My Master's most powerful teaching is in his deeds. I thank God I had been witness to his greatest: the rescue of the slave girl. It is asked about this act, 'why bother?' I know now, finally, the answer to that question: in performing that act, he brought God's will into the world; let those who have eyes to look, see, and those with ears to listen, hear."

The lord of this great house looked at him for a long time. No sound was heard. At length he spoke: "What is your name? — Tomas? — well Tomas, your Master is a holy man who graces our country and you are a faithful and truthful servant who graces my house. I will command more of your time and your teaching."

Since then Tomas' life unfolded under Master's spiritual guidance as it did when they were together in body. At this house there was a learned servant who instructed the children of the household in their lessons. It was he who smoothed the roughness of Tomas' speech and in time he came to speak more ably to his learned listeners, but he never lost the speech that gained him attention from the servants and slaves and destitute who were always close to his heart.

He became known in the city as the disciple of the Galilean, whom he always praised as his Master and the world's Teacher, though none knew of whom he spoke. He spoke of the kingdom of God within and his Master, the chrystos, the king, of this kingdom. Because of this he began to be called "The Christian", after his Master.

One day Jason came to him and told him that Natan, Jason's lord, would have him come to his house and speak to the entire household. Due to Jason's continual urgings, Natan wanted to hear for himself what so many others in the city were talking about.

It was then that the former servant became the teacher, and the former teacher became the servant.

After this, Jason found reason to spend more and more time with Tomas. Natan permitted this, believing that the good offices from Tomas' holiness — a spell that he too came under — that would fall on his servant would also fall on his, Natan's, own head. Jason was able to make Tomas' way easier in the city and in time he, himself, became known as Tomas' man.

But Jason, nevertheless, remained close to Natan and chief among his counselors. When Natan's seers, those sages who were able to read portents according to the location of different bodies in the heavens, came to him and reported dark clouds forming over the Temple in David's city, he called Jason in. Though not wedded to this form of divination, he would not dismiss possible threats to his business. If there was peril for Jerusalem it affected his partners and of course his fellow Jews.

In their consultations both men agreed to inquire carefully and pointedly of the travelers and traders from that country whom they saw regularly about the conditions there. They listened to every shred of news and gossip with heightened awareness, but even so, they could discern nothing untoward.

In the course of time and press of business the worry faded and lay hidden, but never gone. So when a traveler, one clearly just arrived from that country, came to Jason and said he was told that Jason could direct him to one Tomas, a holy man in this city, it flashed in Jason's mind this might have some bearing on the omen they received. Upon inquiry the messenger would only say, "I have a message for him, sir, but it is to him only I can give it — it is meaningless to any other."

Tomas told us what then happened. "I knew immediately the man was from Master. I rejoiced at his speech for it had been a long time since I heard the sounds of my country. But then my heart soared when he told me Master was in his home and he calls his faithful servant Tomas to him. When, how, why he had returned and why I had had no notice of this event were all thoughts that crowded into my mind. But then, these same thoughts instantly left as I heard the echo of his messenger's words, 'Master calls for his servant, Tomas.'"

The messenger went on to say there was to be an ingathering of Master's limbs into their protective shell as a prelude to a coming storm. More than that he could not say but that Tomas' arrival was awaited as he was one of the furthest afield of all Master's servants.

This message, relayed to Jason, then Natan, confirmed their fears and it was decided they would be the instruments to insure Tomas' mission to his Master. It was Jason who contrived to convey him there, convincing Natan that a warning should be sent to their people in Jerusalem by one who would be heeded, if, in fact, they were unaware of the impending trials. In his secret heart, however, he wanted also to make his own pilgrimage to Master, though this was by no means certain as he himself was not called.

This, then, was why they were here. Tomas finished his account and was ready to complete his journey and join Master at retreat. I was to accompany him there. Only we two left that very early morning to complete the assembly. Our faithful and trusted driver who took us was instructed to leave us and return only when summoned. This was the first time in the driver's memory that pilgrims came to retreat with none returning.

We arrived in the late afternoon. It was clear to me even before we came upon the settlement that this conclave was different than all others. The silence of the place was deeper — a quietness with a texture, an alien substance. Neither a stirring soul nor an insect could be noticed. Yet, as I was to learn, there were more present than I had ever before seen in this place.

Tomas and I were greeted by a resident monk who motioned us to silence as he led first Tomas, then me, to our solitary cells. Our instruction, whispered directly into our ears despite our isolation, was simple: "Master is in communion and we await his call." Water was to be left outside our place of respite but I recall no mention of food nor do I recall any being served during that period.

Finally, very early one morning, two, perhaps three days later, I sensed a stirring outside my door. I looked through my small opening and I saw a group of men shuffling toward the common area. I went out and joined them; each was following the one before him, and I easily keeping abreast despite my ungainly stride, so slow was their movement. I realized only then the size of the group and only then understood the many paths there were to Master's door. So many of them did not pass through me by way of Jacob's farm.

As we entered the common room, there was Master sitting in his accustomed place, his eyes almost closed, not heeding the incoming assembly. The men in their practiced way moved slowly to their places forming a semicircle around Master, each one able to have a clear view of him, even those in the rear, as permitted by Master's slightly elevated dais. I took my usual place that allowed me an unobstructed scrutiny of the hall.

In time all sound ceased as the men waited for Master. I saw his eyes sweep the room looking into the faces of each man. He found my eyes but made no notice of it. But for me I could not escape the joy his glance unfailingly evoked in me. Were I told at that moment the sun stopped in its travels, I would have had no doubt of it.

Then Master spoke:

My work is done — I look into your eyes and I know it is done well.

Do not ask why you were chosen; you will receive no answer as I received no answer. Do not search for merit for this work for its merit does not belong to you. It was gained by you in the past, and that is past.

Do the work for the work, not for its fruits. Offer the fruit to our Father to be not a thief. Think of the plants of the field; they offer their fruit to the world and thereby gain their own immortality.

You bring God's will into this world. You till the ground, plant the seed, nourish and protect it. Do not fret that you will not see its harvest in men as you know it in yourselves.

Nor did Moses see the land promised to his people. Yet would any of you yet not be as Moses? None. So know to do this work you are as was Moses. To do this work you are as I am and I bless you for that; for then I become as you are.

I say also to you, as we ready to part: we can never part. For you can no longer not do God's will. Would any of you call again into your lives the suffering you thought man's natural lot? Just one taste of freedom from that suffering opened forever the door to the kingdom, you cannot turn back.

Now return to your homes and keep this lamp lit until in God's good time He blows its light into the hearts of all men. Be content, we have done our Father's wish.

Then Master beckoned the man closest to him. The disciple knelt before him and Master rested his hand on the crown of his head and whispered some words to him that only he could hear. Then the next came and the next until each was seen and given his private blessing.

I was last. As my turn approached I was more and more filled with exaltation. Then to me alone Master came forward and pulled me toward him and kissed my forehead — for me then my life ended, nothing in the world of men could ever destroy his presence in my heart.

I never saw Master again. Nor Sara, nor Jacob, nor Anna, nor any other whose flesh and blood were wedded to mine. I remained at this place awaiting discharge and each morning I arose to a place of fewer and fewer devotees. Then my turn came one early morning just in the depth of night. I was deep in meditation and I sensed a presence in my cell sitting alongside me. I had no fear nor was I disturbed. Of a sudden I heard Joseph's whisper, "Prepare yourself Jonathan," he said, "you must leave. Master wills your safety so this time will be recounted. You can no longer stay in this country." It was then left to Joseph's servants to lead me to this place I now occupy for my rest and final maturation.

THE GREAT MARCH

You never saw Sara again, nor Jacob nor the others?" Aaron asked in wonder. "How could that be? Where did you go, and they? And how did you know their ends?"

In his interest he moved closer to me and when I looked into his face I saw myself reborn in him. All I know he will know, all I am he will be, he draws it out of me like water from a well and it bubbles up ever anew as it is drawn. "I was given this account, Aaron, as I now give it to you. Some day you will look into the eyes of another like yourself and remember me as you tell this story."

I was carried out of this land from that place of the last days hidden in a covered cart driven by the most trusted of Joseph's servants, never again to be in the physical presence of Master. Joseph himself accompanied us some of the way, then he left on his own special mission in these new times. We traveled at night, most dangerous to do but less so than in the daily crowded roads of those unquiet times. And even in the dark on our way to the sea, the sounds and smells and raucous night cries signaled the promised storm had arrived.

During our days of retreat we lived in the unmoving center of the world but it itself continued to swirl around us. Jason came from Jerusalem to a joyful reunion with Jacob, but brought with him the news that the movement of the people had begun. Jason reached our village only weeks ahead of its rising tide. It transpired that though he came from the East to meet with Master and receive his blessing, that was not to be. But his presence was noted and, through Tomas, he was charged a task by Master, a task that changed his first feeling of despair in not receiving Master's glance to a feeling of joy that he had been chosen to do him service.

There are ages, we are taught, in which we suffer the absence of any of those extraordinary people who, by their very presence, maintain the balance of the world. In those times it is the heavenly bodies that outline the destiny of mankind, bringing good or evil, as their placement dictates. There are also times when a deserving people live so well in harmony with God's laws that all good and no evil can be found.

And there are times, such as now, when a Master appears who cannot yet marshal the forces of good to change the world to good. But he can and must introduce into the world the teaching of this vision, that it can be known, that it can be tasted, that it can be lived. Thus to bring forth the consciousness to guide humanity to that final realization. Those who have earned their place as instruments of that beginning are blessed to be able to see this unfolding in their own lives.

In this case, however, it was not the stars people looked at to curse the coming calamity. Caesar Tiberius sent a new man to the Judean procurator's office. It could not have been for reasons of state for the new procurator was ignorant of his own state's history as much as he was of the different civilization he was entering. And though only slightly aware of the needs of Rome, he was thoroughly alert to his own.

As I left not long after he came, I cannot say how I came about this knowledge of him. But it explains the nature of the times. The procurator, Pontius Pilate by name, was an ambitious former soldier of bravery and leadership, qualities loved by Rome. But his Spanish ancestry kept him from the inner circles of Roman aristocracy and he chafed at these limitations. Finally, through much intrigue and betrayal of friends and allies, he won the ear of the Emperor, the hand of his daughter, and the office of the Judean procurator.

Although not stupid, Pilate was woefully ignorant of the special place the Jews enjoyed throughout the empire. Thinking them simply a disobedient, conquered people, not put in their place by less able Roman governors, he was determined to establish Rome's total dominance. Therefore, he confiscated funds from the Temple treasury to finance the building of a 30-mile aqueduct into Jerusalem. First, to provide water to the Roman garrison in the Antonia Fortress, and second, to provoke the violent response he knew would be forthcoming thereby giving him an excuse to show the Roman fist.

The response of the city's Jews was predictable when in their thousands they took to the streets in protest. But they were a disorganized mob and the disciplined Roman army, with its eager German cavalry, were able to contain and disperse them. Though it was not only Jewish blood that spilled and it was not only those that were rioting who were beaten and killed Pilate relished the carnage he wrought, and after peace was restored Pilate considered that a lesson had been taught. Upon the city there descended a quietness which, in Pilate's arrogance, he believed was a sign of surrender and acceptance.

Officers of the previous procurator had given him a number of practices forbidden to him, though he was the occupier and tyrant of this country. These were customs taken for granted by all other peoples who were conquered by Rome and the Roman legions, save the Jews. Among them was the practice of the proud Roman military to march their units into and out of town and city with their martial standards unfurled and embossed with the bust of the emperor. But never in Judea, especially in Jerusalem, was this permitted.

No greater affront could be made against our laws for did not God, Himself, instruct Moses about this abomination? But this particular law specially enraged Pilate, the former soldier, yet basking in his military glory. Still strutting from his first "victory," he decided to again challenge this infuriating Jewish haughtiness.

The opportunity came when a new cohort of troops was scheduled to relieve those serving in Jerusalem. He brought them in under cover of darkness and had them arrange their standards around the walls of the fortress adjoining and overlooking the Temple courts and squares. Surely, they would be in full view of the morning crowds of worshipers, Temple priests and workers, and those with their normal Temple business. Again the alarms were sounded and again the streets teemed with people moving toward the Temple. But this time there was a difference.

In the quiet interlude since the raid on the treasury, sect leaders, disciplined clandestine fighting units, some called in from the countryside and rabbinical schools of all kinds with their young student bodies, had prepared themselves for this further desecration, though they did not know it would take this form. And even those others, the large mass of the people of a more conciliatory philosophy, could not restrain their anger and despair.

They converged in the Temple area with the offending banners clearly in view. But, as if by order, though no leader could be seen, and with no priestly authority in evidence, not a sound could be heard from the thousands. And then, in unison, a multitude of raised fists punctuated the mass of people and many contained clubs and knives, the clearest sign of revolt.

The Fortress commander, new to the area, who had been thinking that twitting the noses of this people was a lark, was now beside himself with fear. He ordered a show of force and displayed a number of fully armed and shielded soldiers, supported by horsemen and local mercenary troops. But it was clear to him that not even the crack legion now stationed in Syria could rescue him from this horde.

In time the High Priest with his entourage emerged from the Temple sanctuary and quiet settled on the crowd as his agent was seen making his way to the commander. Seeing the assemblage under some reasonable authority, the captain gained his composure. But he remained firm in his insistence on displaying the symbols. The procurator ordered them raised and only he could order them lowered, and he was in Caesarea.

When told of this reply some in the crowd shouted, "on to Caesarea", and then in waves the multitude took up the chant until nothing but that could be heard from one end of the city to the other. Thus began the Great March. Its place of origin was the center of the tiny Jewish world and its destination the procurator's palace in Caesarea, the representative of mighty Rome. They had no David to lead them in flesh but for this span of time his spirit was in the heart of each. The High Priest was too infirm to make what became a five day trek, even if conveyed, so his eldest son stood in his place, a fitting selection since he was to inherit the vestments.

But it was not he who led this army, it was the leaders of individual groups, sects, students, and crafts; teachers and preachers and merchants, too, caught up in a cohesion that Jews reach only when God's dignity is besmirched.

The news of this movement flew before it as with the wind and the throng on the Roman highway became as a giant river. Villages and towns along the route fed into it and as Jerusalem was emptied of its population, so, too, were these places. And from the hinterlands came rivulets (how they knew of the travesty none could say) and in their tens and twenties they added to the flood. This was neither sowing nor harvest time so servants and masters, women with their husbands and older children, took their places together.

As they approached the outskirts of the city — Herod's tribute to Caesar, of course, with Jewish money — they founded encampments and resting places though suffering from weariness, thirst and hunger. As the press of the thousands pushed the leading elements of the protesters into the city proper, the residents abandoned their homes and made toward the palace and more secure sections of the city. They looked to Pilate for protection and the procurator, now both enraged and frightened, had reluctantly sent to the Syrian Legate for additional forces but he was not sure of their coming, at least in time.

The Syrians did not originally support the selection of this procurator by Tiberius, and they understood his culpability in this disaster; they could easily allow him to suffer the fate of his own ignorance. They knew, if the Jewish firebrands did not, that Rome was not to be dislodged from this country but the procurator's destiny was not so secure.

Despite the presence of women and children in the march, and many others not inclined to take up arms knowing the consequences, there were militant fanatics who hoped to provoke the soldiers into action, forcing the people into insurrection. Hurling insults, stones and refuse at the horse troops, they created a situation ripe for an explosion. Responding to the demonstration and abuse, one horseman, breaking discipline out of pure rage, brandished a copy of our holy book and using its pages in an obscene manner he flung its pieces into the faces of the crowd.

Nothing now, it seemed, could restrain the people and in one movement they rushed the soldiers trying to seize the offending horseman. But it was his destiny — perhaps the destiny of all there that day — to escape their clutches and the entire troop of horsemen was able to make its way to safety. But news of this transgression swept through the masses and reached the ears of Pilate himself. For a moment the lives of thousands, nay, tens of thousands, were balanced on the edge of a Roman short sword as both antagonists looked into the face of extinction.

In that moment of shocked silence cooler voices were heard speaking of another way and Pilate came to understand there was no halfway ending to this confrontation. These people would resist to the last and accept martyrdom rather than abide this affront. The blood spilled here, he realized, would stain the streets of Rome itself and he was sent here to oversee tribute to the Emperor, not to find work for the Roman army.

He agreed to an audience. For many tantalizing hours they met, the High Priest's son charged with making the most frightful decision of his time, even before his final elevation, and the procurator, caught in the trap of his own arrogance. Finally, emerging from that meeting, alone, the son declared almost unbelievable news: the standards were to be removed. How could this be? The question was: for Pilate, what?

Yes, for Pilate, what? The rumors spread. He desired to spare the people further suffering; it was a reason, though there were few who accepted that. Certainly not the soldiers who felt betrayed.

More to be believed was the later story of his wife's new acquisi-
tion of a villa and property in Rome's developing outskirts. Is it
not said, it is not water but gold that rains on the Judean procurator? But in fact, there was hidden fruit from that audience, fruit
that would not bud until a more quiet time.

The people found their way back to their homes but it was an
eerie quiet that settled on the land. And indeed this quiet, too,
was the signal for a new storm. The demonstrations with their
orderliness and organized components frightened the Temple priests
no less than the Roman occupiers. Their spies had done their work
well over the years and there were few groups and sects not known
to them. But it was now clearer than ever to both secular and
religious authorities that clandestine forces were at work, organizing and planning to subvert their rule.

Starting in Judea, Temple informers began exposing the leaders of the sects, and did not except ordinary members who could
be named and found, who were teaching defiance to Temple law.
Normally, Roman rule was uninterested in these Jewish quarrels,
but after the Great March they came to understand they could
not separate their tranquillity from that of those who collaborated
with them. And they knew also how the people chafed under their
demands for tax and tribute.

An unholy alliance was formed and each did the other's bidding. Roman troops were employed to gather up for questioning
and trial suspects led to them by these hirelings and, as always in
these matters, innocent and guilty alike were confined lest one
dangerous person escape.

Trials were held, and few, once entwined, could loosen their
chains. As the retribution engulfed Judea and then moved into
Galilee and adjoining lands, a forest of shame grew along the Cae-
sarean/Jerusalem highway, the way of the Great March. Like mile-
stones, hanging men were strapped or nailed to their crosses and
terror ruled the towns and countryside. People, once standing in
unison, now turned against each other in a mad attempt to escape.

Tomas' return to Jacob's farm occurred as the first harbinger of this panic came into our village with the returning participants of the protest. His presence signaled the end of the beginning of Master's work. "Master is now preparing," Tomas told them, "to enter into a greater exploration of the myriad environs of God's mansion, places which his heart had always longed to visit, satisfied that the desires of Him for this age have been fulfilled. He remains at retreat, alone now, enjoining all to safety in these perilous times, awaiting what we do not yet know."

Tomas continued, now clearly their new master and guide, and revealed new instructions. All knew he spoke with Master's authority to their secular needs as Master had spoken to their spirits. Jacob's farm could be no more as it was, he said. Sara must leave, her work and life were finished here, remaining meant her destruction. Jason was charged to see to her safety. Jacob would send Anna and Ruth to Sara's home village to her family's farm, which was prepared to shelter them.

As for Jacob, he could still choose ill or wisely his own fate. Tomas would only say, "surrender to Master's will, Jacob, no harm can be suffered through that path." But Jacob did nothing and I cannot imagine his thoughts as he bade farewell to Sara, now in Jason's care, to be spirited out of the country. Nor can I speak of his feelings about Anna and Ruth as he sent them off with his most trusted servant.

Local informers, in their new zeal fed by fear and panic, excepted no one who could be thought an enemy. It was no secret in the village of the strange activities of Jacob's farm, the comings and goings, and the numerous visitors the past years. And of course, Sara's own enemies were quick to denounce her witchery.

One early morning a troop of Roman soldiers led by one such informer circled the farmhouse and entered, seeking its occupants. Only Jacob was there, no house servants, none. Searching the house and grounds proved fruitless and as the day workers arrived for their duties they were questioned and sent away. But Jacob retained his bearing as a man of some substance and although he was kept as a prisoner, a higher-level officer was called to question him.

"Who are you to pester me, a Roman citizen and with high Temple friends, with your questions?" he demanded. "My situation here is my business and if it is to be questioned it will be from those of higher authority." The ploy caused some hesitation on the part of the centurion but he would not be cowed. He insisted on Jacob's detention until that "higher authority" could be located and he accepted Jacob's promise not to flee his small guard.

During the interrogation of the day servants one of them recalled the strange trips into the wilderness that came from Jacob's farm and it did not take long for others to embellish his story. It was said pilgrimages were made to a mysterious place where a holy man resided. Jacob, for his part, acknowledged the presence of such a person but denied being one with him or that he could find him.

A villager reported that Jacob's woman, Sara, was a follower of this man and in Jacob's house lived a gnome, devil's spawn, who, too, it was said, bowed down to this man, and now there was no sign of them. The Temple's agent who accompanied the soldiers demanded a stronger guard be placed on Jacob. Clearly, he said, they could all be sheltered together and this matter was for our people in Jerusalem to deal with.

In time a village man was found who thought he could lead soldiers to that mysterious place where the holy man was said to live. Jacob was to come with them, along with the Temple agent to keep him secure, and the village informants were to join them as well. For the soldiers this was just another wanted man they were pursuing.

Of the villagers, however, there were some who knew something of Master and his followers. As they approached the place, some began to hold back out of fear, but others, disdainful of Master and his disciples, continued and it is from them we know of the events of that time.

They arrived in late afternoon, coming upon the enclave in surprise, suddenly, as they rounded a small hill to enter what they thought was to be another empty valley. There was Master standing in the center of the settlement's courtyard, alone, as if expecting them.

"Peace be with you," he said, first to the soldiers in their language and then to the others now hanging back, with a special nod of recognition to Jacob, not missed by the others. "I have been waiting for you, want do you want of me?"

There were no others to be found in the encampment. Soldiers were sent searching throughout the buildings and the hills around the walls and there was no sign of any other presence. Their order, they told Master, was to bring him to Jerusalem for questioning. But due to the lateness of the day they would not start until the next morning.

They selected a cell for him with only a door for an opening and had him brought to it for safekeeping. A detail of guards was selected and the first watch was posted that very evening. Jacob was placed in full view of the guarding soldiers although he was not shackled.

In the morning when they went to collect their prisoner he was gone. It was not possible, they said, but he was gone. The door was still sealed, the guard was awake and sober but the cell was empty and no sign could be found of an escape. The troop commander could not believe his senses. In his frustration men were questioned and questioned again. The countryside was scoured, but the event was beyond explanation.

In his rage, the commander turned to the accompanying villagers, threatening death to all of them if it could not be said what happened. But his full rage was centered on Jacob, insisting he magically cast spells on the guards, then freed the prisoner, though no sign of how that could have been done was found. Jacob, for his part, was seen unresisting and unprotesting. All were now convinced he was a devotee of Master and responsible for his disappearance, and the villagers encouraged this thought with relief as it deflected the soldier's anger from them.

It appeared Jacob's calmness only further enraged the officer who wanted the prisoner either defiant or browbeaten. But he would say nothing, waiting, one thought, for the centurion's fury to spend itself. Instead, the man reached for his sword but before it could clear its scabbard the Temple agent spoke: "Stay, Centurion, this act will bring disaster on all of us. How could it be explained that a Roman citizen would be cut down so?

'The holy man is missing, true, but he was not your charge, he was mine as agent of the High Priest. Let us take this man to Jerusalem for trial. If he is our blasphemer and your traitor, as it appears he is, he will be delivered up to the punishment he deserves. Simply release him into my custody with several guards to escort him to the Temple. Your role in this matter has ended and has been discharged properly, as I will attest."

The benefit of this course of action became clear to the officer. To his prefect, he could report one man was taken and one not. And since these were men wanted by the Temple guards because of the religious concerns of the Jews, it was not a Roman matter. The officer saw the wisdom of this plan but, still suspicious and frustrated, he ordered Jacob shackled and conveyed to Jerusalem directly.

Although he realized, as he was making his return trip to Jacob's village, that while he could not repeat the strange episodes of that night and morning to his superiors, the villagers who witnessed the events could be depended upon to reveal what they saw. But what they saw was not all and it remained for Jacob, himself, in his time, to speak and reveal the final hours of Master's stay with us.

Jacob was taken to Jerusalem never to return to his farm which now lay deserted once again, as it was before he so proudly and happily brought Sara to it. In Jerusalem he was brought to the Temple and kept prisoner until ready for questioning by the Jewish Council. The charge of blasphemy was a serious one, to the Jews more so than treason, and could mean execution.

Although the Roman authorities would have to approve that fate they seldom opposed such a finding, and surely would not in these days of blood. Jacob was comforted by his many Jerusalem friends, some of whom were members of the council and others of whom had influence with it. Their advice was simple: Jacob simply need deny any association with Master, and since this was the case — was it not — he would leave a free man.

In time, Jacob's turn came. He stood before the council and was charged with being a follower of one Jeshua, a Galilean who set himself up as a Rabbi, but of no recognized school. One who taught the people practices not known by our tradition, who established groups of believers throughout our country, and set the common people against their masters. Moreover, in concert with this man, his wife, Sara, engaged in forbidden practices and witchcraft. How do you answer these charges?

Jacob, looking directly at the High Priest, said:

Your Holiness, some time ago, before the onset of this great commotion in our land, when I was surrounded by my family, and served well by my wife and servants, if I were summoned to this venerable council and asked your questions, I would have answered, "I do not follow that man of whom you speak." I am advised that that simple reply will end this trial for me and ease the way for my friends who have expressed their support for me. Still, I cannot do that. I cannot answer in that way.

I came upon this man many years ago just as he was coming out of his youth into manhood. Even then, his special relationship to our Lord was seen by many, though I was not one of them. Over and over I saw his works and yet found reason to deny his power. He turned ignorant servants into wise men before my eyes. He showed men the nature of compassion and love with his own acts of compassion and love, and when these were asked what did he bring to them they answered as one, "he brings peace into my life, he leaves me without fear." He left us to finish the work of his own life and then returned to bless us with the fruits of that work. And through it all I denied him.

But he never denied me. I do not know, I cannot ever know, why I was chosen to live this life and play this part in his service. But I know that I am now in his service and I stand before you saying these words about my Master without fear and with joy in my heart.

That night he disappeared even as the soldiers had him sealed in his cell in the desert was the time of my own awakening. I was sleeping in the courtyard guarded by the guard that watched over him. And I believed at first, surely as I know I stand here awake before you, it was a dream that night when I rose from my place and saw it as a vision; but it was no dream. The night was quiet and dark but still light from somewhere allowed me to see. I saw the prisoner's cell and I saw the guard pacing in front of its door.

Then, of a sudden, a man, I knew it had to be him, appeared outside the cell — I cannot say how he came from the building but I saw he was there and from him was the light in the night. He beckoned me toward him. As I moved toward him I saw he was speaking to me but I heard no words through my ears but only in my head. "Jacob," he asked, "will you do my work here when I am gone?" "Yes Master," I heard myself answer, "but what work?" "The work will reveal itself, Jacob," he replied, then putting his two hands on my head he said, "remember me."

Then he began to walk into the desert. I watched him as he went further and saw less and less of him until I saw him not as a figure but only as a light and then even that was gone. I came to my senses, awake I would say, though I know it was not sleep I came from. I looked about and saw the dark and heard the quiet night with everything in its place. The guard was pacing as usual and nothing was disturbed. And then I knew finally what the others had meant. I felt his peace within me and the absence of fear, and I knew its cause.

The next morning he was gone. But within me remained his presence and it remains yet. As I stand before you, he stands before you, and I say to you the world you ruled before his coming is not the world you rule now.

After Jacob said his last word a silence never felt before, never felt again, descended on that great hall. But his words fled the hall, its deep walls could not contain them, and they were carried with the wind to the furthest tiny village in Jewish Palestine. And their echoes still sound; as they are not limited by space they are not limited by time.

But in the hall the people looked to the High Priest. He sat motionless, staring down on Jacob. Then, nodding to his servants and seeking their help, he rose from his place to leave the hall. Then, facing the Council, he made a dismissive gesture toward Jacob and those few around him heard him mutter, "Cast him out, cast him out, remove him from our sight."

Thus, Jacob's friends spirited him out of this land to find his way to shelter with those other exiled souls in Egypt, once the land of our suffering, now the country of our redemption.

With these last words to Aaron I felt a burden I did not know I had borne lift from my heart. In Aaron, Master's charge to me had been accomplished. He knows the story of Master's times and will pass them down. I brought him to me and placed my hands on his head in a last blessing, kissed his cheeks and whispered to him my final instructions. As I walked into my mountain shelter, never to again emerge, I felt myself being gathered into the waiting bosom of my Lord.

Hear O Israel, the Lord our God, the Lord is One.

EPILOGUE

Simon returned. Aaron heard his steps and knew it was him from their sound but he made no move to rise from his place directly outside the opening of Jonathan's shelter. He looked up as Simon came into sight, saying nothing, waiting for the older man to approach. Simon, looking quizzically about, made a tentative move toward the dark entrance of the cave. It was then Aaron spoke: "Father is in there but he is gone."

"Gone?" asked Simon, puzzled. "When? In what way?"

"My instructions are that his remains are not to be disturbed, not examined nor covered nor viewed," Aaron said.

"But not to make sure he is dead?" Simon asked, "at least that we must do."

"No, Simon, he was clear at the very end," Aaron said. "We will bring stone workers from the village and they will seal this opening so in time it will not be found. I will bring his last message to the village and tell them that they will ever have his gratitude and blessing. Simon, he accomplished the task his Master, our Master, gave him and he died with peace in his heart."

At these words, Simon gazed thoughtfully at Aaron. This was not the Aaron, the boy, whom he left less than a fortnight earlier. The form was the same to be sure. The cut of the hair, the first showing of the beard, the careless toss of the tunic, would have marked him in any crowd as the Aaron he knew.

But there was a change.

He saw it first in his eyes. Truly, the eyes reveal the soul. And Simon, wise as he was, knew he could not put words to what he saw. No description was possible, he could describe more easily the hidden depths of the sea or the far reaches of the heavens: no, even that is not a fair comparison, since who can enter the deep of the sea or ascend to the heavens? But even to the deepest recesses of our own being, to where entrance meets no obstacle but our own desire, of that, too, there can be no speaking.

But still Simon understood. Aaron truly is one who knows.

Simon now remembered his prophetic words to this lad those few short days ago. "Patience, Aaron, if this man is who I think he is you will be blessed by him and in that blessing your eyes will be unveiled." Yes, Simon realized, Aaron "knows".

And what he knows he can tell. But that telling awaits its own time. First Aaron led Simon to his village below and they too saw in him what Simon detected. Though this seemed the boy they knew, his very being could not be disputed. And when Simon told them Aaron was the last to be with their guardian, their protector, and also their charge, and that he was entrusted with the holy man's last words and blessings, but also his teachings, they looked at the boy differently and saw his authority.

Aaron told them first of his instructions for the entombment. The best stone men in the village were sent to accomplish this and with them village elders to see that the holy man's last wishes were not violated. Then when that was done Aaron told them what he could of the things he was now obliged to pass on.

"At the end," he told them, "he chose me and I became his servant and he my master and through him I became the servant of the Master of us all. I received the story of the Rabbi of Galilee from the mouth of my master who guarded us all these years. And, in ways of which I cannot speak, I learned it from the mouths of those who lived with him, loved him, obeyed him and knew him when he walked among them in body."

They listened silently, intently, sensing holiness in the boy/man before them whom they knew from childhood. He told them of the Galilean, first of his teachings, teachings that they had heard before but never like this, as from the mouth of one who had heard it directly himself

"'I am a man as you are men, yes, and as you are women,'" Aaron said of his Master's words, "'and as I am you are and as I can be you can be.'"

The silence held and the few who would demur could not bring forth their words and they were all held as if bewitched.

"'The kingdom is within you, and without. But the kingdom without is only the reflection of the kingdom within, be not fooled by the image of the world. Be not fooled by the eyes that show you the beauties of the kingdom for even before your eyes the beauties lead you into darkness. Be not guiled by the sweet sounds in your ears, for even as they roar they fade until not the keenest of ears can detect their final whisper."

Aaron paused, looked about him as if waiting for a signal. From them? Who could know? But they made no sound and he spoke again, softly such that they closed in on him so as not to miss a word.

"The one we heard of is truly the one we sought," he began. "The one spoken of in the city, and the one spoken of in the village, and the one spoken of in the desert enclave, is one and the same. He is called by the Nazarenes, the Nazarene; by the Greeks, Christ; by the Jews, Messiah. This is so because he reveals himself according to how one sees: to the small, small; to the great, great; to men, as man; to women, as woman.

"Our father who guarded us these many years, whom we just lost, was truly one with him in the days his Master walked among our people in our Holy Land. This was during the days of the Temple that is no more, and will never be again. His Master and ours was Torah in flesh and blood. He did not teach compassion for the suffering, he was compassion.

"He did not teach truth or justice, he was truth and justice. And he did not teach peace and love, for he embodied peace and love. These dreams took flesh when he took flesh and came into our world as he did, and as they remain he remains. All this I was told and all this I know."

Again Aaron paused. And now there was some stirring from the listeners. "Did our Messiah come and we did not know it?" asked one. "Surely he is not the one for whom we were told to wait?"

"Are the Christian preachers right, then, Aaron?" asked another. "Is this your Master who was hung on a tree to die and rose again in three days in the body as they say? Now do we Jews look away from our Torah for new instructions?"

"Tell us, Aaron," questioned a loud voice from the rear, "if a lad

such as yourself can tell us, who are these other men that this Master came back from the dead to anoint? You tell us to look within ourselves for truth, they tell us to look to them. One man, one Christ, two teachings. What are we to make of this?"

Aaron stood quietly looking at the gathering and each one saw the boy, and each one felt his eyes, and each one saw the presence that belied the youth and marked the authority.

And Aaron said: "I will tell you the words of my Master as they came to me through our late protector whom we nourished and who entrusted me with his message. Beyond that I cannot speak. It is not for me to say yea or nay to the bodily resurrection of another but I can tell you of the ascension of the spirit. Hear in Master's own words as they are engraved on my soul:

"'Your eyes will look upon a world in chaos, tumult, suffering. But they look from a place of tranquillity into which no sorrow can enter. Be of good cheer and know that only you can dispel that darkness in men. It is for each one to witness the spirit within and in that witness will emerge your salvation.'

"As for me," Aaron continued, "I will make my way to the desert enclave of Simon, my friend and benefactor. There I will again repeat the story of my Master and there we will consign it to parchment and memory for all time for that is my task."

And there it began. Aaron did his work and the new evangelists did theirs. What manner of man was, is, this Galilean who lives in spirit yet marks the flesh of generation after generation? Can we ever know? But it is this we do know, his mark is the sign of peace, and where it is, there is peace, and where there is peace, there he is.

Peace be with you.